EVA CHASE

HORRID
CHARMS

ROYALS OF VILLAIN ACADEMY #4

Horrid Charms

Book 4 in the Royals of Villain Academy series

First Digital Edition, 2019

Copyright © 2019 Eva Chase

Cover design: Fay Lane Cover Design

Ebook ISBN: 978-1-989096-48-2

Paperback ISBN: 978-1-989096-49-9

❀ Created with Vellum

CHAPTER ONE

Rory

As prison cells went, I guessed the blacksuits' holding rooms met a pretty high standard. I'd stayed in motel rooms drearier than this.

The space was about twice the size of my dorm bedroom back at Bloodstone University, with a double bed complete with mahogany sleigh frame set in one corner, a chaise lounge against the wall next to it, and a narrow bookshelf with a decent variety of novels and nonfiction offerings beside that. A matching table with three chairs dominated the other end of the room by the tiny bathroom. The soft whir of central air cooled the late summer heat, and it carried a sweet lemony basily scent that I'd probably have found pleasant under other circumstances.

But as cozy as my surroundings looked, this *was* a prison. The walls with their ivory-and-gold wallpaper held no windows. The main door wouldn't budge at my tug. I couldn't attempt any spells on it or anything else thanks to the warded cuffs fastened around my wrists.

On the first morning after I'd been taken in, a faint but persistent itch behind my collarbone reminded me of something else I was missing. I'd heard that a mage would start to feel uncomfortable if they stayed far apart from their familiar for very long. Mine was back at the university. I hadn't been this far away from her for this long since I'd gotten her four years ago.

Would Deborah be okay? She'd managed to find quite a network of passages around the dorm building—hopefully she wouldn't have any trouble finding food and water.

Before I could worry about that for very long, two blacksuits stepped into the room, and I discovered why the table had come with three chairs. One was for me, and the two on the opposite side were for my interrogators.

I hadn't seen the man and woman who came in before, although they wore the same black dress shirts and slacks as every member of the fearmancer law enforcement that I'd encountered. The woman's white hair was pulled back in a no-nonsense bun, and the shadow of a beard on the man's face had a silver sheen. Maybe the older agents handled the talk while the younger ones carried out the activity in the field.

"Please have a seat, Miss Bloodstone," the woman said in a flat voice. "We have a lot to discuss."

I came over to the table as they sat down at it, but after nearly twenty-four hours shut up in this place, I didn't have the patience to wait for them to start the conversation. "I didn't hurt Imogen," I said, grasping the top of the chair. "I wouldn't have. She was my friend."

I'd never hurt *anyone*, let alone killed them. The image flashed through my mind of my dormmate's sprawled body, the blood pooling under her, the lacerations gouging her body. My stomach heaved. Who in the whole school would have wanted to do that to Imogen?

Silly question. It *was* my fault, in a way. My enemies, the rulers of dark magic society and their allies, had set out to undermine me from the moment I'd been "rescued" from the joymancers who'd raised me and brought back into the fold. When I finished my schooling, I'd join the ranks of the fearmancers' rulers, and they didn't want anyone who wouldn't kowtow to their ideals gaining that kind of power. They'd already been responsible for my mentor's death a couple months ago.

And now this. It was the only possible explanation. Bespelling someone into attacking me hadn't done the trick, so they were framing me as a criminal.

"Your involvement in Miss Wakeburn's death is what we're here to determine," the man said. "Please, sit down."

I tugged out the chair and sat. The silver cuffs that diffused my magic clinked as I rested my arms on the table.

I had to remember that these blacksuits might not be cooperating with my enemies. They could be conducting a perfectly legitimate investigation. I'd have a much better chance of convincing them of my innocence if I showed I was willing to cooperate.

The woman had taken out a small tablet. She poised her hand over it as if to take notes, but I wondered if she was making an audio recording of the conversation as well. "Let's start with you giving your account of what happened yesterday afternoon leading up to Miss Wakeburn's death and your arrest."

I'd tried to give my account to the blacksuits who'd hauled me away from the university, but they hadn't been interested in listening. They'd basically ignored me from the moment they'd tossed me in the back of their car with these cuffs around my wrists, other than when they'd escorted me up here to this room.

"I was celebrating my win in the summer project competition at the end-of-term party with my friends and the other students," I said. That interlude of snacking and dancing yesterday afternoon felt like it'd happened weeks ago. "We were in the large gymnasium in the Stormhurst Building. After a while, I left with two of the other scions —Jude Killbrook and Connar Stormhurst. We were going to take a drive before we all headed home for the end of summer break. I went up to my dorm to get better shoes for driving, and they were going to meet me at the garage."

What did Jude and Connar think had happened to me? What did *anyone* think had happened to me? I didn't know who had called for the blacksuits or who might have witnessed my arrest or what they were saying about it. The guys knew me pretty well by now, in... a variety of ways. They had to realize I hadn't actually murdered someone, right?

A pang ran through my chest. God, I wished I had Connar's steady strength and Jude's irreverent humor here to help get me through this new ordeal.

"And then?" the man said.

I wet my lips, my mouth going dry. And then everything had gone to hell.

"I went into my dorm, and right away I saw Imogen on the floor," I said. "I could tell she was badly hurt. I tried to call or run for help, but some kind of spell held me in place. I couldn't talk. And I started seeing images of things that hadn't really happened, of some kind of fight— like her attacker had left an illusionary impression of what they'd done."

The illusionary impression had been structured to put me in the attacker's shoes. It'd felt as if the spell that had sliced Imogen up had seared from my throat.

My interrogators exchanged a glance. "That sounds like a strange thing for a criminal to have done," the woman remarked.

"I'm not saying it was normal. There was nothing normal about finding one of my dormmates dead either. You asked me to tell you what happened."

Her eyebrows arched slightly, but she didn't make any further comment on that subject. She glanced at her tablet's screen. "Our team doesn't report any noticeable magic acting on you when they made their arrest."

"No," I said, my stomach knotting. "The illusions faded away, and the spell that was holding me released right before they got there. As soon as I saw them, I tried to tell them that my friend needed help."

"I don't have any record of that."

"They didn't give me the chance. They cut me off."

"Mmhm." The woman tapped a few things and let out a breath. "How had you and Miss Wakeburn been getting along before this incident?"

"Pretty well. We'd hung out a few times over the summer. She helped me get something fixed for my project." I wasn't sure how much to say about our history. "We didn't argue or anything."

"We've spoken to some of your other dormmates," the man said. "They indicated that there had been tension between you and Miss Wakeburn not that long ago. Because she sided with other students instead of you in a personal conflict?"

Victory or one of her friends had been all too happy to make me look guilty, no doubt. I forced my voice to stay calm even though my mouth tightened. "A few months ago, one of the other girls *blackmailed* Imogen into betraying something I'd told her in confidence. I was upset about it, and I didn't trust her as much afterward, but I mostly blamed the girl who instigated it." They didn't really think I'd killed Imogen over something like that— something that'd happened months before—did they?

"A similar situation could have arisen, then," the woman said. "Another 'betrayal' or conflict of interests, which would have made you similarly upset."

"It's possible that could have happened," I said. "But it hadn't. There wasn't any friction between us this summer. I hadn't even seen Imogen yesterday, let alone talked to her, before I found her body. And even when I was upset about what happened before, I never lashed out at her."

The woman hummed to herself again with what sounded like skepticism. An uneasy prickle ran over my skin.

These people didn't know me at all. They just knew I was a scion and soon-to-be baron, and most of the barons were power-hungry assholes who believed they could get away with whatever they wanted to if they played their cards right. Why would the blacksuits assume I was better than that?

But my position had to come with some privileges. I was the only heir to the Bloodstone barony. They couldn't throw me in their version of jail for years on end without any real evidence... could they?

Or had my enemies managed to produce some sort of evidence that solidified their framing attempt?

The man had tipped back in his chair, watching me. "Can you think of anyone else who would have had a motive to attack Miss Wakeburn?"

I opened my mouth and hesitated. My gut knotted.

I couldn't point the finger at the other barons, claim there was some huge conspiracy they were orchestrating against me, when *I* didn't have any evidence of that. I only knew because of the words of my dying mentor, and no one could ask Professor Banefield to confirm his story now. He'd managed to get a bunch of documents to me that might lead me to concrete proof, but I hadn't fit the pieces together clearly enough yet. I hadn't had time.

If I tried to accuse the barons, I'd only look desperate and possibly insane.

"I don't know," I said finally. "She'd mentioned to me that some of the other students hassled her now and then because she came into her magic late and they didn't respect her father's position as head of Maintenance, but I'm not aware of anyone on campus who would have wanted to really hurt her."

"You didn't notice anything unusual in or around the room when you found her?"

I'd been so shocked by the sight of her body and then panicked as the illusion caught me up that I hadn't had much chance to take a careful look around. "No," I admitted. "I wish I could tell you more."

The woman cleared her throat. "And no one else was in the dorm or nearby outside when you arrived, to confirm that when you went in, Miss Wakeburn was already injured?"

The fifth floor hall had been empty. We'd been the only two people in the dorm—that I'd seen, anyway. No doubt the murderer had taken steps to ensure there were no witnesses. "No, not that I know of."

"Well," the man started, and the door to the holding room swung open again.

The sight of the woman who strode in should have been a relief. Lillian Ravenguard, like a muscular, tawny lioness even with the hint of gray in her hair and the faint lines around her eyes and mouth, had been my birth mother's best friend. She'd come to me a couple months ago offering any help she could give during my transition into fearmancer society, and she'd given me a glimpse into my mother's life through a bunch of letters and media she'd put together for me.

I'd also seen evidence of her collusion with the barons and their allies in the papers Professor Banefield had left me. If she was helping them, she couldn't *really* want to help me.

"All right," she said briskly, setting her hands on her hips. "I think you've badgered Miss Bloodstone enough. She's unfamiliar with our procedures and ought to have a proper debriefing before any interviews are conducted. I'll handle that. You get on with the rest of your jobs."

Even though my interrogators looked old enough to have seniority over Lillian, they leapt from their chairs immediately, a hint of a flush coloring the man's cheeks. As they headed out, Lillian glanced at my warded cuffs and grimaced.

"I'm sorry about those. It's policy. If all goes well, we'll have you out of them and out of here soon. I got here as fast as I could after I heard."

I couldn't take any comfort from her words when I wasn't sure how much I believed them. Had this plot really taken her by surprise, or was she putting on a front so she could screw me over even more thoroughly later? I didn't know what to say to her.

It'd probably be safest for me if I pretended to trust her while I was in such a precarious position.

"This whole situation seems crazy," I said. "I found Imogen's body—that's all. I'm not a killer."

"Of course you're not." Lillian leaned against the side

of the table. "There'll be an official hearing once the agents are finished gathering evidence and testimony, and then we can easily set the record straight. All it'll take is one insight spell conducted by the judge for you to show that nothing violent happened while you were there. Those kind of memories always leap out if they're present."

My heart sank. All at once, the illusions that had battered me when I'd seen Imogen's body made sense.

The tactic wasn't strange after all. The killer had given me images of Imogen angry as if we were arguing, of my own body and voice casting a murderous spell at her. Now those impressions were etched into my memory as if they'd actually happened. From what I knew of insight spells, the sensations that the caster took in were imprecise and muddy even when they were real. Would the judge be able to tell the difference between fact and illusion?

I didn't trust Lillian even enough to ask her that. I wished I hadn't even mentioned the illusions to the other blacksuits. The last thing I wanted was to confirm to my enemies how well their gambit had worked.

"Okay," I said in a voice that felt as if it came from a long distance inside of me. "How long will it be until the hearing?"

"I'll see if I can rush things along. A few days, I think we can hope for. And my colleagues will make sure you're well looked after while you're here, or there'll be hell to pay." She straightened up. "I should appeal to the judge for haste right away. I'll check on you again as soon as I can. You've been through so much already... This just isn't right."

She gave my shoulder a quick squeeze that I managed to restrain a flinch at, and then she swept out of the room. I stared at the closed door with a hopeless sensation expanding inside me.

The barons had locked me up in a trap far smaller than this room, and right now I didn't have even a glimmer of an idea of how to get out.

CHAPTER TWO

Rory

I expected Lillian or maybe the interrogators to return later that day, but no one came through the door except for the impassive woman who delivered my meals and gathered the dishes from the previous one. The blacksuits didn't want me starving, but I couldn't say I had much appetite given the circumstances.

It was almost a relief when the door opened in the middle of the next afternoon, after lunch but way too early for dinner. I sat up on the chaise lounge where I'd been sprawled trying to think my way out of this mess—and immediately stiffened at the sight of the guy in the doorway.

Malcolm Nightwood, the heir to the most powerful baron family other than the Bloodstones, had stopped on the threshold to say something to the blacksuit who'd let him in. He drew his golden-haired head even higher, his muscular shoulders squared with an aura of authority, and the guy nodded and backed away. Malcolm came in alone.

He drew to a halt just a few steps into the room as the door clicked shut behind him. Something in his stance shifted, uncertainty tempering his usual cocky confidence. We eyed each other from across the room.

Malcolm and I... Well, calling our relationship fraught was putting it lightly. He'd struck me as an asshole from the first time I'd seen him, divine good looks notwithstanding, and he hadn't cared for my more compassionate attitude at all. He'd spent most of the last few months trying to bully my defiance out of me by every means at his disposal.

But during the summer, things had taken a turn for the strange. I'd realized he was jealous of the interest Jude and Connar had taken in me, and I'd thought I could turn the tables on him by reminding him of what *he* was definitely never going to have with me. The trouble was, it'd turned out some part of me was attracted to him despite his assholery, and wow, did he know how to fan those flames.

Our attempts at provoking each other to get the upper hand had ended in catastrophic fashion. We'd collided in a sudden desperate make-out session that Malcolm had gotten so wrapped up in, he hadn't registered when my reactions had switched from desire to fear.

He'd backed off when I'd forced him to, and he'd seemed genuinely horrified that he'd pushed things farther than I'd wanted. Ever since that incident, he'd been more careful around me, even intervening when a few members of his unofficial female fan club had tried to hurt my familiar. It had seemed as if he was offering some sort of truce, but I wasn't sure yet how much faith to put in it— or how much I wanted to interact with him ever again regardless. A couple of small kindnesses didn't make up for months of torment.

"What are you doing here?" I demanded.

My voice prompted Malcolm into action. He looked away for a second to mutter a few words under his breath and made a quick sweeping motion with his hand. A quiver of cast magic rippled past me. "To make sure no one's spying on us," he said in reference to the spell, and then, "I told them I had urgent scion business I needed to discuss with you."

That explained why they'd let him in here but not what he actually wanted. "Do you?" I said pointedly.

He gave me a smile with a glint in his dark brown eyes and spread his hands innocently. "It's all scion business between two scions, right? I thought you'd want—" He cut himself off and opened up the messenger bag he had slung over his shoulder. When he drew his hand out, his fingers were cupping a small white form with a black splotch on its hip.

My heart leapt. I jumped up as he held the mouse out to me, and Deborah scrambled from his grasp onto my palm in an instant. She darted up my arm to perch on my shoulder, hiding in the waves of my hair.

She didn't say anything, but then, I wasn't surprised she'd keep quiet while Malcolm was so close. Even the few people who'd met my familiar had no idea that Deborah wasn't just a mouse. The joymancer authorities had arranged for a dying woman's spirit to be transferred into the animal so she could watch over me—and watch out for any threat I might begin to pose if my magical powers awakened.

Deborah's human aspect meant she could telepathically communicate with me in actual words, unlike most familiars, but if the fearmancers ever found out what she really was, we'd both be in deep trouble. My new community saw the mages who worked with happiness instead of terror as mortal adversaries.

"She wasn't all that enthusiastic about coming with me, but I made a case she must have understood the gist of," Malcolm said. "It's ridiculous that you're here at all. I figured you'd at least be able to cope better if you had her with you. I know it can feel pretty awful being far apart from your familiar for longer lengths of time."

I guessed he'd have discovered that from experience. Despite all the things I could have criticized about the Nightwood scion, I'd seen him show real caring for his own familiar, a wolf named Shadow that I'd ended up befriending as well.

"How do you think the blacksuits are going to feel about you bringing her?" I asked.

"Who gives a shit what they want? She's small. I'm sure you can keep her hidden." He paused. "If you're really worried, I could take her back to school."

"No." Every bone in my body balked at the idea of losing this one small ally now that I had her with me. Deborah *was* very good at staying out of sight.

The rest of what he'd said sank in. I sat back down on the chaise lounge, bracing my hands against the firm cushion. "What's ridiculous about me being here?"

Malcolm gave me an incredulous look. "You obviously didn't kill anyone, Glinda."

He'd taken to calling me "Glinda the good witch" after I'd made it clear how much I disliked the way he bullied the other students. If that was the worst way he could insult me, I'd take it.

"What makes you so sure about that?" I couldn't help saying, even as relief fluttered through me. If the guy from school who'd most wanted to tear me down could see that this case was a load of bullshit, I might have some hope of proving my innocence after all.

"Oh, I don't know, maybe the fact that I've never seen you be the slightest bit physically violent with anyone, even when violence might have been sorely deserved." He crossed his arms over his chest, his smile turning wry. "Somehow I doubt that pushover dormmate of yours managed to piss you off *so* much more than any of the rest of us ever have."

I rolled my eyes. "So, you're sure because if I were that kind of person, I'd have already murdered *you*." There was a certain logic to that reasoning, I'd give him that.

Malcolm chuckled, relaxing a little at the mild humor in my tone. "That's one way of putting it."

He grabbed the nearest chair at the table and spun it around to sit on it with his arms resting on the back. When we were on the same level, his presence wasn't so imposing.

"I think the feeling is unanimous within the pentacle of scions," he said. "Declan is running around looking up every court case he can get his hands on, and Jude and Connar insisted on staying at school into the break to poke around for evidence."

I let myself lean back in the chaise, some of the tension wound inside me dissipating when I exhaled. I did have other allies, even if they weren't right here. Declan Ashgrave had been keeping his distance from me because our attraction while I was a student and he was working as a teacher's aide could put his career and his family's security on the line, but he'd spent most of his life using policies and precedents to get his way. If there was anything in fearmancer law that could help me, he'd find it. I didn't know if Jude or Connar would be able to turn up anything the blacksuits hadn't, but it sure as hell didn't hurt having them try.

I rolled the question around in my mouth for a moment before deciding to say it. "What about the pentacle of barons?"

Malcolm's father was the most powerful current baron. Professor Banefield had implicated both him and his wife. How well did they bother to keep their attitudes hidden from their heir?

Malcolm's expression tensed. "I haven't been part of those discussions," he said.

I couldn't tell whether he was dodging the question or just frustrated that he was on the sidelines. He ran his hand through his hair, bringing out the hint of curl in the short locks. Then he glanced around the room, speaking another casting word I didn't know the meaning of, maybe testing the protective spell he'd put up earlier. When he turned back to me, he looked both hesitant and grim.

"Declan suggested your mentor might have been murdered too."

My pulse stuttered, but from Malcolm's phrasing, Declan had been careful to make it sound like the theory was his own idea and not a fact that I'd told him. The Ashgrave scion knew how to be careful when it came to internal politics.

"Are you bringing that up because you're thinking I might actually be a serial killer?" I said with forced nonchalance.

Malcolm made a face at me. "I'm bringing it up because this latest murder makes the possibility sound a whole lot more plausible. That someone else did it, not that you did."

How far had he gotten with speculating about who that someone else might be? Would he have believed his parents were involved? It didn't seem worth taking the gamble that he'd accept my story and not give away to them how much I knew.

"Well, if you figure out who this murderer is and turn them in so I can go free, I'm all for it."

"Rory..." He studied me for a long moment. His smile had fallen away completely, and there was something weirdly vulnerable in his expression with the cocky front stripped down. "I'm not here to hurt you, okay? I know what happened in the boathouse was awful. I never should have gotten so caught up that I wasn't paying attention to how you were responding, and I'm sorry. I'm so fucking sorry. That's not—That was never— I don't want to keep fighting with you. I'm done with that."

His voice had gone raw with the apology. I couldn't cast any spells myself, but even without supernatural insight, I felt the truth in his words. It might be the first time he'd ever been completely honest with me, without any posturing or calculation.

That fact made my heart squeeze in an uncomfortable way, because the apology was completely unexpected and yet wasn't quite enough all at the same time.

"Are you sorry about any of the rest?" I said. "I never wanted to fight in the first place."

"I'm… still sorting all that out. Can we table that discussion for now? Until you're no longer under suspicion of murder, say? I don't expect you to absolve me of whatever all you think my wrongdoings are. I'd just like us to be able to work together while we figure out where we stand on everything else."

He might have had a point. And if he wasn't asking me to forgive him, I didn't see why I should argue about it, especially when "working together" right now was mainly going to mean "get Rory out of this goddamned jail."

I dragged in a breath. "Okay. I accept the apology given and will be patient about the ones that had better be forthcoming eventually."

The corner of his mouth twitched upward, even though otherwise he still looked serious. "Spoken like a Bloodstone." He got up from the chair. "I don't know how long I can get away with staying. Mostly I wanted to deliver your familiar and let you know the pentacle is on the case."

Mostly. He'd also wanted to ask me about Banefield's murder. I hesitated as he headed for the door. I didn't have to tell him anything that would definitely get me in trouble, only enough to plant a seed, if he was already open to it. He'd put himself out there for me by coming here, by saying what he had. I could repay that with a little honesty of my own.

"Malcolm," I said, and he stopped to look back at me. I spoke cautiously but evenly. "What if I told you I *know* my mentor was murdered?"

His jaw tightened. I braced myself, but all he said was, "Then I'd say someone has a lot to answer for."

He let that statement hang, watching me. Waiting for me to offer more detail if I was ready to? I wasn't going to point the finger at his parents right here, right now. I wavered and then said, "If you come up with those answers, I'd be happy to hear about them."

He tipped his head to me. Then he stepped out of the room, leaving me feeling suddenly exhausted.

Deborah scampered from one shoulder to the other with a faint prickling of her tiny claws behind my neck. *Thank goodness. I've been so worried about you, Lorelei. They haven't hurt you?*

I wasn't sure if Malcolm's privacy spell had lingered or how long it would. To stay on the side of caution, I simply shook my head, as if to myself.

My familiar must have caught on to my apprehension. She tucked herself close to the crook of my neck, still enveloped in my hair. *I wasn't sure about that Nightwood boy, but he seemed like my only chance to get to you. Better not to put too much trust in him after the way he's shown himself to behave in the past.*

No kidding. I gave a slight nod to show I'd heard her and agreed. Her dry, steady voice wrapped me in a thin but welcome sense of comfort, even though there wasn't much she could do for me. I lay back down on the chaise lounge, careful not to put pressure on her perch.

Maybe she *could* help. She'd often left my bedroom to scoop out unusual sounds or magic. I groped for the right words.

"I wish I knew what really happened to Imogen," I murmured.

Yes, of course, that's why the blacksuits brought you here, isn't it? I can tell you what I know. I saw a fair amount of the altercation.

My heart leapt with more hope. If she knew what'd really happened...

Deborah snuggled closer. *I heard voices in the common room—not yelling, but they sounded terse. I slipped out to a spot behind the baseboard where I have a view of a good part of the room. Your friend was there, and a woman—she had a shadowy spell around her to obscure the identifying details of her face and body, so sadly I can't tell you anything useful beyond that. If I was near her again, I think I'd know her by smell.*

A woman. One of the barons was a woman—Connar's mother—and there'd been several others on Professor Banefield's list. That didn't narrow it down terribly much.

She forced your friend to stay in one place, Deborah went on. *She must have had some way of knowing when you were on your way to the dorm. All of a sudden she lashed out at Imogen with a spell that hurt her the way you saw. It was only a few minutes before you arrived. She slipped away into one of the bedrooms before you came in. I tried to warn you, but the second you opened the door, this wave of magic hit me…*

"It's okay," I whispered. I hadn't been able to fight the magic that had attached me to Imogen's murder, so I certainly couldn't blame Deborah for being incapacitated by it. I tucked my legs higher, my stomach twisting.

Nothing in Deborah's story gave me much of a lead toward the actual killer. I had a witness to the murder, but she was a witness that no one other than me could interrogate.

One the other fearmancers would have seen as a crime in itself if they'd found out who and what she was.

CHAPTER THREE

Malcolm

Saying I was "home" when I was at the Nightwood mansion never quite sounded right to me. The truth was the first time I'd felt a place was really my own was when my first-year mentor at Blood U showed me to my bedroom in the junior dorm. That room was *mine*, no one dared to even try to breach the spells securing the door, and after a few weeks I finally discovered what it was like to sleep a full night in total relaxation.

Everything in the mansion belonged to my parents. There was no inch of it they couldn't touch if they wanted to. A fact that had been drilled into me to painful and occasionally explosive effect for as long as I could remember. When I drove back through that gate, my armor automatically went up.

Dad and Mom had appeared to be in decently good moods since I'd arrived for this visit during the end-of-summer break, though. As they assembled their breakfast plates from the spread on the buffet before heading to work, I could have sworn I heard my mom briefly humming a melody to herself. A *cheerful* melody.

It was hard not to wonder if the recent incarceration of the Bloodstone heir had anything to do with their sudden high spirits.

I sliced my knife through a sausage as they sat down at the broad dining table. The smells of fried pork and buttery eggs normally would have made my mouth water —we had a damn good cook—but this morning the scents only made my stomach clench up. I forced down the chunk of sausage anyway, savory juices filling my mouth. If I was going to find out anything from my parents, I had to keep every appearance of cool.

If you want to know more about what your father is doing, you should ask him about it, Declan had said when I'd questioned him about the uncomfortable insinuations he'd been making about Professor Banefield's death. *Ask him, and really* listen.

I'd talked with my parents about Rory before. I'd have said I'd been listening. But the events of the last month had proven I'd missed a lot of things I should have seen because I'd been so focused on my own assumptions and goals. What might I have misheard or ignored because I'd taken for granted that my parents were approaching the problem the same way I was—firmly and aggressively but not murderously?

I wasn't getting answers anywhere else, that was for sure.

Things had been less tense with my friends since I'd extended the olive branch for my earlier assholery, but they were still cautious about discussing anything to do with Rory's situation. When I'd asked Connar about his and Jude's investigations around campus, his response had been vague and wary. Which I supposed made sense considering how I'd treated Rory for most of her first couple semesters at Blood U.

That was fine. I'd just have to conduct my own investigations, my way.

"Quite the mess the Bloodstone scion has gotten herself into," I remarked casually as I speared another piece of sausage.

My father sat down with a flick of his napkin over his lap. "I'm sure the blacksuits will sort it out to everyone's satisfaction."

"There are certain standards of behavior even a soon-to-be baron should be expected to maintain," my mother put in, taking the chair beside him.

By which she meant, if Rory had been going to murder someone, she should have made sure she wasn't caught. I swirled the sausage briefly on my plate and wished I had ketchup to dip it in. My parents saw the condiment as too "pedestrian." If I'd brought some with me, it'd no doubt have been rancid before I took a single bite.

"Seems like an odd victim, if she was going to snap," I said in the same offhand tone. "Some of the other girls had really been giving her hell."

Dad made a noncommittal sound. "She was

undisciplined and lacking in training. Justice will be carried out in any case."

"Better we see what she's capable of now, especially after her attempts to present herself as some sort of peacekeeper." My mother sniffed disdainfully.

"A loose cannon needs reining in," my father added, with just the slightest note of triumph.

I looked up in time to catch the glance he exchanged with Mom—a glance with a quick flicker of a smile. My breakfast stirred uneasily in my stomach. Yes, that was exactly why they'd have wanted this to happen to Rory. It offered a perfect excuse to limit her powers and bring her solidly under the other barons' control.

That was why they might have orchestrated the entire situation. It'd be awfully convenient if someone else had framed Rory with no involvement from the people who stood to benefit most, wouldn't it? And the Wakeburn girl made a much better victim than Victory or her friends from *their* perspective. A mediocre mage from a middling family—not someone who'd be especially missed, no risk of pissing off the powerful figures they wanted to maintain good relations with.

Was that what Nightwoods did now? Not just attack our enemies to keep the upper hand, but slaughter random innocent mages if it served our plans? Who the hell wanted to be ruled by barons like *that*?

No one. Which was why they were staying so close-lipped about it even with me.

I had dozens more questions clamoring for attention inside me, but I couldn't ask any of them directly. I did let myself venture a mention of their other possible crime.

"I've heard that the professor who got sick and ended up offing himself was her mentor. Wonder if that really was a natural death or she had something to do with that one too."

Dad had a poker face with the best of them, but I felt him perk up from across the table. "Have you heard someone speculating about that?" he asked.

What, because then they'd try to spin that story around on Rory too?

"No," I said blandly. "It just occurred to me, considering the current situation."

"Well, let me know if anyone else starts talking. If there are leads pointing in that direction, we'd want to know."

Or if he thought they could sway public opinion toward pinning Rory with that death too, he would. I poked at my scrambled eggs before managing to gulp down another mouthful.

What the fuck had happened to family honor? Where was the strength they'd insisted I learn to show from the moment I was old enough to follow their orders? It wasn't *strong* to kill some nobody girl and put the blame on your opponent because you couldn't manage to take the real threat on directly.

They'd decided Rory was too tough for them to handle, so they'd taken a coward's route.

My fingers tightened around my fork, but I plowed through the rest of the food on my plate while my parents cleared theirs. Dad had a new investment to go over with his business partners, and Mom had a meeting for some board she was on. They headed out one after the other before I'd left the dining room.

I wouldn't have considered myself to be under my parents' thumb. I made my own decisions; I had my own mind. But there were some rules I'd never contemplated violating. For example, Dad's home office had been off-limits for as long as I could remember.

Before, I wouldn't have violated that rule out of respect. Now... I was finding I couldn't summon quite the same level of deference I might have in days past.

If Dad really was involved in more horrifying machinations than I'd ever have suspected, I wanted all the proof I could find. He might not have left even a hint around the house anywhere, but if there was going to be some, it'd be in that office.

He didn't simply trust family and staff to stay out of the office. The door had a complicated magical repulsion spell on it too. I cast a quick bit of my own magic to make sure no one was nearby, and then I studied the threads of energy surrounding the doorway. If I stepped more than a few inches away from the opposite wall, a shiver ran over my skin and down into my muscles, urging me to flee.

So I kept close to the wall and murmured a testing word and then another to get a deeper feel for the spell. I'd used something like one part on my dorm bedroom plenty of times. Another aspect reminded me of a project we'd worked on in Persuasion last year.

A small smile crossed my lips. I could disarm it. Dad's

areas of magical strengths were the same as mine, and he'd underestimated how much my skills had grown.

I knew Dad well enough to realize the defenses outside the door wouldn't be the only protections. After I nudged the door open, I identified an alarm spell tied to the floorboards just inside. I didn't need to remove that, only to take a good hop over it. Then I stopped and swiveled to take in the room.

The furniture was styled like the rest of the house—lots of old, fine wood and thickly embroidered fabrics. The space was more open than I'd expected, though. A huge desk dominated one end of the room, backed by a stately wingchair, but the other half held nothing but a rug and a single armchair, with bookshelves along the walls and a heavily curtained window.

No one came in here other than Dad, but I didn't see a hint of dust or smell a wisp of must. He must clean it himself and air it out regularly.

The chair at the desk squeaked faintly when I sat on it, and my nerves jumped, but no catastrophe descended on me. I already knew his computer was a lost cause—I couldn't magic my way into knowing his password, and he'd have chosen something not at all obvious. Like all the other fearmancers I knew, though, he still did a lot of work on paper.

I flipped through his leather-bound agenda, lifting the pages carefully. The meetings and appointments were mostly written in short form I couldn't fully decipher, but it wasn't as if he'd include something like "Frame Rory Bloodstone for murder" in there anyway. I didn't see any suspicious-looking items around the day of her arrest or of Professor Banefield's death.

The document sorter on his desk held various bills and invoices and other business-related paperwork. Somehow I doubted he'd requested a formal receipt for any murders either. I riffled through those quickly anyway and then turned to the drawers.

Nothing in there linked him to Rory or to the professor. Nothing pointed to any violent plans. I grimaced at myself as I pushed the last drawer back into place. Maybe it'd been stupid taking this risk.

My gaze fell on the small metal trash can under the desk. I tugged it out and peered at its contents. The few crumpled papers that I smoothed out, I found unhelpful. Then there was an invitation to some fearmancer gala that Cressida Warbury's parents hoped mine would attend. Obviously Dad hadn't been interested.

I was about to flick the cardstock rectangle with its silvery lettering back into the can when marks on the back caught my eye. I turned it all the way over and tipped it to the light filtering through the window.

Dad must have had this on his desk when he'd taken some notes on another paper. His pen had pushed impressions into the card underneath. I could make out some of the letters just squinting at them.

With a whisper of magic, I filled in the shallow grooves with thicker shadow. The text swam into sharper focus.

Pers — Wed, 2pm
Phys — Thurs, 11am

Illu – Fri, 4pm

I stared at the notes for a moment, my chest constricting. It wasn't hard to guess what this was. He'd been writing down someone's university schedule.

Two of those classes I'd been in this summer. They were the ones I'd shared with Rory. I'd be willing to bet everything I owned in this house the other class was hers too.

At the beginning of the summer, he'd told me to back off her at school. Apparently he'd been keeping track of her movements by other means. For other purposes.

It didn't scream murder, but it wasn't a good sign, either.

I dispelled the magic and tossed the invitation back into the garbage. As I set everything into the right places, the constricting sensation expanded from my chest up to my throat.

Was there really much question? If Dad *hadn't* wanted Rory in the blacksuits' custody, he could have gotten her free by pulling a few strings. He was in on the plot, regardless of his exact level of involvement. I knew that, even if I hated it.

I dodged the alarm by the door again and tugged it shut behind me. As I was rebuilding the repulsion security spell, the floor down the hall creaked. My nerves jumped, and I spat out the rest of the casting as quickly as I could under my breath. I stepped away from the door and started ambling down the hall just as my little sister slipped around the nearest corner.

Agnes slowed, peering at me with her big brown eyes

as she tucked her blond hair behind her ears. Her gaze slid past me down the hall and then back to my face. I tensed instinctively, bracing for questions I'd have to dodge. But she just ducked her head, her own shoulders tense. Maybe she was worried about what *I'd* say to her about her coming down for the morning this late.

She was only thirteen, for fuck's sake. We were in the exact same boat, always on our guard around our parents, always waiting for the next test. I'd never tried to test her too—I'd never wanted to take part in that vicious aspect of our lives... but maybe I should have offered her a little more support along the way. Could I really say I completely agreed to our parents' approach to toughening us up?

Not anymore, not knowing what I did now, that was for sure.

"Hey," I said carefully. "Have you had breakfast yet?"

Agnes shook her head. "I slept in," she said, her voice meek but her mouth tightening defiantly.

She'd definitely picked up a lot of their lessons in caution and keeping one's own counsel. But maybe there were a few things I could teach her that'd serve her better than anything our parents had inflicted on us.

I stepped closer with a tentative smile. "You know, it's been a while since we went to that pancake place you like in town. Mom and Dad went out—they won't even know. You want to go grab a stack?"

Agnes's face brightened in an instant. Our parents disdained the Nary-run pancake place the same way they looked down their noses at ketchup and nachos. I'd always been the one to take her out there when the coast was clear.

"That'd be great," she said. "It's been a while."

It had been, I realized as we headed for the door, Agnes with more of a bounce in her step now. I wasn't sure we'd gone out there since I started in the senior class at Blood U. Our parents' tests had ramped up, and Dad had been watching for the slightest slip to hold over my head... All my attention had narrowed down to surviving and maintaining the authority I had.

Not anymore. I was done dancing to his tune.

CHAPTER FOUR

Rory

I was just getting up from the dinner of roast beef and buttered beans my jailors had brought me when a knock rapped against the door. I froze. No one had bothered knocking before they'd come in before.

"Um," I said. "Come in?" Was telling them to go away even an option?

When the door swung open, I was grateful I hadn't tried that. Declan strode into the room with an authoritative air lent even more power by his tall frame. His bright hazel eyes flashed with a hint of anger as they took in my holding room. Then his gaze came to rest on me, looking me over with obvious concern.

My heart had started thumping twice as fast. I could have kissed him just for being here, except that would have been an exceptionally bad idea with two blacksuits hustling into the room behind him.

"She's been held according to proper procedures," one of them was grumbling.

"Maybe as far as where and how," Declan said, folding his arms over his chest. "As I've already pointed out to your supervisor, any mage never before charged with a crime has a right to continue their day-to-day life with minimal restrictions. She shouldn't be here at all."

"When the crime is murder—"

Declan turned to the man with a glower. "Nothing in the statutes makes exceptions based on type of crime. Do we need to go back and run through the entire law book with your supervisor again?"

"It's fine," the other blacksuit snapped. Apparently having a scion barge in on their operations and tell them how they were doing things wrong had put them in a bad mood. Somehow I couldn't summon much sympathy.

"I can leave?" I said as Declan walked over to me.

He nodded, with a hint of a smile at the relief that must have been written all over my face. "Until your hearing. Which isn't going to happen for at *least* ten more days, because the law also says you're allowed a minimum of two weeks to gather evidence and testimony for your defense." He shot a pointed look over his shoulder at the blacksuits.

"Not when the accused has appointed a representative to investigate in her stead," the first blacksuit protested. "That's already being handled, and her representative—"

"Did you appoint anyone as your representative in this case, officially?" Declan asked me.

"No," I said immediately. "That—I didn't even know it was a thing."

Lillian must have claimed that role without telling me about it or asking whether I wanted her taking charge. I resisted the urge to clench my hands. She'd told me she was going to defend me—all the while speeding my hearing along so there'd be *less* chance to find proof that I was innocent and denying me the chance to look into anything myself.

"There you go," Declan said. "Do the blacksuits have any signed documents that contradict the accused's own statement?"

From the scowls we got, they obviously had simply taken Lillian's word for it. I supposed I couldn't blame them for that.

I rubbed my wrists instinctively, shifting the warded cuffs I was starting to get used to, and Declan frowned.

"Those need to come off too," he said, pointing to the cuffs. "You can monitor her magic usage, but you can't cut it off completely. She'll need it to continue her studies and conduct whatever inquiries she needs to before the hearing."

"That never came up during the negotiations," the second blacksuit protested.

"Because no one bothered to tell me you'd cuffed her like this. I've got photographs of the relevant documents right here." He fished his phone out of his pocket. "And if you need the source material, I've got more books in my car I can bring for you to go over."

The first blacksuit sighed. "You stay here and keep an

eye on things," he said to his colleague. "I'll check with Sootbane."

It didn't seem wise to say much of anything to Declan with the other guy eyeing us. I took the opportunity to sit down on the edge of my bed, tucking my hand slightly behind me.

Deborah, who'd found an opening in the box spring that let her use it as a hiding spot, must have been following the conversation. Several seconds later, her small warm body darted onto my palm. I closed my fingers gently around her and lifted her as if I were reaching to scratch the back of my neck. She scrambled beneath the collar of my shirt where both the fabric and the fall of my hair would conceal her.

I was going to get to leave this place—this prison. I'd have ten days to try to break the case against me. It wasn't a lot, but it was so much more than I'd had before.

The first blacksuit reappeared a few minutes later and beckoned for Declan to come with him. "I'll be right back," the Ashgrave scion assured me. I stayed where I was, with the second blacksuit standing guard, the seconds ticking by with the thud of my pulse.

Finally, Declan and the woman blacksuit who'd been part of my first interrogation marched into the room. She was carrying two cuffs that were slimmer and detailed with different etchings than the ones I was currently wearing. These looked more like matching bracelets.

"Please come here, Miss Bloodstone," she said in a terse voice. I didn't think she was very happy about this turn of events either, but obviously the precedents Declan had presented couldn't be argued away. Thank God I could count on him.

I came over, and she motioned for me to sit at the table. "Lay your arms out," she instructed. When I had, she clicked the new cuffs around my wrists before unfastening the old ones with a couple of quiet casting words. The reduced weight on my arms brought a fresh wave of relief.

"The monitoring cuffs will take an impression of every spell you cast," the woman said. "Certain types of more aggressive magic will set off an alert and result in your returning to custody. Is that understood?"

I nodded, tucking my hands onto my lap. I didn't think that'd be a problem… I'd just have to hope none of my fellow students pushed me into a situation where I needed to use force to defend myself. Lord only knew how the blacksuits would respond to that. I didn't suppose the cuffs conveniently recorded magic that was cast *on* me.

"She's free to go?" Declan prodded.

The woman nodded. "We'll notify you when the hearing date is settled on."

Even more tension stripped off me as I stepped through the doorway into the hall, leaving my lovely but suffocating prison cell behind. I curled my fingers into my palm against the urge to grasp Declan's hand. That wouldn't be a good look here either.

He didn't speak until we'd left the entire three-story facility behind. Outside, evening was falling, a cool breeze washing over the nearly empty parking lot and the shadows stretching long across the asphalt. Traffic whirred by along the highway I could see in the distance.

"I'm sorry it took me this long," Declan said. "I had to make sure I had every possible argument covered, and then it took a whole day before they even gave in to having the meeting." He swiped his hand through the smooth black strands of his hair with a jerky movement.

"You don't have to apologize," I said. "I had no idea there was any way to get out at all. Thank you so much for going to all that work on my behalf."

He looked at me, so much emotion in his eyes in that instant that a flutter ran through my chest. "Of course I did. I know you had nothing to do with Imogen's death. I wasn't going to leave you in there to be treated like a murderer."

"That's what they think I am."

"Well, we'll just prove them wrong."

He opened the passenger-side door of his car for me before going around to the driver's side. As I sank into the leather seat, the familiar cedar-sweet smell of him that lingered inside filled my lungs. I had to work twice as hard not to reach for him as he settled into the seat beside me.

As he started the engine, Deborah scurried down my arm to nestle in my hand. She hadn't spoken to me since I'd picked her up. The truth was, while I trusted Declan more than any other fearmancer I'd met, I still wasn't completely sure how he'd react to the idea that I'd brought a miniature joymancer into their midst. It seemed better not to find out when there was no reason to give away that secret. *I* knew Deborah wouldn't—and honestly, couldn't, seeing as she'd lost her magical abilities with the transition —hurt any of them.

Declan turned the car toward the winding road that led to the highway. "Are you all right?" he asked. "I mean, other than the obvious problems. They didn't push you too hard with the interrogations or anything like that?"

I shook my head. "They mostly left me alone. I think —my mother, the Bloodstone one, had a close friend in the blacksuits. She's been 'looking out for me.' I think she's involved with the barons' plans, though. Part of that looking out for me must have included claiming I'd made her my representative, even though she never told me I had a right to leave."

"They'd need conspirators among the blacksuits to pull something like this off." Declan shot me another concerned look. "I also mean—you found your friend's body—after what happened with your mentor, too, I can't imagine how horrifying that must have been."

"It… wasn't fun." My throat closed up at the memory of Imogen's savaged form. "I haven't had much else to do except come to terms with it, though. And be really pissed off at the people who actually murdered her."

"They won't get away with it," Declan promised, although I didn't think he had any more idea than I did how to make the other barons pay. He exhaled slowly. "You've got a few more days before school's back in session. Did you want me to make arrangements to get you home?"

Home—that big old house in Maine? I hesitated. "If I need to be building a case to prove I didn't hurt Imogen, nothing out there is going to be much use to me, is it? I'll be able to accomplish more on campus. Malcolm came by —he brought my familiar... He said Jude and Connar have stuck around trying to help with the investigation?"

Declan nodded. "They went home yesterday, I think more to see if they'd hear about anything from their parents' circles than because they really wanted to be there, but as soon as they know you're out, they'll come back." One side of his mouth curved up in a crooked smile. "You've inspired a lot of loyalty all around."

I didn't know how to talk about the other guys with Declan. He knew I was... dating them, or whatever exactly you could call what we had. I knew he had similar feelings for me—feelings I returned. But he was the one who'd vetoed any possibility of him and me having a relationship even after he was finished with the teacher's aide job. It wasn't as if I'd picked them over him.

To be honest, I'd have taken all three of them given the opportunity.

That thought sent a not entirely welcome flush of warmth under my skin. I swallowed and groped for a change of subject. "So, we have to assume the other barons are behind this whole setup—them and the 'reapers' or whatever their allies call themselves. Do you have any idea why they'd do something like this? I can't be there to support whatever it is they want to do in the pentacle if I'm in fearmancer prison, can I?"

Declan's smile disappeared. "It actually makes a lot more sense than you'd think. More than I like to think about. We don't really lock people up for extended periods of time—no one's committed a crime the authorities felt warranted that punishment in as long as I've been alive. If you're convicted, the most likely consequence will be that you'll have a spell placed on you that'll restrict your ability to cast."

Uneasiness prickled over me. "Restrict it in what way?"

"You wouldn't be able to cast certain types of spells. There'd be a limit to how much power you could draw on for any individual casting. But that's not the real issue."

It sounded like an awfully big issue to me. "What is, then?"

He was silent, watching the road, for a few moments before he spoke. "Placing a long-term enchantment on a person puts them in a very vulnerable position. Once the spell is attached to you, it'd be easy for the original caster to adjust the workings in various ways without you even knowing. If the person doing the casting is in the barons' pocket... they could use it to control what you do, what you say, what you *think*... and there'd be nothing you could do about it."

CHAPTER FIVE

Rory

The dorm was completely silent. Even after Declan and I walked in and I flicked on the light in the common room, an ominous ambiance filled the empty space. Everyone else in the whole building had gone home for summer break. I hadn't really thought about what that would mean.

As I set Deborah down on the floor, my gaze slid automatically to the spot where Imogen's body had been sprawled when I'd found her. Just as with Professor Banefield, the maintenance staff had removed all traces of her death. I'd never have known any blood had been spilled there if I hadn't seen it a few days ago.

During the chaos of the discovery and my arrest, it seemed the full impact of her death hadn't really sunk in after all. Now it hit me like a punch to the gut.

I was never going to walk into this dorm and see her

careful smile and the flash of her silver hair clip again. Never hear her urge me on in my attempts to push back against the more vicious students. Never head into town together for a little company while we grabbed some groceries or a quick meal.

She might not have been a perfect friend, but she *had* been my friend. Maybe if I'd forgiven her faster for her one betrayal, the barons wouldn't have targeted her. If they hadn't thought they could make a real case for me being angry with her...

I closed my eyes as if that would shut out those guilty thoughts. I couldn't have known my enemies would go this far. If I'd gotten closer with Imogen again, they could have used her in some other way.

Still, the thought of going to sleep amid this silence with the images of her murder floating in my head made my skin crawl.

"Hard being here again?" Declan asked from behind me.

"It just... feels kind of haunted, with no one else here." A lump rose in my throat. "I tried to save her, you know—I wanted to call for help, I fought the spell as well as I could—"

"It wasn't your fault," Declan said firmly. When I drew in a shaky breath, he slipped his arms around me in a gentle embrace. I couldn't help leaning back into the warmth of his body just a little, soaking in the comfort he was offering.

He swallowed audibly. "If it's too much, staying here alone, you could spend the night in my dorm. I mean, there are the couches, and one of the bedrooms has been vacant since that guy graduated in June. But I'd be in shouting distance if you need anything."

The desire to take him up on that offer rang through me from head to toe, but at the same time my throat tightened even more. Already, with his arms around me and his head ducked close to mine, a whole lot more desire was welling up inside me—to be even closer than this, to feel his kiss, to rediscover every inch of the lean frame aligned with mine. How much self-control could either of us really count on alone in the night with only a single thin door between us?

I didn't want to ruin another life.

"I'm not sure that's the best idea," I said. "Even if we stick to different rooms… if someone on staff came by and saw I'd stayed in your dorm… it could still cause a problem, right?"

"It could." He sighed. His head dipped over my shoulder, his breath tickling over my cheek and his arms hugging me a little harder, and for a second I thought he might turn that short distance to brush his lips against my skin. The warmth where our bodies touched flared into a sharper heat.

If he started kissing me here, right now, I wasn't sure my good intentions would hold. I wanted him too much.

His stance tensed, and then with obvious effort he drew away from me. "If you do need anything, I'll be right downstairs."

"Thank you. For everything."

When he left, the space felt even emptier. I hurried

over to my bedroom, where at least I had all my familiar things. And Deborah, who'd squeezed her way in through the various mouse-sized passages. While I pulled the curtain shut against the darkness outside and changed into a pair of pajamas, she curled up in a nook on the bedcovers.

"Do you want anything to eat?" I asked her, able to talk to her freely for the first time since Malcolm had delivered her to me. With Declan's interruption coming right after my dinner, I hadn't gotten the chance to slip her the morsels I'd saved from my prison meal.

I had enough at lunch that I think it'll hold me over, Deborah said. *I can't say this situation has left me with much of an appetite.*

"No kidding." I flopped down on the bed and she cuddled next to my arm. Seeing the blank floor with all trace of the crime wiped away had stirred up other uneasy emotions as well. "I don't know how I'm going to get out of this, Deborah. What evidence am I going to find? Whoever did this will have taken all kinds of precautions to make sure there were no witnesses. And they messed with my mind, so even *I* can't be a witness to my innocence."

The real attacker didn't count on me as a witness, she reminded me.

"Yeah, but it's not as if I can present your observations at the hearing."

She paused for a moment. Her cool nose nudged my skin. *I could present my own observations. You tell them you believe your familiar may have seen at least part of the altercation, and they could take a peek into my memories.*

I tipped my head to look at her. "Do insight spells work on animals?"

Joymancers use similar sorts of magic, and they can allow you to delve into any conscious mind. As I recall, the impressions you get from an animal tend to be vaguer and more jumbled, but that'll be less of an issue in my case.

Or more of an issue. "They'd notice it's strange that your memories are so clear, though, won't they? They might even see something that shows you're more than just a mouse, like a memory of us talking together."

A small risk. If it prevents these barons from putting you under their control... I was made your familiar so I could protect you, Lorelei, and I intend to do that however I can.

She'd always said that, but she knew as well as I did that the joymancer Conclave had assigned her to me more to protect everyone else *from* me rather than the other way around. As much as that fact made my skin crawl, so far it certainly seemed as if I was more of a danger to the people around me than they were to me, if indirectly.

"No," I said. "It's not just a small risk; it's a huge one. The barons are going to be pulling out all the stops to make this charge stick. Who knows how deep they'll poke into your brain if we give them the chance? Then I'd lose you... and I'd still be charged with a major crime. It wouldn't help anyone."

Perhaps you're right. I wasn't thinking about how you would be threatened by the discovery as well. She paused. *I'd do it if you decided it was worth the risk after all, though. I want you to remember that. If those miscreants take you over for their awful purposes, then I'll have failed both you and the Conclave.*

A thought that might have been unfair passed through my mind—was she more worried about failing me or failing the Conclave? I shoved it away. Deborah had supported me as well as she could, stuck in that mouse body and unable to cast.

"I appreciate that," I told her. "We'll just have to find another way." With three—or maybe even all four?—of the other scions working alongside me, I had to have some kind of chance, didn't I?

I nestled my head in the pillow with my hands tucked by my face. The cuffs pressed against my wrists, not letting me forget them even when I closed my eyes to try to sleep. It was a long, uneasy time before I finally drifted off.

The fridge had been cleared out after all the summer students had departed—some of us less willingly than others—and the cafeteria wasn't running during the break, so the next morning I made the twenty-minute walk into the town down the hill to make sure Deborah and I wouldn't starve. I returned to the dorm loaded down with bread, cheese, fruits, and various other essentials, and nearly gave a woman standing in the common room a heart attack.

She flinched at the swing of the door and jerked her hands down from where they'd been raised to cast a spell over the sofa's upholstery. A jolt of fear shot into me from her. When she saw me, her eyes widened. Her stance shifted but didn't exactly relax, smaller whiffs of anxiety tickling past my collarbone from her to join my stores of magic.

"I'm so sorry, Miss Bloodstone," she said. From her simple blue dress shirt and gray slacks, I figured she was part of the maintenance staff. "I didn't know you were back. I was assigned to deep clean the common seating areas today. If you'd rather I came back later…"

"No, no," I said with a wave of my free hand. "It doesn't bother me, as long as it doesn't bother you if I make myself some breakfast."

"Of course not," she said, but I felt her gaze follow me as I headed into the kitchen area.

The woman went back to her cleaning spells, but I caught more than one wary glance aimed my way—and more tingles of nervous energy passing into me—as I toasted a couple slices of bread, fried an egg, and chopped up an apple to share with Deborah. Suspicion wormed its way under my skin.

Was she *really* here just to freshen up the rooms, or was she yet another person the barons or their allies had brought under their sway? They might be setting new plots in motion now that I was temporarily free, even with the hearing looming. She might have intended to cast some kind of harmful spell in here. She might still mean to do it and was worried I'd realize.

I trained my eyes on the back of her head and murmured a general insight spell as I spread butter on the toast, my low voice covered by the scrape of the knife. The woman didn't have much in the way of defenses up. I tumbled into her thoughts in an instant.

As always, the impressions flowed around me without much rhyme or reason. I tasted her determination to see her job done well to make her boss happy… while he was so torn up in grief over his daughter's death. Her boss was Imogen's dad, of course. A simmering discomfort at my presence ran through her consciousness too, but it had nothing to do with any nefarious plans she was part of. Her heightened awareness of the knife in my hand only solidified that fact.

She was afraid she was in the presence of a murderer. And not just any murderer—one who might fly off the handle without much warning.

Nausea gripped my stomach as I pulled back into my own head. I had to force myself to add jam to my toast before I carried it into my bedroom.

Ever since my assessment had shown I was strong in all four domains of fearmancer magic, my fellow students had regarded me with a certain amount of caution. I hadn't *liked* it, but it'd conveniently replenished the fear I relied on to power my magic without me having to actually hurt anyone. Now, though… How many of the students and staff outside the few who knew me well believed I'd killed Imogen in a vicious fury? Was this the kind of reaction I'd have to expect across the board once school was back in session?

I relaxed a little when I heard the click of the main door as the woman left—and tensed up all over again when a knock sounded on it a few minutes later. Then a familiar playful voice carried in from the hall.

"Oh, Ice Queen, don't leave me hanging here."

My spirits lifted in an instant. I leapt up from my desk and all but ran for the door.

Jude's tone might have been light, but when I threw open the door, his green eyes met mine, even darker than usual with worry. I grabbed him in a hug, and he squeezed me back with a pleased chuckle.

"Now that's the kind of welcome I'm talking about. Are you okay?" He eased back just far enough to examine my face. "The blacksuits didn't manhandle you too much, did they?"

Seeing that much concern from a guy who rarely showed he was anything other than absolutely carefree made my heart squeeze. Jude had plenty of his own problems weighing on him, but he'd dashed back to campus to be here for me without me even asking.

"No one hurt me," I reassured him. "It just wasn't exactly a vacation."

"They never should have taken you in the first place," he muttered, and traced his fingers along my jaw. "We'll just have to make whoever set you up like this regret it, won't we?" He gave me a wicked smirk and tipped up my chin for a kiss.

He made it sound so much easier than I could imagine fixing this mess would be, but it was impossible to focus on that with his mouth claiming mine. I kissed him back hard, letting myself get lost just for a moment in all the desire and adoration that radiated from his touch.

Someone cleared his throat from the top of the stairs. I broke from Jude to see Connar watching us with one eyebrow cocked.

"You just had to get in there first," he said to Jude, but his low baritone had a teasing note to it.

He strode over as I turned to meet him, and in an instant I was engulfed in his brawny arms. I lifted my head to kiss him too. Even with the horrible situation I'd found myself in, a wave of gratitude washed through me—that I had these guys who were not only willing to fight for me against my enemies but to share my affections with each other as well.

"All right," Connar said, after pressing another kiss to the top of my head. "Let's see what we can to do make sure justice is served."

As much as I appreciated that sentiment, my gut twisted at the comment. The two scions didn't know yet that any real justice I got for the attacks against me would tear apart both their families.

CHAPTER SIX

Declan

I'd known from the moment I started digging into fearmancer murder law that my efforts wouldn't go unremarked on. So when Ms. Grimsworth summoned me to her office, I had no doubt what the meeting was going to be about. The only question was exactly how it'd play out.

"Come in, Mr. Ashgrave," the headmistress said in her cool voice when she answered my knock. She didn't look especially happy about having to deal with this business before the end-of-summer break was even over, but then, I rarely saw much emotion color her primly professional demeanor. She rarely appeared happy about good news either.

I stepped into her office, the sharp scent of incense tickling my nose, and discovered we had company for this meeting. A blacksuit was leaning against the bookshelves to one side of Ms. Grimsworth's desk—a fairly high ranking one, from the cut of her dark clothes and her apparent age, though I hadn't encountered her during my work to get Rory out of their custody. She didn't say anything as I took the chair in front of the desk, but her intent gaze followed me beneath the sweep of her short tawny hair. Maybe this was the family "friend" Rory had mentioned.

Ms. Grimsworth sat in her usual chair without introducing the onlooker. Apparently the blacksuit wanted to be a relatively silent partner in this conversation. The headmistress folded her hands on the top of the desk and leaned forward. When she spoke, her tone gave the impression that she'd suppressed a sigh.

"Concerns have been raised regarding your involvement with Rory Bloodstone. You've assisted with her Insight seminar in your capacity as teacher's aide as well as offering her tutoring, if I'm correct?"

"That's right," I said calmly, although my stomach had knotted. I'd expected this, but I also didn't know exactly how the accusations might play out. The last I'd heard, Rory's paternal grandparents had fled the country in the wake of the criminal investigation I'd set in motion, off to Europe somewhere to hope they could simply wait out the inquiries. That didn't mean they couldn't have tried to take one last jab at me by sharing their theories about my and Rory's personal relationship as they'd left. Hell, for all I knew, someone else had witnessed an incriminating interaction between us without us even realizing.

"It appears you've gone to great lengths to assist Miss

Bloodstone in the face of her recent incarceration," Ms. Grimsworth went on. "Certainly beyond what we'd consider in the scope of a teacher's aide's responsibilities to one of his students. Questions have been posed about potential bias interfering with your ability to do your job."

That all sounded pretty vague so far—and while it was difficult to read Ms. Grimsworth's mood, my increasing impression was that she found this entire interview rather ridiculous. Not that I could afford to relax with the blacksuit looking on.

I schooled my expression into one of bemusement. "I can understand why that issue might be raised, but all I can say is that I don't see my efforts on Rory's behalf as having anything to do with my role as teacher's aide. Regardless of our positions within the school, we're colleagues within the pentacle. I supported her as a fellow scion."

The blacksuit opened her mouth for the first time. Her voice had a slight edge to it. "You'd go to these lengths for your other 'colleagues' as well?"

I shifted my gaze to her, my shoulders squaring. "I would. Thankfully, none of the other scions have been involved in a crime on this level, so I can't point to direct evidence of that fact, but if you look over my history, you'll find plenty of instances when I've used my understanding of our laws and formal procedures to help them in smaller ways."

I didn't know whether she'd already investigated that history, but if she hadn't, she'd find out it was true soon enough. Of all the questionable things I might have done when it came to Rory, defending her legal rights wasn't one of them. When it came to those actions, at least, I stood on perfectly firm ground.

Unless the blacksuits had something else up their sleeves. Or unless my fellow barons had decided to throw me under the bus along with Rory. Apprehension prickled down my back.

Ms. Grimsworth shifted back in her chair. She glanced at the blacksuit. "I can confirm that Mr. Ashgrave has generally led any petitions involving formal policy when it comes to the other scions, here at the university at least."

"It seems to me there is some conflict of interest there all the same," the blacksuit said.

"School wasn't in session at the time," I said before she could go on. "And if it would be a problem for me to continue contributing to Rory's case once classes start up again, then I'll resign as teacher's aide. I'm sure the blacksuits would agree that the pentacle must come before a temporary teaching position."

I said the last bit as evenly as everything else, but it was meant as a parry. No blacksuit would want to suggest, especially in front of a respected witness, that they opposed solidarity among their future leaders.

The woman frowned, but she mustn't have had any other ammunition—or none that she was prepared to use just yet. "I don't think that will be necessary," she said. "At least not from our perspective."

"Nor from ours," Ms. Grimsworth put in. "The matters appear to be quite unrelated. Though while you're particularly engaged in Miss Bloodstone's legal affairs, I expect you to ensure that any evaluations of her class performance are conducted by Professor Sinleigh rather than yourself."

"Of course," I said, and with that, it seemed the interview was over.

I only had a few minutes to feel relieved. As I headed out of Killbrook Hall, my phone buzzed in my pocket. I pulled it out, and my heart sank.

I'd gotten a single, brusque text from Marguerite Stormhurst—Connar's mother and the Stormhurst baron. *Urgent meeting, 1pm, the field. Your presence is mandatory.*

That was less than an hour from now. Which wouldn't have given me enough time to drive out to the Fortress of the Pentacle if the barons had tried to hold the meeting there... and perhaps they hadn't wanted there to be any risk that what we were about to discuss could be overheard or recorded by the pentacle's official administrative employees.

I'd only met the other barons at the isolated field where we occasionally assembled for emergency meetings twice before, once while I was still technically only in training with my aunt Ambrosia as acting baron. The only good thing about the way they'd called this get-together was the fact that she'd almost certainly been left out. On the other hand, if they didn't like the answers I gave them today, they might be inviting her back into the position that should be mine soon enough.

I switched directions to veer toward the garage, ignoring the impulse to text Rory—or, hell, even Jude or Connar—and tell them why I was leaving campus. It wasn't as though, if the barons decided to turn their murderous intentions on me, the other scions would be able to do anything about it without putting themselves in even more danger. And I didn't really think my older colleagues would go to those lengths just yet.

That didn't mean this conversation was going to be at all enjoyable, though.

The possibilities of what they'd say and how I'd answer whirled through my head as I drove, although I'd already thought through my arguments before I'd first contacted the blacksuits on Rory's behalf. The issue wasn't so much what I'd say as how the barons would take it… and if the last few months had taught me anything, it was that for all I knew about them, I was still capable of underestimating them.

The field in question lay a few miles from any habitation, stretches of pine forest shadowing either end. The country road that led to it was full of potholes that jolted my car's suspension. An even rougher lane branched off, petering out into overgrown grass after some ten feet. It was there that three other cars were already parked when I pulled into the field. The three full barons—Julian Nightwood, Edmund Killbrook, and Marguerite Stormhurst—were leaning against the hoods. Their gazes followed me.

I stopped the car with the uneasy impression that they'd been talking for quite a while before I'd turned up. That they might even have already been together when Baron Stormhurst had called me to this meeting. Together and discussing *me*.

"Ashgrave," Nightwood said the moment I'd opened the door. "Glad you could make it." His steady voice was laced with just enough venom for me to register it, but hardly enough that I could have called it out.

"Of course," I said. "The pentacle calls, I answer." They weren't going to dock me any points on loyalty to *this* job, that was for sure.

I came around the front of the Honda and propped myself against the hood as the others had, keeping my movements as loose as I could manage to despite the tension wound inside me. Nothing would be worse than revealing *I* knew I'd done something they wouldn't approve of.

Distant thunder rumbled in the cloud-choked sky, and a damp wind licked over the field. If we didn't keep this meeting short, we'd all end up soaked.

"What do we need to discuss?" I asked, as if I had no idea.

Killbrook narrowed his eyes at me, which only amplified the serpentine impression his angular face always gave me. "We were informed that the Bloodstone scion has been released from blacksuit custody, on your request. Something you should have discussed with *us* before going ahead, don't you think?"

I blinked at him as if startled by the idea. "I was simply ensuring proper procedures were followed. I didn't realize there'd be any debate about that."

Nightwood shifted, with a tiny gesture of his hand that might have signaled something to his colleague. "Naturally we expect the law to be followed," he said. "But

I would trust the blacksuits were in the process of handling it. Bloodstone has finally made a misstep that may benefit us. Surely you could see that?"

A "misstep." As if murder were a simple mistake. As if they hadn't orchestrated the entire thing rather than Rory stepping wrong.

I reined in my irritation. "Of course that factor occurred to me," I said, letting my voice get slightly tart. When dealing with venomous snakes, sometimes you had to show you could respond in kind, or they'd take your apparent weakness as an opening. "It also occurred to me that convicting the sole heir of a barony might be a rather difficult task. If she's given the full amount of time to mount a defense and still can't establish her innocence, the judge will be even more… open-minded in the extent of the sanctions, don't you think?"

He'd be more inclined to lay down harsher punishments—and to give the barons more rein to impose them, I meant.

The other barons were silent for a moment. Stormhurst cocked her head. "How can you be so sure she won't manufacture some proof in her favor while she's walking free?"

I raised my eyebrows at her. "Considering the blacksuits are tracking every bit of magic she casts, I'm not sure how she could manage that. If she tries to, she'll only dig the hole even deeper. I can't imagine how she'd start even if she had unrestricted use of her magic. With the carelessness of the crime, there must be ample evidence against her already, assuming she's responsible."

I watched the faces around me carefully. Killbrook exhaled wearily and rubbed his mouth. Nightwood only kept his usual imposing demeanor. Stormhurst gave a snort that sounded just a touch forced. The figures in front of me had far too much practice at holding their cards close.

"She has dug herself quite a hole," Stormhurst said. "Her access to the barony will depend on our good graces once she's convicted."

"As it should have all along, considering the outside influences that have muddled her understanding of the world," Nightwood put in, the closest he'd likely ever come to admitting he'd not only wanted but intended for this outcome. "The balance will be right within the pentacle, and we can move forward without further distractions." He fixed his dark gaze on me. "As long as your gambit doesn't backfire in some way you haven't anticipated."

"I'll be right there to keep an eye on her process," I said. "I can't see any way she'll get herself out of this fix unless somehow she's honestly not guilty. How much chance is there of that?"

The question might have been a smidge too pointed. Nightwood's mouth tightened, and Killbrook shot me a brief glance that was just shy of a glower. I kept my expression impassive as if I'd meant it as an honest question.

"I expect we have no need to worry about that," Nightwood said. "But we *would* like to be kept informed of any further action you take as it involves Bloodstone. All of our fates are connected to hers."

"I'll take initiative as I see the need," I said. "But I'll make sure you stay updated."

Stormhurst's voice dropped low, to almost a growl. "Before you take any more initiatives on your own, remember *you're* not quite full baron yourself. Your fate depends on us as well."

"I'm only attempting to live up to the role," I said with a smile, but my stomach balled tighter as I got back into the car. That was as close to a direct threat as I'd ever gotten from them. The line I walked had just gotten twice as precarious.

But it still wasn't anywhere near as fraught as the path Rory was on. I tried to stir more sense of triumph in me as I started the engine, but it was weighed down by the dread pooling in my chest.

As much as I hated it, what I'd told the other barons was true. If Rory couldn't prove she hadn't hurt her dormmate even with the time and freedom I'd bought her, she'd be worse off than if I'd left her to stew in the blacksuits' holding room.

CHAPTER SEVEN

Rory

"If only the school had bothered to invest in security cameras," Jude lamented, stroking his fingers over my hair where he was sitting next to me on the sofa in the scion lounge.

"They wouldn't have done us much good," Connar pointed out at my other side. "Anyone who could pull off the level of magic needed for the rest of the crime could have blocked them off or cast an illusion to change the recording."

Jude hummed to himself. "True. All right, scratch that complaint, let's keep all cameras away."

I resisted the urge to pull both him and Connar closer, to snuggle into them like a shield against the awful situation I was facing. Just because Declan accepted that I was involved with other guys didn't mean I liked the idea of rubbing it in his face. Besides, the four of us had come down here to the private basement lounge area to figure out the right strategy to tackle that situation. I had to stay focused.

Thankfully, Malcolm wasn't back from the break yet, so we didn't have to deal with any interruptions from him.

Declan shifted in his armchair with a frown. "The two of you didn't come up with anything useful when you were poking around while I was researching the legal aspect?"

Connar shook his head. "Nothing that would prove Rory wasn't behind the attack or that someone else was." He gave my knee a gentle squeeze. "What about Victory and her friends? They've had it in for you for a while, haven't they? And they knew about the tension between you and Imogen—they had easy access to the dorm…"

I took a sip of the Coke that Jude had poured for me, the fizzing of the liquid going down my throat sharpening my focus. "They *were* at the party in the Stormhurst Building."

"I stayed longer than you did," Declan said. "I remember seeing Victory and Sinclair there afterward—I was keeping an eye on them in case they tried something. But Cressida…"

I'd seen Cressida, I realized. She'd bumped into me, literally, in the first floor hallway when I'd been heading for the stairs that led to the dorms.

A chill washed through me for just a second before I remembered Deborah's account. She'd said the real attacker had still been in the dorm room when I'd come in.

"Cressida couldn't have been involved either," I said. Besides, I knew I hadn't been framed by students, although I guessed it was possible the barons had made use of them somehow. I hesitated, debating for the hundredth time whether this was the right moment to drop that revelation in my lovers' laps.

Declan redirected the conversation before I had to decide, maybe sensing my discomfort. He didn't appear to be in any hurry to accuse his friends' parents of treason either. "If it wasn't for the illusion spell, your memories would be enough to absolve you," he said, and rubbed his mouth. "Will you let me do an insight spell on you—just to look at that moment? Maybe there's something about the illusion that we'll be able to point in comparison to your actual experiences, so we can prove it isn't real."

My spirits leapt with a jolt of hope. "Okay. I couldn't really tell if there was anything really off about the illusions—but I was pretty distracted in the moment, panicking over Imogen."

With a deep breath, I willed down the mental shields that had become instinctive. Even though I was surrounded by people I knew wanted nothing more than to help me, my pulse thumped a little faster as Declan leaned forward, his gaze intent on my forehead. Through everything that'd been thrown at me since I'd entered the fearmancer community, I'd managed to keep my thoughts and memories reasonably secure. Leaving myself vulnerable made my nerves jitter.

"*What happened when you found Imogen Wakeburn's body?*" Declan asked with the slight lilt of a casting. A tingle raced through my head as he must have delved into my thoughts. I had no sense of what he was seeing. Jude took my hand as if suspecting I needed the extra reassurance.

All I could do was sit still and wait for Declan to finish sorting through whatever impressions had risen up to meet his question. When he sat back with a sharp exhalation, my mental protections sprang back into place before I even needed to think about it. A ripple of relief passed through me having that wall of defense around me again.

Declan's expression had turned pensive. "It's going to be hard," he said. "That was a skilled illusion—it mimics actual memories too well to distinguish the difference with insight. The whole process is always so jumbled as it is…" His gaze rose to meet mine. "There might be something, though. Most of the words were blurred, but with the spell—you haven't been using your own casting words yet, have you?"

I shook my head. "It's easier using actual words. I haven't been confident enough to start making things up on the spot or relying on invented phrases. There's a word I've been using for general insight spells, but that's it."

"And your professors would be able to confirm that?"

"They should. They've all seen me cast for classwork recently—honestly I've felt a little embarrassed that I'm still using literal words."

The corner of Declan's mouth crooked upward. "You should be thankful for it. It might help solidify your defense. Whoever cast the illusion clearly didn't realize that about your own magic use. The spell that appears to kill

Imogen in your memories was directed by a word I've never heard before."

"Really?" The hope I'd felt before bubbled higher. I hadn't noticed that aspect in the chaos. "That's pretty good evidence that I didn't cast the spell, isn't it?"

"It should be," Connar said.

"It *should*," Declan agreed. "And I expect it'll help sway the judge. I don't think it'd be smart for us to assume it'll be enough on its own. Your accusers could argue that you purposefully came up with a casting word for that kind of spell to sow doubt if you had to use it."

Jude made a face. "That's a huge stretch. If Rory supposedly lost control in a fit of anger, why would she have a spell for that situation?"

Declan held up his hands. "I know it's ridiculous. We all know it's ridiculous to think that Rory would have attacked anyone in the first place. But we also know that scheming isn't exactly an uncommon occurrence among fearmancers, don't we? It wouldn't be a hard story to sell. *If* that's the only proof we offer. We've got at least a week to come up with more."

"They could use insight to help determine whether she planned a casting word in advance, couldn't they?" Connar said.

"Maybe," Declan said. "It'd be hard to phrase a question that specific in a way that gives definitive proof. Especially when the truth is that she didn't."

And I didn't really want the judge poking around in my head any more than he or she needed to. The fear that had gripped me when Lillian had talked about the judge viewing my memories shivered through me again.

"They'll probably want to use a lot of insight on me at the hearing, won't they?" I asked. "It'd be hard for me to refuse without looking guilty."

Jude elbowed me teasingly. "If you don't have any murderous secrets to hide, I think you'll be fine. You put the rest of us to shame."

"Not by regular fearmancer standards, though, right?" I looked at each of them. "There are things I've thought, things I've said, that the authorities might see as treason. I still miss my joymancer parents. I still... I still wish I were back with that community instead of here sometimes."

A lot of the time, even if not quite as much now that I had the support of these three guys. And then there were the plans I'd made to bring down the whole school, the conversations I'd had with Deborah that would reveal who she really was... My mind could incriminate me of crimes the judge would probably see as worse than a murdered friend.

"I've never seen a judge request an all-encompassing insight spell during a hearing," Declan said softly. "But it's true, we don't know for sure what questions they'll ask—and it's possible they'd ask something that would brush up against those feelings. They'll be looking for signs of animosity..."

Connar sat up straighter, his expression fierce. "We'll make a good enough case that they don't have any grounds to do an extensive insight interrogation."

Declan and I exchanged a glance. We both knew that

the people pulling the strings behind the scenes would take the opportunity of the hearing to undermine me any way they could. I couldn't count on any amount of evidence sparing me that intrusion.

But maybe there was a defense I could use that didn't involve any magical shields. If my enemies could mess with my memories using an illusion... there were other ways I could disguise the reality of my thoughts, weren't there?

"Just in case," I said to Declan, "why don't— Before, you passed on some reports to me about cases involving the joymancers, conflicts between them and the fearmancers. I'm guessing there's more material like that you could give me? If I've been reading that stuff before the hearing and have it fresh in my mind, it should help cloud any of the positive feelings I have about them."

Declan paused. "There is more. If you're sure you want to read it. The joymancers... I don't doubt that your adoptive parents treated you well, Rory, but you didn't know any of the others. The reports I gave you before were true. Their community has done some pretty awful things."

Awful by fearmancer standards, maybe. I still wasn't convinced there was no bias in the accounts I'd read. Even if the Conclave had been afraid of me and denied me my magic... even if the circumstances of my birth parents' deaths had been questionable... how could anything they'd done compare to the horrors the fearmancers had treated me to in just five months?

"That's fine," I said. "I want to know the truth. If it

unsettles me, well, then it'll stick in my mind even more, right?"

Jude chuckled. "That's the spirit," he said, ruffling my hair.

By the time we headed up to the main floor, we each had tasks to do, if not a definite plan for proving my innocence. Declan went off to get those records for me, and Connar gave me a quick kiss before heading into the library, where he was going to look up some advanced physicality approaches that he thought might reveal something in the crime scene. Jude ambled out onto the green with me, intending to chat up the few teachers currently on campus.

My job was to take a walk around the university and see if anything jostled free a memory that could point me in a useful direction—something I might not have noticed the significance of before Imogen's murder. It didn't feel like a lot, but it was a starting point, anyway.

As we came out of the building, one of the general education professors was leading a small group of students our way. The glints of the leaf pins by their shirt collars revealed that they were all scholarship students: Naries. Blood U admitted a handful of nonmagical students each year to give the rest of us practice at keeping our magic secret—and easy targets for generating the fear we needed to fuel that magic.

"This is Ashgrave Hall, where you'll be staying," the professor was saying. "Each of you should have received a dorm assignment with your letter."

"The new batch of senior Naries," Jude said by my ear

as the professor led the group into the building. "Or at least the newly senior ones. They always start their school year here in the fall to mimic the regular school system. The staff have them arrive a little before classes start to get settled in… so they have a little time to acclimatize before the mage students will really go after them."

"Lovely," I muttered.

"Hey, they'll have more of a respite this term thanks to you."

I'd almost forgotten the summer project I'd been celebrating right before Imogen's death. With my help, a group of Naries had designed and overseen the construction of a clubhouse solely for the scholarship students. The wards I'd laid down with Connar and Jude's help would give them one place safe from malicious castings.

That victory seemed like a small one in the face of everything that had happened since.

Jude leaned in to kiss me, letting his lips linger a few seconds longer than Connar had—maybe on purpose—and shot me a grin before setting off toward the teachers' offices in Killbrook Hall. The guys might have been willing to share my affection, but I didn't think their competitive instinct had completely faded.

I was about to meander toward the Stormhurst Building, figuring I should retrace my steps from right before the murder first, when a few more figures came around the hall from the main parking lot, one of them a completely welcome sight.

Shelby, the Nary girl from my own dorm room and

the first person on campus who'd been truly friendly to me when I'd arrived, was hauling a small wheeled suitcase over the grass to the paved path. She had her cello case, which was nearly as tall as she was, slung over her shoulder. Her mousy brown hair bobbed in its usual ponytail, and her expression was as earnestly determined as ever. Keeping her spot at the music program at this school meant the world to her, especially since she'd nearly lost it once.

My first impulse was to hustle right over to welcome her back, but something in me balked. I didn't know what she'd heard about Imogen and my supposed involvement in the murder. The Nary students had left the morning before it'd even happened. Maybe she had no idea? But surely the administration would have notified them somehow, if only to pre-empt the talk that would be circulating among the fearmancer students on their return.

Shelby spotted me right then and bounded toward me as fast as her luggage allowed with a smile that didn't leave any room for doubt. Whatever she *had* heard, she was still perfectly happy to see me. I let a smile stretch across my own face as I met her halfway.

"I'm glad you're already here," she said after we exchanged a quick hug. "Weird as it might sound, I'm glad to be back."

"Even when you've got more hassling from people like Victory to look forward to?" I said.

"Ah, really, there are people back home who can be just as mean. At least here I'm making sure I'll have a good enough career that eventually I'll never have to go back." She gave a sheepish laugh. Then her smile faltered. "Is it really true—the school sent around this official notice that Imogen *died*?"

My chest tightened. "Yeah," I said. "They're still investigating exactly what happened." She obviously didn't know the whole story. I fumbled for the right words. "I— People are saying, because I was the one who—"

"I didn't know they allowed murderers to come back to school," someone said from across the green.

I stiffened, my head jerking up. It wasn't only Naries arriving today. A few of the senior fearmancer girls, ones I didn't know that well, had just come onto the green, carrying their posh tote bags. If they had larger luggage, no doubt their chauffeurs or the school staff would be carrying that.

The three of them were staring at me, hostility in their eyes, fear wafting off them to congeal in my chest. The aggressive posturing was a front. They saw me as just as dangerous as the maintenance staff woman had the other morning.

"I didn't hurt anyone," I said, willing my voice not to shake. "I found her body—that's all."

"That doesn't seem to be what the investigators think," one of the girls said. Her gaze dropped to my arms, and I could tell she'd noted the recording cuffs, although she couldn't comment on them in front of Shelby. "I think I'll steer clear, thanks."

She raised her chin with a faint sniff, and the girls started to march on, giving me a wide berth. I'd have left it at that, but Shelby took a step toward them, her voice unexpectedly taut.

"You obviously don't know Rory at all," she said. "She's the last person who'd ever attack someone, let alone —let alone *that*."

"Shelby," I said quietly, even though her defense made my heart squeeze with gratitude. The last thing she needed was for her friendship with me to make her an even bigger target.

"What the hell do you know?" the first girl snapped.

"A lot more than you do. She's the only non-scholarship student in this place who's *never* been an asshole to me." Shelby gave the girls a pointed look as if to remind them of the times when they'd probably been assholes too. "So why don't you shut up about things you don't know anything about?"

The girls looked from Shelby to me, and another quiver of fear seeped into me. They turned and went into the building with an audible huff but no other comment. Shelby drew herself up a little straighter.

"That felt good," she said. "I'm tired of just putting up with them talking crap—especially when it's about you too. How could anyone think *you'd* murder someone?"

You have no idea, I thought but couldn't say. I wasn't allowed to tell her anything about magic or fearmancer politics… and even if I could, at this point my life was such a mess I wasn't sure she'd have been able to wrap her head around it.

"People look for the easiest person to blame," I offered, and she nodded as if that was explanation enough. As she hefted her cello, I noted the silver chain with the violin charm I'd given her still hanging around her neck. I'd warded that charm to defend her from any spells cast her way.

"Let me help you with your stuff," I said, reaching to grab her suitcase. As I bent down, I murmured a few words under my breath to propel more magic into the charm. After a week away, its effects would have faded.

And as much as I appreciated Shelby's growing confidence, I knew just how much trouble it could get her into too.

CHAPTER EIGHT

Rory

I discovered Malcolm was back in residence when I stepped out of my dorm room that evening. He was standing in the hallway outside, in the process of cuffing a boy who didn't look more than sixteen across the head while two other junior students looked on.

My lips parted with an automatic protest. The juniors had all glanced up the second the door had opened, even the one Malcolm was harassing, and three waves of terror coursed into my chest. At that sensation, my mouth snapped shut before a sound had left it.

"I'd better not see you skulking around the senior dorms again," Malcolm said, aiming a menacing glower at all three of them. With bobbed heads and meek postures, the juniors fled for the stairs.

By the time they'd disappeared from view, my nerves had settled. I gave Malcolm a skeptical look. "Is it really necessary to resort to physical violence just because they wanted to check out the place?"

I got the impression he'd only just held himself back from glowering at me too. "That's not all they were doing, Glinda. I caught them whispering to each other about some big plan to see if they could provoke you. Two of the nitwits had dared the other to bang on your door and pick a fight."

To see whether they could get me to attack him like I supposedly had Imogen? My stomach turned. I guessed I shouldn't be surprised. It was just like fearmancers to goad each other on like that, and the juniors weren't quite as careful in their attempts at bravado.

"Well, you didn't need to step in," I said, pulling the door all the way shut behind me. "I'm pretty sure I could have sent them off no problem on my own, without maiming anyone in the process. Or are you rethinking your stance on my innocence and you were hassling them for their own protection?"

Malcolm's jaw worked. "This is my job as the heir of Nightwood. I know you don't like it, Rory, but the scions are meant to exercise their authority—to keep the rest of the community in line. If you don't start now, no one's going to listen to you when you take your spot at the barons' table."

I wasn't in the mood to get into an argument with him about this of all subjects. "I think I'll find other ways to 'exercise my authority'," I replied, and headed for the stairs.

"It's for their good too," Malcolm called after me. "If

no one lays down the law when they're breaking it in small stupid ways, imagine how much trouble they'll get into the next time around."

Unfortunately, that logic did have at least a little sense to it, even if the last thing I wanted to do was *agree* with Malcolm on his approach to student relations. I settled for ignoring him as I left him behind.

Jude had texted me asking me to meet him in "the music room." Nightwood Tower, which held all of the university's classrooms, had at least a few different spaces for rehearsing music, but I knew from past experience which one the Killbrook scion would have meant.

The room with the piano was right up near the top of the tower. A graceful melody seeped out as I nudged open the door.

Jude was already sitting at the piano, his fingers dancing over the keys with an easy confidence. He didn't look up in acknowledgement, but a few additional flourishes crept into the tune with my entrance. A satisfied smile curled his lips. I leaned back against the door and let the music wash over me. It was a shame, really, that he kept this talent a secret. He was very good.

He finished with a chain of finger work that sped through the notes so quickly his hand became a blur. Then he turned with a little bow. I laughed as I gave my applause. "Show off."

"If you've got it, flaunt it," Jude said with a wink. He scooted over and patted the bench beside him. "Come here?"

I sank down next to him, and he tucked his arm

around my waist. Sitting there in the small but airy room, I couldn't stop my mind from slipping back to the last time I'd spoken to him here. The time when he'd confessed that he knew he wasn't really the heir to the Killbrook barony—that he wasn't a Killbrook at all. When his parents had failed to produce an heir, they'd arranged for his mother to get pregnant with another man under the influence of magic.

And now his parents were expecting a new baby, one that would be the real heir. One that made Jude not only expendable but a liability. His father wouldn't want anyone finding out about his deception.

I was the only person Jude had dared to tell. Not even the other scions knew. Being with me wasn't just about having a good time for him, despite the carefree airs he feigned so well. I might be the only fearmancer he knew who wouldn't shun him when they found out the truth of his parentage.

Maybe Jude had guessed the direction my thoughts had wandered in. He rested his free hand lightly on the keys and played a few soft notes. "If I've got any natural talent, it came from my real father," he said, looking at the piano rather than me. His floppy dark copper hair fell forward to shadow his eyes. "That's actually why I started teaching myself in the first place. I figured out who he was not that long before I started here, looked him up, and found out everything I could about him."

I scooted closer and tipped my head to Jude's shoulder. "Do you think you could ever tell him what happened—who you are?"

He shook his head. "It'd just make a bigger mess. And I don't think he'd want to know. He was married when it happened—he's got his own kids. I don't want to ruin his life, for what? He'd probably hate me because of what my parents did to him to make it happen."

"It wasn't your fault."

"No, but it's the only reason I'm here." He reached and shut the keyboard cover before turning to me. "Let's not dwell on that, though. I had much more enjoyable reasons for asking you to meet me here."

I raised an eyebrow. "Did you?"

He smiled slyly and touched his nose to mine as his breath warmed my lips. "Who do you think you're talking to?" His fingers teased into my hair and traced over my scalp, sending a giddy shiver through me. "You've had to spend your summer break worrying about all kinds of crap. I think you deserve a chance to leave all that behind." He brushed a kiss to my cheek, then my jaw, then the corner of my mouth, until my lips ached for contact. His voice dropped to a murmur. "I've never been with a girl up here before."

"No?" I said, just barely holding back a gasp when he nipped the crook of my neck.

"You're the only one who's ever gotten to see my musical side." He paused and looked me straight in the eyes. "The only one I would have wanted to share that side of me with."

The emotion in those words made my pulse skip a beat. Before I could answer, he was kissing me the way I'd wanted, his mouth capturing mine, his hands in my hair and on my waist pulling me even closer to him.

Jude had bragged to me once about his extensive experience in this area, and while I couldn't say I enjoyed thinking about the many other girls he might have gotten hot and heavy with, I had no complaints about benefiting from all that practice. With each kiss, my lips tingled hotter. They parted, and his tongue slipped past them to duel with mine. An eager flush was already spreading through my entire body.

Maybe this was only a temporary escape from the problems looming over me, but damn, it was a thrilling one.

Jude turned his attentions to my neck, making each inch of my skin light up with pleasure. His fingers danced up my side as if playing a melody on my ribs and stroked my breast through my silk blouse. A whimper worked from my throat at the rush of sensation.

I slid my hands up under his shirt, ignoring the wobble of the thin silver cuffs at my wrists, wanting to feel as much of him as I could. His lean muscles shifted at my touch. I swept my palms over his nipples, and he groaned with a sear of breath against my neck.

"I never knew it was possible to want someone this much until I met you," he said in a rasp.

My agreement came out as a shaky chuckle lost in the crash of his mouth against mine. As we kissed even more hungrily, his hand eased my skirt up my thigh, his fingers tracing patterns on the sensitive skin as they climbed. A throbbing heat built where my legs met.

An urgent sound escaped me that was almost a growl, and Jude grinned against my lips. He cupped my sex, somehow relieving the ache of need and sharpening it at the same time.

With each swivel of his fingers, bliss pulsed up from my core. My breath trembled between kisses. Jude rose off the bench, tipping me over so I lay on my back and tugging my panties off at the same time. He bent over me to claim my mouth once more, but before I could do more than run my hands down his chest, he was pulling back.

"I haven't gotten to taste you yet," he said with a mischievous gleam in his eyes. Tugging at my hips, he slid me to the far end of the bench. My knees bent to keep my feet on the wooden surface for balance—and splayed around his head as he knelt between my thighs.

"Fuck," I muttered as he pressed his lips to a tender spot just inches from my sex. Jude hummed with satisfaction and charted a scorching path the rest of the way to my core. His mouth closed over my clit with a skillful flick of his tongue, and I couldn't hold back a moan.

My hips rocked with the movements of his mouth. Every thought fled my mind except the awareness of the waves of pleasure rushing through me. He sucked hard on my clit and then grazed it with the tips of his teeth, and I outright bucked with a cry of longing. My head tipped back against the bench.

Jude devoured me with renewed intensity, his tongue slicking right inside me, and I came apart with a shudder of limbs and breath. The ecstasy rolled through me all the way up to my head and down to my toes.

It wasn't enough. When he raised his head, I tangled my fingers in his hair and urged him back up over me. "I want everything," I said.

"Who am I to deny you?" he said with a rough laugh. He snapped his belt open and made short work of his pants, leaning over me. As he kissed me again, my taste tart on his lips, his hand slid under my ass to pull me even closer to the edge, raising my hips at the same time. My ankles crossed behind his waist instinctively. He dipped his head just long enough to speak the quick protective casting, and then he plunged into me so hard and fast I moaned again.

I was so ready, and the angle he held me at sent his cock through me with the perfect sear of pleasure. He kissed my mouth, my shoulder, my breasts through my blouse, his free hand branding me everywhere as the other held my hips in place. I caressed his lean body everywhere I could reach, but it was hard to focus on anything except the peak I was hurtling toward with each thrust.

I arched into him, he adjusted my hips against him just slightly, and his cock hit a spot inside me that set off an even more electric burst of pleasure. "Faster," I pleaded. He complied with a groan. He filled me again and again, pressing that blissful spot over and over, and I lost myself completely.

My back bowed, my legs quivered, and pleasure crashed over me so forcefully that sparks went off behind my eyes. "Oh," I mumbled, with another quake as Jude came shuddering with me.

He rocked to a stop, still holding me to him, bent over me where I lay on the bench. Pleasure had hazed his eyes and softened the sharp angles of his face. I touched his cheek with a rush of affection. He gazed down at me with a smile I couldn't have called anything but joyful.

In an impressive show of physical maneuvering, he managed to collect me against him so he could sit down on the bench with me straddling him, barely breaking the contact between our bodies. He leaned back against the closed piano and wrapped his arms around me. I nestled my head against his shoulder with a contented sigh. His arms tightened.

"I know we talked about it before," he said quietly, "but I want to say it again, just to be clear. I don't care about being part of the barony. I just want you in my life, any way I can have you. If some secret Bloodstone sibling appeared tomorrow and proved themselves the real scion, that wouldn't change a thing. If you ever have any doubts —if you need to look inside my head—"

The earnestness of his tone made my heart skip a beat. I lifted my head to meet his eyes. "I believe you. *You* don't have to prove anything to me."

A look came over his face that was hopeful and hesitant all at once. "That's why— Everyone and everything here is bullshit. *I've* been bullshit my whole life. But now, being with you… I feel like I'm figuring out how to be someone real." A tiny bit of fear shivered from him into me. His voice came out even lower than before, "I love you, Rory."

An ache spread through my chest at the nervousness he'd felt admitting those three words. My emotions were too cluttered for me to say them back with the certainty he'd have deserved, but I answered him the best way I could, with a kiss so tender it took my own breath away.

Jude kissed me back, holding me close, not seeming to need more than that. As he adjusted me against him, my sex brushed against an unexpected hardness in his lap. I kissed him once more and eased back with an amused smile. "Ready to go again already?"

Jude beamed at me, any anxiety he'd been feeling before gone. He shifted his hips so his erection slid against me again. "I do bring a *few* talents to the table, if not a title."

A giggle tickled up my throat. I leaned close, slipping my arms around his shoulders, and murmured in his ear, "Then make love to me."

He laughed a little breathlessly. "I've never wanted to do anything more." And as he slid inside me, I couldn't let myself believe that I'd ever have to give this up.

CHAPTER NINE

Rory

Being back in class should have made my life feel more normal, but reminders of how much had changed in the past week surrounded me. Except for Connar, the students in my current Persuasion seminar reacted with varying tremors of fear when I walked into the room. The girl at the desk next to the one I took scooted farther away on her seat. I heard someone behind me murmuring to a friend that they didn't need to worry because of the blacksuit "bracelets" I had on.

And then there was our teacher. Professor Crowford strode in looking like his usual aging ladies'-man self, his mostly silver hair falling artfully on either side of his heavy-lidded eyes. In his particular case, the problem wasn't that anything about *him* had changed. I simply knew more about him than I had before. Like that he'd thought it was a great idea to encourage all the fearmancer students here for summer term to manipulate the Nary students as far as they could.

Like the fact that Professor Banefield had included him on a list of people involved with my biggest enemies, the barons.

Crowford didn't appear to pay any special attention to me when he came to a stop in front of his desk. He leaned against it and rubbed his hands together with a smile of anticipation.

"Good to see you all back. I hope you enjoyed your break—longer for some of you than others—and that you're ready to dive back into your learning."

Heads nodded along the rows of desks. Crowford pushed off the desk again and started to pace at the front of the room. I let my gaze follow him, which was totally normal for a student. What I'd really like to learn today was not his lesson but what was going on inside his head. But a man adept in Persuasion must have also built up some pretty solid mental walls.

"I thought we'd try something a little different today," he said. "All of you are more than familiar with the most common use of persuasion spells, which is to influence another person's mind. But for those of you who aren't particularly strong in some other domains, you may be interested to hear that a talent in persuasion can be adapted to compensate for certain other skills. For example, you may not be able to conjure an object out of thin air, but with enough practice you can 'persuade' something already there to move or alter its shape in basic ways."

To supplement a person's abilities in Physicality. I had to admit that was kind of interesting, even though I already enjoyed working in the Physicality domain more than Persuasion. That kind of flexibility must apply to other skills as well. Jude had told me he was only actually strong in two areas, not three, but he'd managed to convince the professors that he had the same three strengths as the other scions all this time.

As Crowford drew in a breath, I said my insight casting word under my breath with just the slightest nudge of power. I wasn't launching an assault yet, just testing the terrain.

My awareness tapped against a barrier around the professor's mind. To my careful prodding, it felt firmer than any I'd encountered before.

I drew my focus back. Getting in there, especially getting in unnoticed, would take a lot of work. Maybe not something I could risk while the blacksuits' cuffs were recording every spell I cast.

Crowford motioned to us. "Let's start with a small test you can all participate in. Take out some small object you have on you—a pen, a coin, a keycard—and set it on your desk. See if you can persuade it to move from one side of the desk to the other, using *only* your persuasive abilities. No physicality spells allowed."

The first thing in my purse that my fingers closed around was a pack of gum. That seemed small enough. I set it at the left side of my desk and considered my approach.

A pack of gum didn't have a mind to cast on. How was I supposed to direct my spell?

Professor Crowford chuckled. "I see many of you looking puzzled. As an additional tip, let me remind you that all magic is about the transfer of energy. When you persuade someone's mental state, your magic is acting on the energy in their brain. Every object contains a certain amount of energy down to its atoms. Convince that energy to act."

Right. I frowned at the pack of gum and drew some of my magic into the back of my throat. When I concentrated, I could sense a faint hum of... not awareness, but *presence* from the little cardboard case.

"*Slide*," I ordered it in my best persuasive tone, willing the energy be inclined to shift sideways. The box twitched and traveled half an inch to the right. A smile crossed my lips. Not bad for a start.

It took ten minutes or so, but I managed to compel the gum all the way across my desk. From the whispered voices around me, everyone else was intent on the assignment as well. Professor Crowford strolled between the desks, offering words of encouragement and assistance as needed. When he reached me, he watched for a few seconds and then said only, "Nicely done."

As the rest of the class finished with their attempts, he took his position at his desk again. "Let's try something a little more substantial. Miss Scarlow, you've worked from this angle before, clearly. Would you like to show the class just how large an effect you can pull off. Say..." He glanced around and pointed to the wooden cabinet in the corner. "Lift and rotate the cabinet."

"I think I can do that, sir," the girl said, her cheeks flushing eagerly at having been singled out as a worthy example.

I guessed she'd have to persuade the air around the piece of furniture that it was meant to push upward and then around? Using that type of magic to move something that big and heavy seemed absurd to me, but presumably showing the limitations of this kind of spell was the point of this lesson.

It was possible to move that large an object, in any case. The girl said her casting under her breath, and then added a few more words, and the cabinet wobbled a few inches into the air. It edged up inch by inch until it hovered a foot off the ground.

Triumph lit her face as she spoke again with more casting words that meant nothing to me. The cabinet swayed and began to turn in a slow but steady circle. Someone behind me drew in a breath in awe.

Then the classroom door opened with a squeak of the hinges and voices in mid-conversation.

Everyone startled and looked over. Professor Crowford made a cutting gesture with his hand, and the girl who'd been casting blanched. The cabinet thudded to the floor as she released the spell. We all stared at the four figures in the doorway who were now staring back at us.

They were Naries. I recognized a couple of the guys from my summer project activities, and there was Shelby just behind them with another girl. All Naries... and they'd almost walked in on us in the middle of a magical demonstration. My heart started to thud almost as loud as the cabinet's fall. Weren't there supposed to be protections against that kind of intrusion?

"I believe you've come to the wrong room," Crowford said in a cold tone.

"I—the schedule said—" the boy at the front of the group stuttered. He looked down at the paper in his hand and winced. "Crap. I could swear I re-checked this three times because we don't usually go to this room. I'm really sorry about the interruption."

They retreated together, Shelby shooting me a quick smile when she spotted me just before the boy yanked the door shut again.

"*That* could have been disastrous," the professor muttered, which didn't do anything to settle my nerves. Or those of my classmates, from the look of the faces around me. "They're getting awfully bold."

I didn't see what boldness had to do with it when it'd been a mistaken reading of a schedule. But a shadow flickered across most of the other mages' faces at those words. "Should we do anything?" one of the guys asked.

Crowford cocked his head. "Perhaps it would be good to leave them with a negative impression of this intrusion, if anyone has an appropriate idea?"

"I'll knock one down the stairs," another guy volunteered, sounding way too eager, and leapt right into his casting. My pulse hiccupped for a totally different reason. Any of the Naries could get really hurt if he pulled that off.

There wasn't time to protest. As soon as he used his magic to sense their position, he'd attack. I swiped my hand across my mouth to hide the word I spat out in a whisper with a sharp breath. "Shield."

With every ounce of my concentration, I flung my protective spell through the door, willing it to fill the entire stairwell. It snapped into place an instant before the guy's casting hurtled into it. A jolt ran over my skin as the contrasting magic dissipated against each other.

The guy sat back in his seat with a smirk. Clearly he hadn't been able to tell that his spell had been blocked before it'd reached its target. Better for me.

Crowford gave an approving nod that made my stomach turn. "We offer them so much already," he said in apparent scorn, and switched back into teaching mode.

As he talked further about the manipulation of inanimate objects using persuasion, I stayed tensed in my seat. The entire sequence of events ran through my head on repeat. With each iteration, my heart sank a little more.

When class let out, I hung back so I could leave with Connar, who'd been sitting in the back. He caught my eye with a slight tip of his head in acknowledgment. I walked slowly to give the other students the lead, waiting until they'd disappeared around the bend in the stairs.

"That was weird, right?" I said in a low voice. "The Naries coming in—the way Professor Crowford reacted… I know I haven't been here that long, but it's been a couple terms, and that's the first time I've seen something like that happen."

"I've never seen a mistake like that either," Connar

said. "I guess everyone makes mistakes from time to time, and it isn't surprising that Crowford might have forgotten to put the protections in place at the beginning of class…"

His doubtful tone bolstered my conviction. "But it'd be an awfully huge coincidence for him to forget at the exact time a Nary somehow repeatedly misread the number on his schedule, wouldn't it? And… it all happened really fast, but I'd swear he motioned for what's-her-name to drop the cabinet before he had a chance to see who it was. Why would he have assumed the people at the door were Naries?"

Connar considered me. "Are you saying you think that he knew it would happen ahead of time? That he *meant* for it to happen?"

"I don't know. That seems awfully weird too." I rubbed my arms, even though the dry tower air was only pleasantly cool, not cold, compared to the lingering summer heat we'd face outside. "I just don't like it. It felt… like it happened as an excuse to hurt them."

"Yeah," Connar said quietly. He scowled at the steps. "You've got enough to worry about as it is, Rory. I'll keep an eye on him and watch for anything else that seems strange. I don't think that incident had anything to do with you, at least."

Thank God for small mercies? I forced a smile. "True. What are you doing now? Maybe we could—"

We stepped out into the sunlit green outside, and my voice halted at the sight of the woman waiting just beyond the tower. Lillian Ravenguard had been standing with her hands on her hips, her stance poised but not tense with that leonine grace of hers. She moved to meet me the moment I came into view.

"Rory," she said with a warmth I no longer trusted. "I was told you should be out of class soon. Can I talk to you for a few minutes?"

Her gaze passed over Connar's brawny frame with what looked like professional attention, as if she were sizing him up. Even though he could have handled a hell of a lot more fight than I could, I bristled instinctively inside. I didn't want anyone targeting my guys in the plot against me.

"Sure," I said, and shot Connar a quick smile. "I'll see you later."

He nodded with a wary glance toward Lillian. I suspected he wasn't going to stray too far from where he saw us go.

Lillian started to amble toward Ashgrave Hall, and I fell into step beside her. "What's going on?" I asked. "Is there news about the hearing?" A nervous quiver raced through my chest. They hadn't arranged it early despite Declan's efforts, had they?

"It's been set for next Wednesday," Lillian said. "You'll have a little more than your two weeks to prepare... however you intend to prepare." She peered at me sideways. "Are you sure coming back to the school was the wisest idea? I wouldn't tell you what to do, of course, but I promise you my own investigations will cover every aspect of the situation."

She wouldn't tell me what to do, no. She'd only lie to me about the authority she was claiming and what my rights were. I caught myself before I gritted my teeth in annoyance.

"Even if I can't find anything useful myself, I'd rather be living life as normally as possible as long as I can rather than be shut away in that holding room."

She chuckled. "Spoken as your mother would have. Fair enough. That wasn't actually the main reason I wanted to talk to you. Have you experienced anything unusual in the last few days?"

Was that question some new part of their plot to establish my incompetence? "Unusual how?" I asked.

"Just a sensation in or around your body, maybe quite faint, that you didn't recognize and couldn't see a cause for. Maybe something you'd have taken for a spell."

My brow knit as I thought back. "Not that I can remember. Why? Do you think someone might have been casting on me?" Had they and she was confirming that they'd done it subtly enough that I hadn't noticed?

Lillian didn't look comforted by my answer, though. She rubbed her mouth. "You never know, when you've drawn this much attention... Have you seen any other illusions, even if not on the same scale as the ones around the murder, that appeared to be aimed at you?"

"No, nothing like that either." My throat had started to tighten. I stopped before we'd finished passing the hall. "Is there something I need to be worried about—to watch out for?"

I wasn't sure she'd tell me if so, but I got the impression she was actually bothered by this line of questioning. She might have wanted to help speed along my downfall, but only her way. If someone had other designs on me, she could very well decide to protect me from those.

But Lillian shook her head. "I just wanted to be sure. If anything like that does come up, you get in touch with me right away, all right? And I'll keep tracking down our leads to make sure you come out of that hearing with the right verdict."

She turned and patted my arm. Her hand brushed my skin with a faint prick as if from the rough edge of a ring. It faded before I'd even registered it, and then she was hurrying away with one last wave.

I studied my forearm, but the skin appeared unbroken. There wasn't even a pink spot as if it'd been pinched. I might have only imagined the hint of pain after all her talk about odd sensations. Given the circumstances, though, I'd ask one of the guys to check my arm just to be sure she hadn't cast some covert spell on me.

Whatever that sensation had been, I had no doubt at all that she hadn't told me the real reason behind her questions.

CHAPTER TEN

Jude

I 'd never enjoyed calling home—really, I'd avoided doing it unless absolutely necessary. Since my mother's announcement about her pregnancy, any contact had gotten even more uncomfortable, on my end at least. So, I might have procrastinated for around a half hour, tidying my room and reviewing my most recent class assignment, before I finally convinced myself to pick up the phone. But I did pick it up.

My body sank into the plump feather pillow I'd braced against my bed's headboard. The fresh breeze slipping through the half-open window carried a pleasant hint of the autumn to come, but every muscle in my body tensed as I placed the call.

It was Mom who answered, of course. If Dad was in the vicinity of a phone, he'd have taken one look at the call display and promptly turned away. I was counting on Mom to get me access.

"Jude!" she said in her typically over-exuberant way. "I didn't expect to hear from you so soon. Is everything all right?"

She'd always acted as if she thought she could make up for Dad's coldness by showering me with appreciation, and that hadn't changed even with the baby on the way. Had she even thought about what the new arrival was going to mean for me? She'd stuck with Dad all this time despite what he'd made her do and how he'd treated her and me afterward... Had she convinced herself that they'd somehow quietly swap heirs without any harm coming to me?

"Nothing's wrong," I said. No need to make her anxious. "School's the same old school. How are you doing?"

I didn't really *want* to hear about my impending sibling, but showing an interest would make her more likely to advocate for me after.

"Oh, you know, this is the easy part, really. The baby's been kicking a little harder the last couple days. She's obviously a strong one."

I had to partly tune out her voice while she rambled a little more about the kid who was essentially my death sentence, but I needed that space anyway to gather my resolve. My mind traveled back to yesterday night with Rory, to the terrifying but exhilarating release of telling the heir of Bloodstone how much she meant to me.

Our interlude in the piano room had been amazing in

so many ways. The truth was, though, that the moment I thought back to with the most satisfaction was simply holding her in my arms and feeling her relax in my embrace. To know that she trusted me to support her, that I'd somehow *earned* that trust… No sexual bliss could top that.

I could do this for her. Even if it made me feel sick to my stomach; even if it was going to take every ounce of my self-control. She needed me to fight for her in every way I could. I might have let down an awful lot of people in my life, but she wasn't going to be one of them.

When Mom's chatter fell into a lull, I drew in a breath, my free hand clenching around the bedspread.

"Could you get Dad? There's something I wanted to ask him about."

The question startled Mom into a few seconds of silence. I was pretty sure I'd never asked to speak to my father in all the years I'd boarded at the university. "Yes," she said, wrenching herself out of her shock. "Yes, of course, I'll— I'm sure he'll have a moment. Let me go get him."

She hadn't been able to hide the uneasiness in her voice. She knew as well as I did that it didn't matter how many "moments" Dad had, he wouldn't want to give any of them to me. I was counting on her being tenacious enough—and him being softened a little by the heir on the way—to get him on the line.

The dead air while I waited stretched across one minute and then another. I shifted restlessly on the bed. I didn't have much of a backup plan if he refused to talk to me at all.

There was an abrupt rustling as the phone on the other end was lifted. Dad's voice carried to my ear, distant and brisk. "Your mother said you wanted to speak to me."

With less than ten words, he could make me feel like I was barely worth the dust on his shoe. I closed my eyes and reminded myself of why I was doing this. Of the caramel sweet smell of Rory's hair and the way she smiled at me.

To her, I was someone who mattered.

"Yes," I said in my most pleasant tone. "I mean, we haven't really talked since…" *Since ever.* "…since all the plans for the new baby started. How was your tennis match yesterday?" I might not have a remotely close relationship with my father, but I still listened well enough to know what he was up to.

"Fine. I'm assuming there's something else."

Okay, so making friendly conversation wasn't going to get me anywhere. I hadn't figured it would, but it'd been worth a shot. Down to business then.

I sat up straighter, as if I could convey my posture over the phone. "Yes. But it's not for me. You know I handle my own affairs just fine." As he preferred. "It's about Rory Bloodstone."

"What about the Bloodstone scion?" Dad asked, sounding more attentive all of a sudden. That seemed like a good sign.

I launched into my pitch. "Obviously you know about the accusations she's facing. I've gathered since she's been released temporarily to the school that there are complications with proving her innocence. From what I've seen of her, there's no way she could be responsible for the attack, but she doesn't have many resources on her own. If one or more of the barons spoke up on her behalf, I'd imagine—"

Dad cut me off, twice as cold as before. "If she's to be baron, she needs to learn to fend for herself too."

My throat tightened. "She's only known fearmancers *exist* for a few months. Her entire family is gone. The barons have gone to bat for each other before—it's hardly unprecedented. Wouldn't it be better for all of you to have her unencumbered by—"

"What makes you so concerned about her future?"

I'd been prepared for a question along that line, but my back stiffened anyway. If he thought I was asking for personal rather than professional reasons, he'd never want to agree.

"I'm concerned about the barony," I said. "Shouldn't I be? It's my future too. Strong, united leadership is what keeps our society in line."

Either Dad didn't buy that explanation or he didn't care what my reasons were—it only mattered that I was the one asking. "If Bloodstone has the strength to be part of that unity, this hearing will determine that," he said firmly. "No scion or baron should need to send others begging on their behalf."

"I'm not— She didn't—" I started, but the phone hung up with a definitive click.

My fingers squeezed around my own phone. I forced

myself to lower it without hurling it across the room in frustration, glaring at the wardrobe across from me the way I should have been glaring at my father.

The barons had the perfect opportunity to solidify Rory's role in their midst. If they stood up for her now, she'd see being part of the pentacle had some benefits, the way she'd come to trust me after I'd shown I'd be there for her. How the hell did they expect to accomplish anything if they never found a way to accept her into the fold?

But I'd heard it in Dad's voice. He cared more about thwarting my request than about what it would mean for his career. Fuck, I might even have made him *less* inclined to help Rory by asking.

Even with a real heir on the way, even when he was the one who'd created our family situation in the first place, he hated me that much.

I dropped my head into my hands and pressed my palms to my forehead. Why did I even let myself care what he thought? I knew who he was and what he'd done. I'd tried my best… and this was where it got me.

Why was I waiting around for him to sever me from his life when I could decide what I did with mine all on my own?

A tenuous but hopeful sense of resolve rose up inside me. I didn't have a solution to any of the larger problems Rory and I were facing, but I could at least pull myself completely out from under Dad's thumb for as long as I had until he upped the ante.

I got off the bed, glanced out the window, and was diverted by a scene that appeared to be in the process of unfolding. A couple of Naries were just heading out of view in the direction of Rory's clubhouse… and a few of my fellow fearmancer students were slinking along a careful distance behind. I didn't like the look of that at all.

When I strode out of the building, the mages I'd seen were still lurking several feet away from the clubhouse. Connar and I had checked the wards Rory had buried beneath the place when we'd returned to school, so I knew their magic had been holding steady, but they were still small in the grand scheme of things. A concentrated assault could break them.

I sauntered over to the other students—seniors, but newly promoted ones, the guy on the right sporting straggles of hair he must be attempting to call a moustache. I didn't think any of them had been here for the summer session.

"Hey," I said in a casual voice as I joined them. Their murmured conversation fell silent as they all turned wary but respectful gazes on me. I might not know them well, but they knew who I was. Everyone recognized the scions.

I nodded toward the clubhouse. "You know that was Rory Bloodstone's summer project, don't you? If you mess with it… you're messing with her. Maybe not the wisest idea, just as a tip."

I didn't like the fact that my warning would have twice as much impact given the crime Rory had recently been accused of, but the end result was worth it. The guys paled, mumbled acknowledgment, and backed away with enough wide-eyed worry to convince me they wouldn't be striking at the Naries' new safe spot any time soon.

Footsteps hissed through the grass behind me. I looked around to see Sinclair coming over. She glanced after the retreating guys and gave me a tight smile.

"Still fighting her battles for her, huh?" She flicked her sleek black bob back from her shoulder. "You've made yourself into a real knight in shining armor. It's kind of pathetic."

Did she really think I'd ever cared what *she* thought of me? We'd barely talked outside of our occasional tumbles into bed. At most we'd been acquaintances with benefits, and since I'd set my sights on Rory, even that small connection had ended.

"You're entitled to your opinion," I said nonchalantly. "In my role as knight, I should probably let you know that you and Victory and the rest had better keep your distance if you want to keep *any* favor with the pentacle."

She let out a huff. "You don't want to worry about that. Malcolm made it very clear to Victory that he expected her to back off, and you know what she's like about him. She still thinks she's going to marry him someday." Her tone made it clear how ridiculous she found that idea.

I hadn't known that Malcolm had not only reconsidered his approach to Rory but been publicly enforcing a cease-fire too. With a jab of uneasiness, my mind tripped back to the claim he'd tried to stake on the Bloodstone scion not long after she'd arrived here. Even when he'd been determined to tear her down, he'd wanted first dibs on picking up the pieces and winning her heart.

He'd torn into me when I'd made my intentions to pursue her clear.

Rory had only proven herself more spectacular since then. What were the chances he didn't still want her? Ha. The question was more… what were the chances she'd want him, if he made his amends thoroughly enough? She'd forgiven *me*, after all.

How much room would be left for me if he made a move? As an actual fucking scion, with all the strength and clout that came with that, he had a hell of a lot more to offer than I did. And I didn't think he'd like the idea of sharing.

I shook those worries away. Rory would do what made her happiest, and that was the way it should be. I couldn't dwell on uncomfortable hypotheticals.

Especially when I had a very definite malicious force right here in front of me.

I studied Sinclair. "And you'd never go behind Victory's back?"

"No," she said tartly. "I wouldn't. I happen to know what loyalty is."

Was that supposed to be a jab at *me*? I raised my eyebrows as I crossed my arms over my chest. "I didn't make you any promises I didn't mean, Sinclair. I didn't make you any promises at all. We had a little fun—and you were having plenty of fun with other guys at the same time—and now that's done. I never owed you more than that."

She sniffed. "I guess I just expected that if you ditched me, my replacement would meet a higher standard."

A flicker of anger shot through me at the implication that Rory was somehow less than the girl who'd made the remark—or that what I had with her was only a replacement for the scrap of a relationship before. I held it in check with a sharp smile of my own.

"All that proves is you don't know very much at all, Sinclair. I'm so glad we could have this chat."

I set off for the hall that bore my father's last name without a backward glance. If Sinclair wanted to stew in bitterness, let her, as long as she left Rory alone.

It'd been months since I'd last paid a visit to the professor who was assigned as my mentor. Regular meetings were only scheduled during a student's first year, and after that you talked only as either party deemed necessary. I hadn't made much use of that opportunity in general. It was no wonder that surprise was the first reaction that flashed across Professor Burnbuck's face when he saw me at his office door.

The senior Illusion professor recovered quickly. "Mr. Killbrook," he said, motioning me in. "To what do I owe the unexpected pleasure?" Burnbuck could give all due deference without being afraid to work in a subtle criticism about my neglect of this resource. That was one of the reasons I liked him, as much as I liked any of the staff.

I dropped into the seat in front of his desk and folded my hands in my lap. "One time you mentioned a friend of yours who does independent work with her illusion magic. I was hoping you could tell me more about that."

Burnbuck gave me a curious look. "Any particular reason why?"

I shrugged and grinned at him. "Let's just say I was thinking it might be good to expand my horizons."

And if those horizons didn't involve Baron Killbrook being anywhere in sight, so much the better.

CHAPTER ELEVEN

Rory

I settled in on the scion lounge sofa, my legs stretched across the pliant cushions and the welcome silence of the basement room wrapping around me, and for the first time I felt like the space could really be mine. I'd avoided coming down here for most of my time at Blood U because it'd been too much Malcolm's domain. Too much a reminder of the other scions' initial hostility.

But most of that hostility had transformed into anything but animosity by now, and even Malcolm appeared to have suspended his campaign against me. There wasn't any better place on campus to meet up with other scions in private. And, hell, I *was* a scion too. I had every right to use the lounge.

I got to enjoy that comfortable sense of confidence for about two minutes. Then Malcolm walked into the room.

I tensed automatically. He blinked as if making sure he was seeing right but then strolled on past me without any further indication that he thought it was strange I was down here. I watched him make his way to the bar cabinet, tucking my feet closer to me so I could easily jump up if I felt the need to escape.

"What are you up to down here?" he asked in a mild tone. Ice from the little freezer next to the cabinet rattled into his glass, followed by a hiss of poured alcohol.

"I'm supposed to be meeting Declan," I said. "He wasn't sure exactly when he'd get back."

"Am I allowed to ask what you're meeting him about?"

Declan had said he'd have some reports on the joymancers for me—hard copies, like before, so there wouldn't be any electronic trail suggesting I'd had to work to skew my testimony. Knowing how Malcolm felt about the magical opposition, I wasn't inclined to find out what he'd think of my current strategy. For all I knew, he'd tip off his dad.

"It isn't any of your business," I said.

He turned with the glass in his hand and took a sip of the amber liquid. "Fine. You don't have to sit there all tense like I'm going to spring an attack. I told you, I don't want to fight anymore—and I remember very well what you said you'd do if I so much as touched you again." He gave me a wry smile. "But I'm also not going to leave just because you're here."

I guessed that was fair. And I cringed a little remembering my threat to break every bone in his hands.

We'd *both* gotten carried away that day in the boathouse, and with everything that had happened after, I didn't really believe he'd intended to force me into anything I didn't want.

It was kind of hard to hold the intensity of that moment against him when half of the reason his presence unnerved me was how much I'd enjoyed... well, having him against me, for the brief time before logic and panic had set in.

I let myself sink into the back of the sofa, but I kept my legs bent close. "I'm not asking you to leave, but I think I'm justified in a certain amount of caution, no matter how many white flags you're waving. You've put me through a lot more than just that moment by the lake. I hope you don't think my memory's that short."

He shrugged and, with a casual ease that made my skin itch, sat down at the other end of the sofa. It was a three seater, so a few feet of empty space remained between us, but I'd have preferred a few dozen.

"You came into the university guns blazing, insulting me and everything I care about," he said. "I can admit that I should have realized sooner that you didn't understand what you were getting into. Like I said before, we can hash out what I should be apologizing for when everything's simmered down. But I'm *not* going to apologize for defending myself, the scions, or fearmancer society in general when it seemed necessary. Just so we're clear."

Damn it. With every word he said, I wanted more and more to smack the cool self-assurance out of him, but at the same time he made it sound so fucking *reasonable*. As if he hadn't already proven himself to be an asshole before I'd said a single word to him.

"You can see it however you want," I said. "But I'll just point out that the first time I ever insulted you, it was after *you* had just mocked the people who raised me—my parents, who I'd watched murdered in front of me that morning. I wasn't exactly in the clearest state of mind, and I don't see why your insults get a pass while mine were some horrible offense."

Malcolm's expression darkened for a second. He turned his gaze to his glass. "So, you're still calling the joymancers who stole you your 'parents'."

"They *were* my parents." I pushed myself straighter, keeping my eyes trained on him. "Do you still think they kept me in a cage and tortured me or something like that? The worst thing they did to me was suppress my magic and not tell me that I had it. Otherwise, as far as I can tell, they did a hell of a lot better by me than the parents of most people around here. They took care of me like I was their own kid, they comforted me when I was sad, they celebrated everything I accomplished, they tried their best to make sure I was happy and safe. I never, for one second, doubted that they loved me and wanted me to have the best life they could give me."

Malcolm's head had come back up. He stared at me for a long moment, apparently lost for words. Then he made a pained grimace and took a bigger gulp of his drink. "Well, no, I wouldn't have expected that's how they'd have treated you."

Because his own parents didn't treat him anywhere

near that well? I'd been horrified by Connar's story of how his parents had compelled him and his brother into a near death match to decide who'd inherit the barony, and he'd indicated that he thought Malcolm had it even worse. I'd only met Malcolm's dad once and briefly, but he'd struck me as brutal in that short time.

If it was normal for fearmancer parents to be harsh on their kids—whatever excuses they gave about preparing them for the wider world—why would any of them imagine their enemies would treat a fearmancer with more kindness rather than less?

I didn't want to delve into the fraught relationship Malcolm might have with his parents. Maybe he could shed some light on the less personal dynamics I was still grappling with, though.

"My parents were the only joymancers I knew," I said tentatively. "They always talked positively about the magic they worked and the mages they worked with, but I never met any of the others—not while I was aware of it." Representatives from the Conclave might have observed me from afar surreptitiously. "So while I can speak up for the two of them, it's true that I don't really know their community all that well. Why do you hate them so much? Have joymancers actually *done* anything to you, or is it—"

Malcolm interrupted with a rough chuckle. "Have they done anything? Rory, they killed your fucking parents —your real parents."

My stomach twisted at the memory of the burnt bodies in the photograph. "We don't know exactly what went down that day. Maybe my parents were planning to do something harmful and that was the only way the joymancers could stop them. It's not like the barons always tell everyone else what their real plans are."

"I don't know whether they were doing more than they'd told people they were. But it wasn't just them. Declan's mom was there, and she wouldn't have been scheming with your parents. From what I've heard, the other barons saw her as a pain in the neck, always arguing against any harsher policy they were considering. And *you* were there. Maybe our ideas on parenting are different from joymancer ones, but I can tell you there's no way in hell a baron would bring her only heir into a remotely dangerous situation at two years old."

I thought of the video Lillian had shared with me of my birth mother cuddling my infant self, of the gold-encased baby shoe I'd found in the Bloodstone mansion's storage room. No, I didn't think the former Baron Bloodstone had seen me as expendable.

"My mother must have been involved in other questionable plans before," I said. "The joymancers might have gotten the wrong idea, but not out of nowhere."

"They still didn't have to kill them. They didn't have to kill Declan's mom. How the hell do you think he feels every time you sing their praises, by the way? And they didn't have to drag you away and raise you on lies. No matter how nice the people who raised you were, they stole your power and your heritage from you. That's sick."

I didn't totally disagree—and the comment about Declan made me wince. "Is there anything else?" I had to ask. "In your whole lifetime, is that the only way the joymancers have attacked fearmancers?"

Malcolm snorted. "Are you kidding me? No matter what we do, even the mages as powerful as the barons have to take all kinds of precautions to make sure the joymancers don't interfere. They cost my dad a major business deal just last year. There've been skirmishes—I'd swear the blacksuits spend at least as much time protecting all of us from joymancers as they do policing within the community. The 'Conclave' always has people skulking around up here, trying to figure out what we're doing and messing it up any way they can, even when it's totally legitimate work."

"Well, what have the fearmancers been doing to them at the same time?"

"Nothing," Malcolm shot back. "That's the one principle all the barons have agreed on for as long as I can remember. We don't engage. We stick to our territory up here and leave them to do whatever they want off at the other end of the country. If they left us alone, there'd be no fighting at all."

I wasn't sure I totally believed that. There'd been other things Malcolm hadn't known about his father's activities. But... I couldn't think of any good reason to keep it *secret* if the fearmancers launched a counter-attack. It sounded like pretty much every mage around here would have cheered on an assault.

"They've decided everything we do is evil, and that any means are acceptable when it comes to screwing with us," Malcolm went on. "You have no idea... My grandfather, the baron before my father, he's got a huge scar where his eye should be." He drew his finger from his brow down to his cheek. "Joymancers caught him when he was coming out of a consult with his *accountant*. The fact that we exist at all is a crime to them. So, who are the really bloodthirsty ones?"

I was saved from having to try to answer that question by the soft squeak of the door's hinges. Declan stepped into the lounge and paused at the sight of us in what must have been an obviously tense conversation. He caught my eye with a questioning look as if to ask if I needed help.

Malcolm shoved himself off the sofa, setting his glass with its remains of ice on the coffee table. "Don't worry, no one's been eviscerated. A little faith would be nice."

"I didn't say anything," Declan said calmly.

"Doesn't take any insight to read that face sometimes." Malcolm gave him a light clap on the shoulder as he passed the Ashgrave scion, with no sign of being actually offended. "I'll leave you to your 'meeting'."

As soon as Malcolm was gone, Declan turned to me. "Was he hassling you?"

I shook my head. "No. He was actually… okay for once. I was just asking him what he knows about joymancers."

"Ah. I'm sure he had plenty to say about that." Declan drew out a thick envelope from his shoulder bag. "I've got plenty of official material for you to look through. Take it slow. There's some stuff in there that's pretty… upsetting."

So considerate of my feelings even when it came to the people who'd murdered his mom. I swallowed hard as I stood up to take the envelope. Malcolm had made a good point on that subject. In his hostility against my parents' people, he hadn't just been defending fearmancer ideals but his closest friends as well. Maybe I'd been a little callous when it came to the Ashgrave scion's past.

"I hope you know—no matter what else I think about joymancers, I hate what they did to your mother," I said. "I'm not absolving them of that. It was awful."

Declan's mouth twitched with a hint of pain. "I know, Rory. And I'd never say every one of them is a horrible person. Your parents obviously raised you well. I just think... it's good for you to understand exactly where you came from."

"Yeah." I looked down at the envelope, its weight ominous in my hand. "I guess I'd better get on with that."

When I'd retreated to my bedroom, though, I didn't open the envelope right away. I lay down on the bed and let my thoughts stew about the information I'd already gotten from Malcolm.

Deborah's furry body scurried along my arm, coming to a stop by my shoulder. *Hard day, sweetheart?*

"You could say that." I frowned at the ceiling, debating even asking the question. But if anyone could give me an answer unbiased by fearmancer principles, it'd be her. "Deborah... The joymancers do come up here to the northeast and try to meddle with fearmancer business quite a bit, don't they?"

Well, I suppose a few take up that duty at any given time. It's not something the Conclave talks about widely. But it's the only way we can stay abreast of what they're planning and intervene as necessary.

As necessary. How did the Conclave define that? Deborah had admitted to me that they'd wanted to take down this school for as long as she could remember... but did they even *know* how the place worked if they'd never been able to observe it, or were they simply operating under that principle that all fearmancer things should be shut down?

"What about the other way around?" I said slowly. "I mean... Did the fearmancers ever come to California or wherever to attack the joymancer community down there? Other than when they found out where I was and came for me? I don't remember my parents ever seeming nervous, like they'd heard about some altercation and were worried my real people might be coming for me."

Deborah made a dismissive noise in my head. *The fearmancers know better than to tackle us on our home ground. Perhaps the Conclave became over-confident because of that, and that's how they ended up finding you. The attack on your home is the only breach of our security I know of.*

She sounded proud of that fact. Even though, from what Malcolm had just told me, the success wasn't because the joymancers were so good at protecting their own... It was because the fearmancers hadn't *tried* to break down those defenses until they'd had an unavoidable reason to.

I rubbed my forehead. I didn't even know if I objected to people interfering with the fearmancers in general. A lot of them did do a lot of awful things. But... how did killing the ones who actually pushed for moderation, like

Declan's mom, or throwing off legitimate business deals do anything other than stir up more resentment?

What if my parents hadn't been typical joymancers? What if their attitudes of compassion and acceptance had made them as much outliers in their community as Declan's family was in his?

CHAPTER TWELVE

Rory

With no one but the four of us in it, the main gymnasium felt twice as big as usual. Our voices bounced off the high ceiling as we walked over the colored lines marked on the wooden floor.

"I checked with all my usual professors," I said. "They'll all confirm that I haven't been using my own casting words with my spells." I'd half expected my current mentor, Professor Viceport, to refuse. She'd acted chilly toward me since I'd started at Blood U for no reason I'd been able to determine. But she'd actually been the most emphatic in her agreement. Maybe she was finally getting over her grudge now that she'd talked with me more and seen my skills develop over the summer.

"That's something." Declan stopped where the platform had been set up on the day of the summer project announcement and turned on his heel. "You'd have had the best view of the room when you were up here getting your certificate. See if you can settle right into that memory—watch for anyone you didn't recognize, especially someone who couldn't have been a student."

I let my mind slip back to that moment, my senses detaching from the present the way Declan had coached me. It wasn't exactly a spell, but the technique was related to Insight—a way of sharpening one's own mental impressions.

"I recognized all the teachers," I said, my voice sounding oddly detached as I focused on the memory. "And all the students there looked familiar. I don't remember seeing anyone else. I was looking pretty carefully too, because I was wondering where Imogen was."

"I didn't see anyone unexpected either," Connar put in from where he stood at my other side. "I was keeping a close eye out in case anyone tried to interrupt Rory's moment. If there was someone who didn't belong, I think I'd have noticed."

Declan sighed. "It was a long shot. It wouldn't have been smart for the culprit to make an appearance here."

We'd already tried the same trick with my memories outside and by Ashgrave Hall, on the theory that someone might have been standing watch to alert the murderer of my impending arrival. But if that'd been the case, they'd kept themselves well out of view.

Jude caught my attention with a trailing of his fingers halfway down my back. "You're still owed a prize, aren't you, Ice Queen? Unless you claimed it without telling us about it."

"No." I let out a raw laugh. "I almost forgot." For winning the summer project contest, I had the right to pick any object in my possession and bring it to the professor of my choice to ask for them to use their expertise to imbue it with a spell. I'd been caught up in the murder before I'd had much time to think about my options. "I don't suppose there are any innocence-detecting spells I could ask for?"

"Wouldn't that make life easier?" Declan gave me a crooked smile. "I'd already been considering whether your prize might come in handy, but I can't think of any spell you could request that'd make a difference to your hearing. There are ways of identifying illusions, for example, but they only work in the moment, not from memory."

"Save it for when you're sure of how it can help you the most," Connar suggested.

Lord knew there'd probably be some new problem I could use help with soon enough.

"Do you know who the judge will be now that the hearing date is set?" Jude asked Declan as we meandered back toward the entrance. "Anyone we could find some way to sway toward more sympathy?"

Declan shot Jude a look. "I don't think we want to get Rory off the hook through bribery or threats. Something like that could come back to haunt her so easily."

"I know, I know. I'm just tossing ideas around." Jude grimaced. He paused for a few seconds and then met my eyes. "I tried to convince my dad to step up on your behalf

—for the good of the pentacle and all—but he was being his usual asshole self and didn't want to hear any ideas coming from *me*."

My heart skipped a beat. He'd gone to his dad asking for support for me—his dad who was part of the conspiracy to see me sanctioned in the first place?

But Jude didn't know that. Because I'd balked at telling him—my chest clenched up at the idea even now. I wasn't even sure why anymore. It wasn't as if he or Connar could have much worse opinions of their parents than they already held. Did I really not trust them with the information, after everything?

I had to trust them. I couldn't let them keep fighting for me without knowing exactly what—and who—we were up against.

"It wasn't because of you," I said. "I—There's something we really should talk about." My gaze found Declan's. His jaw had set, knowing what I was about to do and maybe dreading it, but not objecting. "Not here in the gym, though." Was even the scion lounge secure enough to have this conversation?

"I know a good place," Declan said. "Somewhere no one would expect students to bother with."

He led us down the hall and around the corner toward the change rooms that led to the pool. A faint chlorine scent laced the air. He murmured a quick spell to open a maintenance door halfway down the hall, and the smell thickened as we descended a set of stairs into a dim room full of pipes and valves and a mechanical hum. Declan spoke another few words that I assumed were intended to guarantee our privacy and nodded to the space.

"One of the benefits of having studied the school blueprints, among many other things."

Jude touched one of the larger pipes gingerly to make sure it wasn't hot and then propped his shoulders against it, crossing his arms loosely over his chest. "What's all the secrecy about?" His tone stayed light, but a worried crease had formed on his forehead. No doubt it hadn't been lost on him that I'd mainly reacted to his comment about his dad.

I looked down at my hands and then at Jude and Connar. The Stormhurst scion had stayed near the bottom of the steps as if to guard the door.

"I wasn't sure how to tell you this, and I wasn't sure it was even a good idea, so… maybe I let it go longer than I should have." I swallowed thickly. "You know that my first mentor, Professor Banefield, died. I was there when it happened. It was a spell that'd been cast on him—first to make him sick when he tried to warn me about people who were out to hurt me, and then to make *him* attack me when I managed to dispel the first part. He killed himself because it was the only way he could stop the magical compulsion."

Jude's eyes flashed. "It must be the same people who set you up to take the fall for Imogen's murder. Fucking bastards."

"That's what I'm assuming," I said quietly. "And that's the part I haven't known how to bring up with you. Banefield was able to tell me who'd cast the spell on him before he died. He said it was the older barons. And some people called the reapers, who I guess are working with them."

All other emotion vanished from both guys' faces in the wake of stunned shock. Connar recovered first, the muscles in his arms flexing as fury radiated through his voice. "You're saying our parents are behind all this—that they tried to have you *killed*—"

"I don't think they want me dead," I interrupted. "Not that it makes things much better, but they might have even bigger problems if the Bloodstone line passes to someone they can't predict. Banefield said they wanted him to destroy my magic. I guess... to hurt me enough so I couldn't really cast anymore, like what happened with your brother."

Connar winced at the comparison, but his anger didn't fade. "Competition within a family in the pentacle is accepted. Barons trying to sabotage an heir to another family on that level, especially conspiring together, is the worst kind of treason. If they were exposed..."

"There's nothing to expose at this point," Declan said as the other guy trailed off. "I've been watching for the slightest hint, but the barons are keeping their cards close even when they're talking with me. It's no wonder they haven't let anything slip to either of you."

Jude's hands were clenching and opening at his sides. "I thought I knew just how low he'd stoop. Fucking hell. He doesn't deserve the goddamn barony."

"If it helps at all, I don't think your mother has been part of the plots," I said. "Banefield was able to leave some papers for me, including a list of people I'm assuming are these 'reapers'… and the barons. Both of Malcolm's parents are on there, and both of yours." I tipped my head to Connar, and then turned back to Jude. "But only your dad. Whatever meetings they were having to plan out this stuff, he never saw her getting involved."

"She wouldn't stand up to him if she found out, though. She's never been able to argue with him." Jude kicked at the floor. His expression stiffened. "You don't think—will it have made things worse that I talked to him about you?"

"You didn't mention any of the ideas we've talked about for proving my innocence, like the casting word, did you?"

He shook his head vehemently. "Even without knowing he's a full-out traitor, I wouldn't have trusted him with that."

"Then I think it should be fine. For me." My heart squeezed as I gazed back at him. "If he thinks you're on my side, I'm not sure what that'll mean for you—or you, Connar."

Connar's face was grimmer than I'd ever seen it before. "If my parents want to take me to task for standing by a fellow scion, they can try. I don't think they'll enjoy the results."

"I doubt my father believes I'd be able to accomplish much anyway," Jude said with a flippancy I could tell was forced. "He may use it as an excuse to turn on me later— but if he didn't have that one, he'd find something else.

Don't worry about that when you're the one on the chopping block."

I choked up for a second before I managed to speak. "I just don't want anyone else getting hurt because of me."

"Hey." Connar stepped forward and set his hand on my waist, looking down at me intently. "It's never been because of *you*. It's because they're power-hungry jackasses."

It was hard to shift the blame that easily when I'd had to watch blood spill from so many people I cared about. I closed my eyes and dragged in a breath. "Whatever it is, both of you should be careful how you talk to them about the case and about me… Until we have real evidence that they're scheming against me, they have so much more power than we do." And even if we got that evidence, would the blacksuits really act against three of their rulers? I had my doubts.

Connar made a disgruntled sound, and Jude grasped my hand to give it a squeeze. "I'm not sure I'll be speaking to my father ever again," he said. "But I'm still here for *you*, whatever you need."

Declan exhaled slowly. "Right now you need to be getting to our Insight seminar, Jude." When the other guy started to protest, the Ashgrave scion held up his hand. "If they can make a case for Rory being a disruptive influence when it comes to our studies, do you really think they won't make use of that?"

Jude muttered a stream of scathing words to himself, but he followed Declan in tramping up the stairs. Connar and I trailed behind them, out of the Stormhurst Building and along the path to the main triangle of the tower and the two halls. He took my hand, running his thumb over my knuckles in a gentle caress.

It was getting late in the afternoon, though the late summer sun still shone brightly, and the green was bustling with students heading to their last class of the day or chatting with friends after just having gotten out. Walking among them, apprehension prickled over my skin. I shifted my hand away from Connar's instinctively.

Jude had declared his affections in public before, but Connar hadn't made any romantic gestures quite that overt. If word got back to his parents that he'd not only defended me to Malcolm but was actively intimately involved with me…

Connar caught my hand before it'd strayed more than an inch from his. He glanced at me and tugged me around to face him when he saw my expression.

"Listen," he said, leaning close. "I've spent too much of my life letting other people decide what I should be doing, what I should care about… And that's led me to making the worst decisions of my life. I'm with you, no matter what my parents will think about it. That's *my* decision. Let me have it."

I choked up all over again. "Of course," I said.

He touched my cheek and closed the last short distance to kiss me, there in the middle of the green with at least a dozen spectators. My pulse thumped, but it was at least as much giddy as it was nervous. I kissed him back hard. If he wanted to show everyone what I meant to him, let them see that I returned those feelings without reservation.

He drew back just a smidge, his nose bumping mine, and gave me a smile that was almost shy. "I told you ages ago that I wanted to take you out someday. It's really taken me too long to follow up on that idea. Can I treat you to dinner in town?"

I had to smile back. "Are you asking me on a date, Mr. Stormhurst?"

"If you can't tell, then I'm obviously doing a bad job of it."

A laugh spilled out of me, a little bittersweet because of the circumstances but happy all the same. "Not at all. I think that's just what I need right now."

I needed the reminder that people could change. That no matter how awful a situation seemed, it could still turn around into something wonderful. Even if I couldn't see just yet how either of those facts would apply to the murder charge hanging over me.

CHAPTER THIRTEEN

Connar

Heading up to the dorms after our date, Rory and I had to part ways in the Ashgrave Hall stairwell at my floor. I wasn't ready to let the evening end just yet. I guided her past the door and nudged her up against the wall as I kissed her.

Rory smiled against my mouth with a pleased hum. The sweet smell of her and her soft form against mine returned me to the backseat of my car less than an hour ago, when her breath had broken as she'd arched beneath me.

A twinge of longing to do that all over again shot straight to my groin. I willed my desire to stay in check. I had no problem being open about my feelings for this girl, but getting caught in the act in the dorm stairwell wasn't a good look on anyone.

At least I'd taken her away from all the stress that had

been dogging her for a little while. I'd given her a little slice of normality in the middle of the chaos. That was what mattered more than anything.

I kissed her again, catching a hint of the red wine we'd had with dinner still lingering in her mouth, and then forced myself to draw back. Rory beamed up at me, even more gorgeous than usual with her eyes bright and her cheeks flushed. I couldn't resist leaning in to claim her mouth just once more.

"I'll see you tomorrow," she said like a promise as she headed for the stairs up to her own floor.

"As much as I can," I replied. I watched her disappear up the steps before pushing past the door to the hallway outside my dorm.

The common room light was on, but none of my dormmates were around. The first week back at school, it wasn't unusual for most seniors to stay out late enjoying the freedom of being away from home before the workload started to pile up. On the other hand, a droning snore carrying from one of the bedrooms told me at least one of the guys had already crashed for the night.

I ambled over to my corner room, said a few quick words to disable the security spells I had in place, and stepped inside.

I froze on the threshold with my hand halfway to the light switch. The moonlight seeping past the window silhouetted two figures standing by my desk. Figures familiar enough that I knew them before I flicked the light on, but that didn't stop my stomach from sinking.

"Hello, Connar," my mother said in a low, blunt voice. "Let's take a walk."

When I'd talked to Rory about my parents this afternoon, I'd dismissed them completely. It was a lot harder to summon that certainty facing them just a few feet away.

These two people had witnessed me at my absolute worst. They'd *pushed* me to my worst… and I wasn't completely sure they couldn't do it again. Baron Stormhurst was used to getting things her way, regardless of who fell beneath her feet.

Whatever they wanted to say to me, I at least agreed with them that it was better to do it away from here. I didn't need my dormmates hearing the way they'd speak to me.

"Sure," I said, keeping my cool as much as I could. With a burst of confidence fueled by my growing sense of conviction, I added, "You could have just called."

"I felt this discussion would be best had face to face."

They followed me out of the building, my mother stalking after me and my father striding along with heavier steps. Even though he was built like I was and she was much thinner, her wiry frame exuded even more power than his bulky body. I might be able to look down at her from a few inches, but she hadn't lost the ability to make me feel small with one cutting glance.

When we'd left Ashgrave Hall, my mother took the lead without hesitation, knowing I'd come along. She veered across the east field, considering the Nary clubhouse with narrowed eyes, and marched straight into the thicker darkness within the forest. I followed her more by sound than sight as the cool night breeze shivered past us. It wasn't that cold, but goosebumps rose on my bare forearms.

It didn't take long to figure out where she was going. She stopped and motioned my father and me past her, and then activated the key ward that protected the Shifting Grounds. Physicality had been her primary strength too, the talent running in the family as magical skills so often did. I'd never seen her shift forms, but no doubt she'd made plenty of use of the private clearing when she'd been a student here some thirty years ago.

No one except one of the two Physicality professors could disable that ward once activated. We'd have no witnesses for this conversation.

Dread swelled in my gut as we walked the rest of the way to the clearing. The moon was only half full, but it cast enough light across the cleared circle of grass for me to see my mother's expression when she spun on me. Her sinewy features were tensed.

"I hear you've taken up with the Bloodstone scion," she said. "Some sort of romance? Really, Connar?"

The things Rory had revealed to me about my parents tickled through my mind, making my jaw tighten. My gaze slid away from my mother for a second, taking in the clearing.

Not that long ago, I'd been here with Rory. I'd let her watch me shift, trusted her not to be unnerved by my dragon form. And she hadn't been. She'd shown so much faith in me, then and since… I had to be worthy of it.

I met my mother's eyes again. "Is there any particular reason I shouldn't get involved with her? It's not as if I'm going to let it interfere with my duties as scion."

"Oh, no? So you haven't forgotten that you can't have her if you still want to be baron."

"Of course not." That fact weighed on me every time I looked at Rory.

"The girl is a threat to the stability of the pentacle and your mother's work there," my father said darkly. "You know we want to see her beaten down, not *wooed*."

"I thought you were taking care of that aspect yourselves now."

That tossed-out comment might have been too careless. My mother's gaze sharpened. "What exactly do you mean by that?"

If she knew that Rory had found out about the barons' involvement, they'd pull out all the stops to utterly crush her before the hearing even happened. My pulse hiccupped.

"I understand the barons are all refusing to support her in challenging the charges against her," I said, fumbling for an answer she'd believe. "Normally you'd stand by a fellow baron."

"She's not baron yet." My mother sucked in a sharp breath. "Has she been speaking against the rest of the pentacle, then?"

Shit. "No," I said quickly. "Jude mentioned that his father said something along those lines." And hopefully I hadn't just landed my friend in a heap of trouble too. I might have the physical strength and the magical power to more than hold my own among my peers, but I'd never been known for quick wits. I couldn't match my mother in verbal sparring. How the hell could I get through this confrontation without turning it into a catastrophe?

The answer came to me in a rare flash of brilliance—so brilliant that I hesitated as I turned the idea over in my head to make sure I wasn't tricking myself. But no, that should work to get my parents off my back *and* protect Rory from their prodding. And the strategy was simple enough that it only required one lie.

I adjusted my stance, cocking my head to one side. "I thought you'd be happy about the progress I've made. I'm in the perfect position, don't you think?"

My mother raised her eyebrows. "The perfect position for what?"

"To find out what Rory *is* thinking about, how she plans to fight the charges—what she decides to do afterward. To undermine the decisions that would put her in a better position to oppose you. She trusts me now. She'll listen to me. I can get a lot more mileage out of that than bullying her."

A slow, cruel smile crept across my mother's face. I had to restrain a shudder at the sight of it. She glanced at my father. "Look at our heir, coming into his own. I was starting to think I wouldn't see the day."

The implied criticism in those words would have stung more if I'd actually wanted to live up to their example. With everything I knew about them, after everything they'd put me through, I was happy to be charting my own path.

I would have felt satisfied that the gambit had worked so well if my mother hadn't turned to me a moment later with a calculating gleam in her eyes. I'd learned a long time ago to be on guard whenever I saw that expression on her face.

"You can do something for us right away, then," she said, raising her chin. "Put a worm in your new girlfriend's ear."

I hadn't bargained on having my bluff called this quickly. But maybe I could still work around her request. "What kind of worm?" I asked.

She ambled a little ways into the clearing and then back toward me, the strength in her movements turning the stroll into more of a prowl. "The barons *have* discussed lending our support to Bloodstone's cause, *if* she concedes to our very reasonable requirements. Baron Nightwood will be coming to put the proposal to her tomorrow. It would be in everyone's favor, including hers —and yours—if she accepts the deal. So use this influence you've gained to advise her in the right direction. That shouldn't be too difficult for you, should it?"

The slight edge in her voice told me she hadn't totally meant her praise about me coming into my own. She might believe I'd seduced Rory with malicious intentions, but she wasn't confident I could follow through. She knew I wasn't a skilled schemer just as well as I did.

"Encourage her to take the deal?" I said. "I should be able to manage that. She doesn't want to have to go through with the hearing as it is." That much was true but vague enough that I couldn't see it hurting Rory any for me to have said it.

My mother's smile grew. "Excellent. Let's see how well your powers of persuasion—magical and otherwise—have grown. And here I was thinking you might need a little more motivation to really find your footing as scion."

Something in her tone turned my blood cold. "More motivation?"

She nodded casually and rested her hand on my father's arm. "We've worried that you've been held back by qualms about the past. You won your position fair and square. There's no shame in how it happened. But maybe it would be easier for you to focus on where you are now if the last traces of that past were gone. We've been looking into facilities that take people like Holden when it's no longer ideal for them to remain at home."

Every particle in my body stiffened in resistance. "I don't think that should be necessary," I said carefully. To my relief, my voice came out steady, even though my heart was thudding. "I barely think about Holden anymore as it is."

Please, let them not know about my periodic visits to my brother's quarters in the Stormhurst home. Please, let this be only a threat they don't see the need to follow through on. Lord only knew what would happen to Holden if they decided to cut him off from the family completely.

"I'm glad to hear it," my mother said. "In that case, I suppose there isn't any rush. It's an option we can keep on the table if it seems necessary in future." She nodded in satisfaction. "I'm so glad we could have this talk."

I wished I could feel half as pleased with it. As we set off back toward campus, the full impact of the threat sank in.

I'd bought myself a little time with Rory—but how long would I need to pretend to be double-crossing her to ensure my brother's safety? And what would happen to all of us if I couldn't pull the ploy off convincingly enough?

CHAPTER FOURTEEN

Rory

The only thing worse than having to get up for an early class after a fantastic date was having that class with your most disapproving teacher. I showed up for the Physicality workshop with a minute to spare and my clothes and hair pretty well in order considering I'd only woken up half an hour ago, but Professor Viceport followed my trek to the last remaining worktable with a look of disdain. She might not have been eager to see me convicted of murder, but she still didn't exactly *like* me.

She cleared her throat to begin class, but a guy farther down the same row as me raised his hand in the air with a question. One of Viceport's eyebrows arched, but she nodded to him. "Yes?"

"I was trying to fix something in my dorm this morning using a Physicality spell," the guy said, "but I had to stop because the feeb who's—"

"I'd prefer we stay above base slang in this class," Viceport interrupted. "You mean a Nary dormmate of yours?"

The guy gave a brief grimace that could have been in embarrassment at a misstep or annoyance that he wasn't allowed to use the insult—it was hard to tell. "Yes. Exactly. Because he was hanging out in the common room, I had to stop. It got me wondering about why we try so hard to keep our powers secret from the—from the Naries in the first place. I know all the stuff everyone says about caution and so on, but we're way more powerful than they are. Would it really be so awful if they knew that?"

Viceport offered a considering nod, leaning her slimly elegant frame back against her desk. "An interesting question, Mr. Cutbridge. Somewhat beyond the usual scope of my teaching, but certainly relevant to every area of magic. We can take a little time to discuss it."

My back stiffened at his name. *Cutbridge.* There'd been a Cutbridge on Professor Banefield's list of the barons and their allies. Could it have been this guy, even though those notes had gone back years and he didn't look any older than me? Probably not, but almost definitely a relative— his dad or grandfather or an uncle... even an older cousin.

Which didn't mean my classmate necessarily had nefarious intentions, but his use of the derogatory term for Naries and his general attitude had already raised my hackles.

Professor Viceport glanced around the room. "Can anyone share their understanding of our policy of discretion?"

At the back of the room, Victory raised her hand. My long-time nemesis hadn't spoken to me—had barely looked at me—since Malcolm had told her off a couple weeks ago, but her presence still made my skin twitch warily.

"We have more freedom if we don't have to navigate Nary rules or expectations about magic," she said in a pert voice. With the teachers, she was always on her best behavior. "Our powers allow us to work around them pretty easily, and if they knew about us, it'd just cause a whole lot of extra stress."

"Yeah, but we're letting that policy restrict us too," the Cutbridge guy said. "Families aren't supposed to have more than two kids so our society doesn't get too big to stay hidden. We're always having to keep a look out and disguise or hold off on using magic if we're anywhere outside fearmancer properties."

"Both of those points are true," Viceport said. "It's very rare that there's one obvious right way of handling a societal issue. What usually happens is we decide on what causes the fewest problems for the greatest number of people, and staying hidden has accomplished that goal so far. If we *were* to start using magic openly, how do you think the much larger Nary population would respond?"

"They'd be scared," the girl behind me said. "They'd think we're monsters or mutants or something like that."

"Yeah," the guy beside her piped up. "They'd try to… to exterminate us or at least imprison us to make sure we couldn't hurt them."

"I'm pretty sure we'd come out of that fight on top," Cutbridge said. "I mean… we do have magic."

"But why have some big war at all?" Victory asked. "And then, what, we'd have to be constantly watching our backs afterward in case they tried to attack us again?"

Cutbridge shrugged. "We could convince them it's in their best interests to let us do our thing. Then we'd be the ones in charge, calling the shots. We wouldn't have to hide from anyone."

Professor Viceport gave him a wry smile. "I'm not sure the scenario you're proposing would be all that simple to achieve. And many of us have no interest in ruling over the entire population of Naries. Let them live their lives, and we live ours, governing our own. If the barons felt we'd be better off otherwise, I'm sure they'd propose as much."

Her gaze slid to me for just a second, as if she thought I might contribute some political comment. I was still getting used to *being* a fearmancer—I wasn't really qualified to weigh in on global issues just yet.

"Well, *I* think it'd be amazing," Cutbridge said, apparently needing to get the last word, and then let the subject drop so Viceport could get on with the actual class. I made a mental note to pay extra attention to what he was up to around campus.

The workshop was almost over when Viceport's phone pinged with an alert. She took a brief glance at it, and her mouth tightened.

"Miss Bloodstone," she said, shooting me a narrow

glance with no effort at all to keep the message private. "Ms. Grimsworth would like to see you once class is out."

Why would the headmistress want to see me right now? I fumbled my final conjuring a little in my distraction, which didn't win me any points with the professor. As soon as she dismissed us, I hurried over to Killbrook Hall.

Ms. Grimsworth had generally been a supportive if distant figure since I'd arrived on campus. I hadn't seen any reason to consider her an outright enemy. So I wasn't feeling *that* nervous until she answered her office door and I saw it wasn't just the two of us.

Malcolm's dad, Baron Nightwood, was standing by the other side of her desk, his arms folded over his chest. Seeing him was just as disorienting as the first time. He looked so much like his son, only a little tighter in the face and grayer in the hair with age.

The last—and first—time I'd talked to him, he'd frozen me in place and made it clear he intended to make me regret any disrespect. And since then, of course, I'd found out he was part of, if not the leader of, the plot to crush me into subservience. If I were making a list of people I least wanted to talk to, he'd be right at the top.

I gave him a slight dip of my head as I came in, figuring a minor show of respect couldn't hurt anything, anyway. I was hardly in a position to do battle with the most powerful fearmancer in the country, as the thin weight of the silver cuffs on my wrists gave extra evidence to.

"Thank you for coming so quickly, Miss Bloodstone,"

Ms. Grimsworth said. "Baron Nightwood wished to have a conference with you, and I'm lending him the use of my office." Her tone gave away no sign of whether she liked the idea of this meeting. She turned to the baron. "Naturally, the room is fully warded to ensure all conversation within stays private."

"I'd expect nothing less," Baron Nightwood said.

He waited until she'd disappeared into her private quarters before sinking into her chair behind the desk. I wavered on my feet, not sure whether I should sit too or keep standing there awkwardly. At least standing I could more easily make a run for the door if I felt the need to flee.

"It appears you've found yourself in something of a quandary," the baron said, leaning back in the chair in a casual pose. His expression was contemplative but not hostile. "Have you made much progress toward building a defensive case for your hearing?"

As if I intended to discuss my progress with him of all people. "I've gained some ground," I said vaguely. The truth was I still wasn't sure I had a hope in hell of getting through the hearing unsanctioned, especially with him and the other barons pulling the strings behind the scenes, but I wasn't going to admit that.

The baron hummed to himself as if he could guess what I wasn't saying. "It does seem to be a rather complicated situation. Unfortunate that you've made so many enemies in your short time here that someone would go to such lengths to besmirch you, assuming that's your story." Even though it was just the two of us, and he knew I was innocent as well as I did, he worked a clear note of skepticism into his voice.

I fought to keep my teeth from gritting. "I didn't kill anyone."

"The other barons and I don't much care whether you did or not," Baron Nightwood said. "The Wakeburn girl was no one of consequence. Your carelessness, if you were responsible, is a separate matter. Our main concern is for the pentacle. So, I've come in my official capacity to extend an offer of support."

I controlled my reaction as well as I could, but I was pretty sure my eyes bulged. "I—what?" Hadn't Baron Killbrook just dismissed Jude's request for help? There had to be a catch.

And here it came. Baron Nightwood smiled coolly at me. "We're willing to intercede on your behalf to ensure the hearing is decided in your favor. However, in consideration of those efforts and in light of your potentially reckless conduct, we would expect you to make some concessions to us in return."

Of course they would. I finally let myself sink into the chair across from him. "And what concessions would those be?"

"Nothing all that involved. As is reasonable regardless of the charges, given how new you are to the community, we'd ask that you pick one of the three of us established barons as an advisor, established by official contract, for the next five years. Your decisions as baron would need to be discussed and agreed on with that advisor."

How very convenient for them. They wouldn't be able

to force me into a ruling I didn't want, but I wouldn't be able to outright object to or present proposals of my own unless they approved. Fuck that.

"And?" I prompted, because he had said "concessions," plural.

He nodded to my arms. "And you would continue to wear those cuffs for the next year, with the monitoring of your magical usage handled by us."

So they'd also be able to keep track of every spell I cast, even those I was using to protect myself. My stomach knotted.

"It isn't very much compared to what you'll face if you're judged guilty of the murder of a magical peer," Baron Nightwood said without any apparent concern. "But if we're going to intervene, we have to begin proceedings now. So I'll need your answer before I leave."

My pulse stuttered. They were really putting the pressure on. I looked down at my hands, willing my mind to focus despite the whirling of my thoughts.

What he'd said was true. Giving one of the barons veto power and letting them monitor my magic for a set period of time was a hell of a lot better than the fate Declan had described, where they might take over my thoughts and actions completely. I *didn't* have much of a defense yet. What if I gambled and said no, and then I lost? Wouldn't it be smarter to take the safe route?

But every part of me balked at the idea of giving in. They'd set me up in this situation, and now they were going to play savior?

Why would they be making this offer at all if they were sure I couldn't prove my innocence?

I grasped onto that thought with a surge of resolve. They *weren't* sure. That was the only explanation. They were worried I'd come out of this scenario without any sanctions placed, free to keep doing things my way, so they were willing to take a lesser advantage to ensure they won something.

They'd orchestrated the trap. If they thought there might be a way out... I had to believe there was too. I still had a week to find it.

I raised my head and looked Baron Nightwood straight in the eyes. "Thank you, but if I'm going to be judged innocent at the hearing, I'd prefer it to be because I proved I actually am."

A hint of surprise flickered across the baron's face. He hadn't really expected I'd decline.

"Wait a moment," he said. "I don't think you've fully thought this through."

I got up from the chair. "I have, and that's my final decision. When I'm absolved of the crime, then we can discuss my place in the pentacle."

Before he could argue more, I walked out of the room with a thudding heart, hoping I hadn't just risked my freedom and my magic in vain.

CHAPTER FIFTEEN

Rory

S helby was in the dorm room kitchen when I came in. She startled at the sound of the door so badly the glass in her hand slipped. It hit the counter with a thunk, water splashing out. She checked it for cracks and let out a sigh of relief.

"Sorry," she said. "I guess I'm a little jumpy this morning."

I frowned, coming over to join her. "Is everything okay?"

"Yeah. I mean, it's pretty much normal." She grabbed a dish towel from the knob of a cabinet and swiped it over the puddle on the counter. "I feel like the regular students are being a little more… pushy than before with people like me here on scholarship. Maybe they don't like that we have the clubhouse now? I don't know. It's nothing major, more just a vibe."

I didn't think "just a vibe" would have her flinching at the sound of the door. Shelby had a habit of downplaying her problems. And between the weird incident in Persuasion class and the discussion that guy in Physicality had brought up today, *I* was also noticing some kind of shift in attitude toward the Naries compared to the past two terms.

It could be about the clubhouse—that made a certain kind of sense. Seeing the Naries have a safe space to escape to could have rubbed a lot of the fearmancer students the wrong way, diminished their sense of power. I really hoped my attempt at helping the Nary students hadn't backfired spectacularly.

"Let me know if anyone in here hassles you, all right?" I said, motioning to the bedroom doors around us. "You shouldn't have to put up with that kind of crap, and… they're all a little scared of me because of the rumors about Imogen. I might as well put that nervousness to use getting them to back off on you."

I didn't like the way most of my peers looked at me now, but at least that way I'd get something good out of the whole mess.

The corner of Shelby's mouth twitched with what looked like amusement, but she shook her head. "I think it's better if I fight my own battles—or don't, when it's better to keep my head down. They'll just be worse when you're not around. That's what bullies are always like."

Having been homeschooled most of my life before now, I didn't have much direct experience to go by, but she sounded as if she did. "Fair enough. If you change your mind, just give me a shout."

"For sure." She perked up. "Oh, one of the guys came around looking for you about an hour ago. Connar? I told him I was pretty sure you'd gone to a class. He wanted me to tell you to meet him at the 'lounge' if I saw you before he did." She gave me a speculative look.

That request sounded more urgent than him just wanting to spend time together. "Thanks," I said to Shelby. "I'd better go find him now."

When I opened the door to the scion lounge, Connar was standing by the pool table with Jude and Declan, his expression stormy. "I know it can't be anything—" he was saying. He stopped and turned at my entrance, relief washing across his face. Jude set down the pool cue he'd been fiddling with.

"Hey," I said, taking in the worry they were all exuding. "What's going on?"

"Malcolm's dad is going to come to make you an offer to do with the murder charge today," Connar said. "I'm not sure exactly what the barons are going to try to arrange, but—"

Was that all? I gave him a wry smile. "I know. He was already here. I talked to him after my class."

Connar tensed. "What did you tell him?"

I waved off his concern and walked over to the alcohol cabinet to grab a pop. It was way too early in the day still for anything alcoholic. "It's fine. I told him thanks but no thanks. They wouldn't be trying to bargain with me if they didn't think there's a decent chance I could pull through this, right?" I hoped I sounded more confident saying that than I felt.

"What did they want?" Declan asked, putting his own cue back on the rack.

"For me to hand over veto power for my decisions as baron to one of them for five years, and let them monitor my magic through these for one." I wiggled one of the cuffs. As I took a gulp of the tart cola, the fizz bubbling down my throat, I glanced over at Connar. "How did you know Baron Nightwood was coming?"

His chiseled jaw tightened. "My parents paid me a visit last night. They were hoping I could help convince you to take the deal. The fact that it mattered that much to them makes me pretty sure that going along with it would have been a bad idea."

His parents had dropped in out of the blue last night —rather than just calling him or something. I studied him. "Is that all they wanted to talk about?" Yesterday had also been the day of his big public show of affection toward me. It was possible word about that had gotten back to them quickly.

He shrugged. "Nothing else worth mentioning."

I'd take his word for that. I dropped onto the sofa's cozy cushions with my drink. "I know the barons think I can beat the murder charge… but *I* still don't know how I'm going to do that. I've only got a week left before the hearing. What else is there we haven't tried?"

Jude took the chair next to me, his eyes bright. "I've been doing some additional research on illusions," he said. "Tricks for differentiating between magic and reality. There are a couple factors I hadn't realized that might apply even via an insight spell into your memories."

My spirits lifted. "Like what?"

"Did Imogen have any small but distinctive features the illusionist would have had to duplicate? Like… a dark mole on her face, or an obvious scar, or maybe she was wearing something that day that had a pattern or image that wasn't totally symmetrical?"

I knit my brow as I thought back to the memories, fighting the urge to cringe at them. "Nothing on her body or her clothes that I noticed, but she was always wearing a silver hair clip on one side."

Jude leaned forward. "How big?"

I formed an oval between my thumb and forefinger. "Around that size. Not tiny."

"Hmm. That might not be small enough. Apparently when casting under stress—which I'm going to assume the mage who was working against you was operating under, at least a little—there can be a faint mirror effect in an illusion meant to copy an actual being or object. But it centers on small, high-contrast details. The pins wouldn't have been that much lighter or darker than her hair either, would they?"

"No. I don't remember seeing any mirroring of the pin, but I was probably too distracted to pick up on things like that."

Declan sat down on the sofa beside me. "I can take an objective look at the memories again, if you're okay with that, and see if anything shows up to an outside viewer."

He tipped his head to Jude. "You said there were a couple factors."

"Yeah. The same thing with stress and copying an existing thing—there may be a small vibration visible on areas of fine detail—like hair, or eyelashes, or if she had a particularly intricate design on her clothes." Jude motioned from his head to his shirt.

My hopes had started to deflate. "All of this is assuming the murderer was feeling stressed. The barons would have sent someone who'd be cool under pressure for a job like this, wouldn't they?"

"It can't hurt to try," Declan said. "Will you let me take a look?"

"Of course." It was easier the second time around. I exhaled slowly and willed my instinctive shields down at the same time.

As before, Declan asked about what happened when I'd found Imogen, and a faint tingle rippled through my head with his intrusion. It felt like even less time had passed than before when he pulled back out. His frown told me enough.

"I didn't pick up on either of those effects," he said. "I don't think we're going to make a case that way, at least not from Rory's memories."

"Who else's could we use?" Connar muttered. "She was the only one there."

No, I wasn't. I had to catch a laugh as a rush of inspiration hit me.

Deborah couldn't act as a witness at the hearing. Her perceptions of the illusion wouldn't help me. But she'd told me that a mage could look inside an animal's head using insight. Just as Declan had been peering inside my memories to get a more detached outside perspective... maybe *I* would recognize something from my familiar's memories that would connect a few dots. There were all sorts of fearmancers I'd met that she hadn't. Spells I'd seen cast that she wasn't familiar with.

Jude was watching me. "You look like a lightbulb just went off in that head of yours, Ice Queen."

I wrinkled my nose at the nickname—and to deflect from the point he'd made. The truth about Deborah was the one secret I still had to keep, for her sake more than anyone's.

"I just remembered a technique I read about a while back for clarifying memories," I improvised. "I should go back to the scene and see if I can prompt anything else loose by looking around my dorm." I pushed myself onto my feet.

"Do you want us to come with you?" Connar said from where he'd stationed himself behind the sofa, looking like he very much wanted to be with me on guard duty.

"You all aren't really supposed to be in the girls' dorms, are you? Maybe there are other illusion clues you can find, or—" I glanced at Declan. "Professor Crowford is involved with this group somehow. I haven't gotten a good opportunity to take a peek inside his head, but maybe you'd be able to."

He nodded. "I'll watch for an opening. You let us know if you turn up anything you think we could work with, okay?"

"Of course."

As soon as I'd left them behind, I dashed up the stairs to my dorm room. Deborah must have sensed my urgency, because she came scampering out of one of her nooks in the wall seconds after I'd burst into my bedroom. I sat down on the bed, and she scurried up it to hop onto my palm.

Did something happen, Lorelei?

"Not exactly," I said quietly, mindful of the thinness of the walls now that the other girls were back in residence. "I just realized there's one important avenue I haven't tried. You said you'd let a judge use insight on you to view your memories of the murder—will you let me see them?"

Deborah answered without hesitation. *Of course. I've told you everything I saw already, though.*

"Yeah, but... we're not always the best judges of our own memories. And I've met a lot of fearmancers you haven't had any contact with. Maybe I'll recognize the murderer, or see some other clue that'll help us prove my case. It's worth a shot, right?"

It certainly can't hurt. You go right ahead, whenever you're ready. Without my magical abilities, I couldn't block anyone from taking a peek even if I wanted to.

I peered down at her furry white head. *Please* let this get me somewhere. I couldn't let the barons take total control over my life. I couldn't be branded as a murderer.

"What did you see when Imogen was murdered?" I whispered, and fell into my familiar's head.

As expected with an insight spell, the impressions that washed over me were jumbled rather than a clear replay of those events. I tasted the dry, woody air from the tight passages inside the wall, heard the faint squeak of the dorm's door opening and a startled gasp. I saw a figure cloaked in shadow, even her edges blurred so it was impossible to tell her height or much about her frame other than she had a woman's shape, whipping a spell that sliced into Imogen's skin. I watched the figure duck into one of the bedrooms as footsteps sounded outside the door.

The fragments jumped back and forth. I was dashing to the opening to see what the fuss was. Then blood sprang from the wounds all across Imogen's body. Then she was uninjured again, protesting in a choked voice. Then she fell and hit the floor with a limp thud.

And something thumped faintly in the distance, like an echo.

The disjointed memories swept over me again. I could piece together the sequence in my head. The murderer had taken too much care to ensure she couldn't be identified on the off-chance someone was watching. But there was that distant thump again, just after Imogen's dying body slumped on the floor.

I yanked myself out of Deborah's mind and swayed with momentary dizziness.

Did you notice anything? my familiar asked anxiously.

"I think… maybe." I gathered my thoughts. "After Imogen fell because of her injuries, there another sound, farther away, like something being hit or dropped. Do you remember that?"

My familiar rubbed her paw against her nose. *Yes. Now*

that you mention it, I did catch that at the time. It came up through the floor—someone in the dorm below, I assumed. Not anyone who could have seen or heard anything from your room, I don't think. Those floors are quite thick. I barely heard the sound from down there even with my sharper hearing.

"It came *right* after, though," I said. "There's a chance someone heard something. If they could even cast a little doubt on when Imogen was attacked—if their testimony could suggest it happened before I was even at the room—I've got to find out who was down there."

CHAPTER SIXTEEN

Rory

M y eyes popped open, and I gasped for air. For the
first few seconds, I couldn't seem to pull more
than a fragment of a breath into my lungs. My pulse
thundered in my chest, and my mind scrambled to make
sense of the shadowy room around me.

Lorelei?

Deborah's familiar dry voice penetrated the haze of
panic. I clenched my hands and found them grasping the
sheets on my bed in my dorm room. My breaths started to
even out as the pressure on my chest eased.

Nothing was attacking me, at least not right in this
moment. I was here in my bedroom alone, other than my
familiar. It'd just been a nightmare.

A nightmare like the ones Malcolm had used to send
into my head: dark and formless, shot through with terror

but with no sense of what was so terrifying when I woke up. A chill ran down my spine.

I didn't appear to have torn up anything like I often had in those fits during spring term. "Deborah," I whispered. "Was I yelling?"

No. My familiar's voice became clearer as she scampered across the bed to rest her front paws on my arm. *You murmured a little in your sleep—you sounded distressed—but I don't imagine anyone heard you other than me.*

Thank God for that. I gave her a quick stroke of my thumb down her back and slipped out of bed to my open window. Leaning out, I checked the stone wall of the building between my room and Malcolm's at the opposite end. The early morning light was thin but bright enough for me to see no unusual protrusions had appeared. Last time, he'd been using an amplifying piece to store and intensify the spells he'd been aiming at me in my sleep.

All that meant was he'd decided to be more subtle about it. My jaw clenching, I yanked myself back into my room and grabbed the first halfway decent outfit I could assemble out of my wardrobe. With a rake of my fingers through my hair, I pulled the messy waves into some kind of order. Then I marched out of my dorm and across the short hallway to Malcolm's.

The guy who answered the door was tall and freckled with a mop of dark brown hair. He blinked at me over the top of the toasted wrap he was in the middle of eating, and a quiver of fear shot into me. He recognized the supposed murderer from next door.

I gave him a tight smile. "Is Malcolm here?"

"Just a second." He dashed across the common room as if I'd threatened to fillet him if he didn't hoof it fast enough. The other two guys eating breakfast at the dining table watched me with equal wariness. I decided I didn't much care whether they saw me as some horrible threat if it meant they cared more about appeasing me than potentially pissing off Malcolm by summoning him.

The Nightwood scion emerged from his bedroom a minute later in a shirt and slacks that looked just thrown on, with a frown and slightly bleary eyes. He gave them a quick rub when he saw me and drew his posture straighter as he sauntered the rest of the way over.

"What's going on, Bloodstone?"

My awareness of our audience prickled over me. I backed up, and he followed me into the hall. As soon as the door had shut behind him, I jabbed a finger at him.

"It's not much of a truce if you're still messing with my head."

Malcolm's expression turned puzzled. "What are you talking about?"

"Those nightmares you sent at me before—I just had another one."

His frown came back. "I didn't have anything to do with that. I haven't cast any magic at you since... since that day when we were in the lake." He gathered his composure after that momentary faltering. "I didn't hear anything from your room."

"I didn't freak out the same way," I said. "I just—I woke up in the same kind of panic, without remembering the dream at all—that's not how my regular nightmares usually go."

Something shifted in his face at my comment about "regular nightmares." Maybe he hadn't realized how many others I had to compare to. He looked down at his hands and then at me again, his eyes searching mine. "I don't know what to tell you. I honestly had nothing to do with it."

He sounded genuine. Maybe it was just a coincidence that this nightmare had felt so much like those past ones. Maybe it'd been inspired by those past ones rather than directly caused by the same source. In which case I'd dragged Malcolm out of bed for nothing.

On the other hand, he could be lying. It wasn't as if he hadn't jerked me around plenty of times in the past.

I crossed my arms over my chest, just shy of hugging myself. "How do I know I can believe that?"

Malcolm opened his mouth with an exasperated look and then closed it again. His brow knit. He contemplated me for a moment, possibly realizing what a tall order proving himself would be considering our history.

"Ask me whether I cast any magic at you. Or when the last time was. Or however you want to phrase it," he said abruptly. "Make it an insight spell. I've got nothing to hide. I *am* telling you the truth."

I stared at him. *Malcolm* of all people was voluntarily letting me inside his head. Of course, I had to assume that if I tried to take a more general dip into his thoughts and memories, he'd punt me out faster than I could blink. But even for a specific question, it was a greater show of trust than I'd have thought he was capable of.

The fact that I'd misjudged him sent a twinge of guilt through me, but I had to take the opening he'd given me, just to be sure. "All right," I said. "Ready?"

His jaw tightened, but he nodded. If he was going to offer me this much trust, I could show him I wasn't the kind of person who'd abuse it. I fixed my gaze on his forehead and said, "When was the last time you cast any kind of magic to affect me?"

My awareness flipped and mingled with his. The impressions washed over me in a shifting wave of images and sensations. I caught a glimpse of me bobbing in lake water up to my neck with my hair slicked wet and sleek, a flash of desire, a murmured spell shaping the currents in the hopes of stirring the same desire in its target, the flush of my cheeks and an answering flare of heat in Malcolm's body—

I jerked myself out of his head, my face flushing too. A tingling that was awkward but not entirely uncomfortable spread through my chest and farther down, to all the places that wouldn't have minded indulging in that sensation again if I'd been willing to let myself.

He hadn't been lying, anyway. It took me a second to find my tongue. "Okay. Thank you. I'm sorry I jumped to conclusions."

Malcolm shrugged, his gaze a little more intent on me, maybe a little more heated with the thought of the memory I'd just dipped into. "I suppose I can't really blame you. I did do quite a number on you with those spells before." He paused. "I'm sorry about that. I think it's safe to say that was one tactic I took too far. I thought... I don't know." He rubbed his forehead with a grimace.

A second apology from the heir of Nightwood in as many weeks, on top of the vulnerability he'd just offered in opening up his mind to me? I found myself speechless again.

The other scions had assured me that Malcolm had plenty of positive qualities, but it'd been pretty hard to see them in the midst of his campaign against me. Now that he was lowering his guard, trying to make peace and even understand where I was coming from... It was hard not to wonder how much differently our association might have played out if I'd gotten this version of him to begin with.

I still disagreed with plenty of his ideas, but less of them than I'd have expected. I couldn't claim anymore that he was a full-out villain. Who was to say how I'd have acted if our positions and histories had been reversed?

As I groped for an appropriate answer to his apology, one of the dorm doors behind me opened and a couple of the other senior students ducked out, talking quietly as they walked to the stairs. People were starting to head off to classes or whatever other responsibilities they had this morning. A different sort of panic jolted through me.

I turned on my heel. "Well, I— I've got to get going."

"What's the big hurry all of a sudden?" Malcolm took a step after me. "Is something else going on?"

It might have been the way he'd just opened up to me or the fact that he sounded honestly concerned—probably some of both. Before I could second-guess the impulse, I told him the truth.

"I wanted to talk to the guys in the dorm under mine. It occurred to me that one of them might have been in the room when Imogen was attacked and could have heard something that would help my case."

Malcolm gave a brisk nod, looking completely alert now. "I'll come with you. I can encourage them to… speak up if any of them aren't so keen."

That wasn't the outcome I'd been going for. "I'm sure if I need any help, Declan—"

"Declan will already be off in the library or consulting with Professor Sinleigh or God knows what," Malcolm said dismissively. "The guy has never heard of the concept of sleeping in. Come on. Let's see who's around. I don't know all his dormmates off the top of my head, but when I see them, I should be able to at least tell you who was around for the summer session."

That could actually be useful. I wasn't sure I trusted my memory with the students I didn't know all that well and hadn't known for very long.

"Okay," I said. "But let me ask the questions. It's *my* case."

A teasing note came into Malcolm's voice. "If you insist, Glinda."

We tramped down one flight of stairs to the hall beneath ours. True to his word, Malcolm hung back a couple steps behind me as I knocked on the dorm door.

I *did* recognize the guy who came to answer it: Alex Rutland, who'd tried very ineffectively to ask me out a few months back, after everyone had found out I was the most powerful mage currently attending the school and before anyone had thought I was a murderer. I suspected the new development might have put a damper on my marriage prospects. An unexpected bonus.

He paled a little when he saw me, as if he thought I might be going to murder him for daring to flirt with me two terms ago. I fixed him with a firm look. "Rutland, get all your dormmates who are around into the common room. I need to talk to everyone. Scion business." If that excuse had worked for Malcolm with the blacksuits, it'd damn well better work for me here.

"Yes—yes, of course," Alex mumbled, and hustled across the common room, leaving the door open for us.

A couple of the guys were already sitting on the sofas, and a few more were at the dining table. Alex rapped on two of the other doors to bring the inhabitants out and stopped a guy who'd just emerged from the bathroom in a bathrobe.

Malcolm had been right—Declan, who had the bedroom right under mine, was gone. I knew he'd still been at the end of summer party when I'd left it anyway, and it wasn't as if he'd have failed to mention he'd come back to the dorm during the time of the murder.

I scanned the faces in front of me. Alex had been around during the summer, and I was sure two of the other guys had been in some of my classes. The other five I couldn't have said.

Malcolm leaned closer and spoke under his breath.

"Mr. Bathrobe, the two on the sofas, and that guy just coming out of his room weren't here for the summer."

I tipped my head in acknowledgment with a rush of gratitude. "You four don't need to be here for this," I said, pointing to them. Even the ones who'd already been out in the common room when I'd arrived scattered to their bedrooms at my dismissal. My chest jittered with fresh jolts of fear. I was building quite a store of magic today.

In the momentary silence as the remaining guys gathered warily, I couldn't help noticing that no sound at all traveled to me from the room above. My own dormmates must be walking around up there with their morning preparations now, but I wouldn't have known it from down here. *Was* there any chance someone had heard Imogen's fall—and that they could say exactly when it'd happened?

I had to try.

"You were all here for the summer session," I said, looking at the four guys still in front of me. "What time did you each of you leave the end-of-term party?"

"I was there until the end," Alex said. From Malcolm's nod at the corner of my vision, he remembered well enough to confirm that.

"Same here," the second guy. Another nod.

"I left right after the prize announcement," said a guy holding a mug of coffee. His gaze darted nervously not to me but to Malcolm before he added, "My parents wanted me home right away for a family business meeting."

"I left somewhere in the middle," the last guy said. "I wasn't really paying attention to the time."

I focused on the final two. "Did either of you come back to the dorm after you left the party?"

They both hesitated. Malcolm cleared his throat, and the coffee guy shook his head with a jerk. "I'd already packed the things I needed in my car. I went straight to the garage and drove home."

The last guy sighed and offered a crooked smile. "Eventually, sure, but by the time I got here there were blacksuits all over the place. I took a detour with my girlfriend into the woods."

The room had been empty until after the murder, then. Except—it *couldn't* have been. I didn't know whether anyone down here could have heard what was happening over their heads, but Deborah had definitely heard a noise from down here.

"Thanks for your time," I said quickly. "That's all I needed to know."

"You're giving up just like that?" Malcolm asked when I'd retreated into the hall.

I shook my head. "There was someone in that room when Imogen was attacked. I—I was able to figure that out." Regardless of the new side of him I was seeing, I sure as hell wasn't telling *him* Deborah's secret. "Would the cleaning staff have started work before the session was even over?"

"Not likely," Malcolm said. "They have a whole week afterward to get everything in order. Maintenance prefers to keep out of students' way as much as possible. But you're thinking too much like a good witch." He raised his hand as if to tap my head but stopped just shy of brushing my hair. "You're assuming whoever was in there was supposed to be. Breaking and entering is fair play around here."

My heart sank. "Then it could be literally *anyone*. If I just had some idea—"

I cut myself off in mid-sentence as the pieces clicked in my head.

I did have an idea. I'd dismissed the possibility that Cressida knew anything because I'd seen her leaving the stairwell before I'd even started up from the first floor, and the real murderer wouldn't have shown herself to anyone in my dorm.

But... if Imogen's attacker had been holding her in place for a little while before I even showed up, like Deborah had said, then Cressida couldn't have gotten into *our* dorm room in the first place. So where had she gone up there? What had sent her hurrying out of the building so quickly she'd practically run into me?

"What?" Malcolm said, studying my expression.

"I know who else to ask," I said, without much boost to my spirits. "But even if she does know I'm innocent, I think she might be happy to see me go down for the crime anyway."

CHAPTER SEVENTEEN

Jude

I t was a long drive to the main Killbrook home from
Blood U, but I jumped at the first chance I got to
make the trip. The funny thing about coming to a major
decision was that once you'd arrived there, no matter how
gradual the process would be, the impatience to get on
with it would keep itching at you. I was going to make a
clean break, and I wanted it to start now.

I had no classes after my morning seminar until my
business course the next afternoon, so I didn't really need
to hurry. The Mercedes's engine purred as I zipped along
the highway past trees and farmland. My familiar, who I
hadn't wanted to leave cooped up in my dorm bedroom
for ages, bounced between the floor and the passenger seat
with ferret chortles that were a lot more pleased than I felt.

After a while, to distract myself from thoughts of the
task ahead, I put on my playlist of my favorite modern

piano tracks. Too bad the music industry was even more of a clusterfuck than the fearmancer community, or maybe I'd have considered trying to build a career for myself there.

The complex melody that filled the interior of the car didn't quite overwhelm my nerves. I drummed my fingers against the steering wheel. Mischief cocked her head at me with a questioning sound, and I reached over to give her a quick scratch under her chin.

"It'll be fine," I told her and myself. "In and out. No big deal."

This early in the afternoon, I could hope no one would be home except the staff, who wouldn't hassle me. Dad should be off tending to his various business concerns, and Mom often visited with her friends or looked in on the local shops she'd invested in during the day.

Still, my chest tightened when I finally turned down the winding drive that led to the mansion. The tall gate with its dark bars loomed ahead of me. I punched in the code on my dashboard control that would unlock the gate and drove on in toward the sprawling stone building beyond.

One of the grounds staff was trimming the hedges along the driveway. Otherwise there was no sign of activity. I parked the Mercedes in the loop outside the front door, not bothering with the garage. "Wait here," I told Mischief, who for once in her life decided to be obedient and curled up on the leather seat. Lord only knew how much of my uneasiness she was picking up on.

Ideally this really would be a quick in-and-out. I didn't have much here I was interested in hanging on to.

"Hello, Mr. Killbrook," our butler said as I crossed the foyer to the stairs. A look of consternation crossed his face. "We weren't expecting you home."

"Don't worry, Cravers," I said. "I'm not staying for dinner. I'll be out of your hair in less than an hour."

I jogged up the stairs and veered across the expansive hallway to the east wing. My shoes thumped against the worn but polished hardwood. It was a familiar sound, but the matching thud of my pulse turned it somehow ominous.

I threw open the door to my set of rooms and paused for a moment when the door closed behind me, letting out my breath. A faintly floral smell tickled my nose—the housekeeping staff had come through with their cleaners and air fresheners. Otherwise, the sitting room attached to my bedroom and private bathroom looked the same as it had when I'd left last week: cushy leather couch across from the huge TV, shelves packed with an equal number of books and video games, the old arcade consoles I'd been collecting standing along the opposite wall.

The other scions and I used to have a blast here when I'd invite them over. I hadn't done that in a while. Not since I'd realized how little this all belonged to me, actually.

But I figured my father who wasn't really my father owed me a few things for dragging me into this world and this wretched situation. I just had to figure out what in this place I cared about enough to bother taking with me.

I didn't have the means to transport large items, and anyway, the apartment I'd managed to rent on short notice came furnished. Better not to have any major reminders of my old life there anyway. The whole point was to leave this all behind.

Wandering the room, I grabbed the newest game console and my favorite games. The rest I could live without. I tossed those into one of my suitcases and took another look around the room. The tightness in my chest dug in little claws.

How much had *any* of this stuff really mattered to me? It'd all been its own kind of distraction from my dad's chilly treatment and the reasons for it I'd discovered.

I left the sitting room for my bedroom and checked my closet for any clothes I'd want to hold onto that I hadn't already brought with me to school. This formal suit had always suited me particularly well, if I ever had a good occasion to wear it again. I tossed a few sweaters and thicker pants for the winter after it. A nice pair of Oxfords that felt too fancy for most school functions. My wool coat. Some diamond cufflinks I doubted I'd ever wear but that might be useful if I burned through my money too quickly.

There really wasn't much else. I stepped out of the bedroom with an empty feeling expanding inside me, just as the door from the hallway opened.

"Jude." My mother stopped on the threshold, staring as she took in me and then the suitcase, her eyes widening. "The staff said you'd come home. What's going on?"

At five months along, her pregnancy was starting to

become obvious. The silk blouse she'd chosen flowed over her rounded belly. The life growing in there had the potential to utterly destroy mine—through no fault of its own, of course. I focused on Mom's face, on the red hair just a couple shades lighter than my own falling in loose curls around her features. My stomach clenched.

I didn't want to blame Mom for her part in the conspiracy to bring me into this world. She loved Dad; she'd only been trying to make him happy. She'd believed him that producing an heir by whatever means necessary would accomplish that. She'd showered me with affection when that promise had proven to be a lie.

But she had to have realized that eventually the truth would come out, one way or another, and I'd pay the consequences. She'd never stood up to him about the way he'd treated me. And how could she not realize what her current state meant for my future? Was she just willing that knowledge away, letting herself pretend it wasn't true because as far as she knew, I didn't have any idea?

"I'm just getting a few of my things," I said in a voice that came out oddly detached to my own ears. "I decided to get a place of my own."

She blinked at me. "A place of your own? But—if there's something you're unhappy with at the house— You can always make use of one of the other properties—"

"I wanted a place that's just mine," I said, calmly but firmly. "That's all. You can tell Dad not to worry—I'm not going to come asking for anything. I can handle it all on my own."

I'd already spoken to the bank to make sure my account there was only in my name. My parents couldn't touch my accumulated "allowance" and the chunk of my inheritance that had transferred over to me at eighteen. The funds in there should last me a good long while, definitely long enough to finish school and establish myself in some kind of paying work.

My parents would never need to think about me again. I'd fade right out of their lives… and maybe Dad could let that be enough.

Mom's mouth twisted at a pained angle, and her hand came to rest on her belly, as if somehow my soon-to-be baby sister was affected by this situation. "I don't understand. Did something happen, Jude? Please, if something's wrong, you can tell me."

Looking back into her worried eyes, I was struck by the urge to take her up on that offer. To tell her just how much I knew and how scared I was. To go back to those childhood years when getting a hug from her was almost enough to offset the sting of Dad's cold shoulder.

It had been a long time since then, though. I wasn't sure I'd even get a hug. More likely, her stare would turn horrified, and she'd plead with me to stay… so that she could contact Dad and find out how *he'd* want to deal with me.

I swallowed hard. "I'm fine, Mom. Just feeling the need for a little independence. *You* don't need to worry about me either, I promise."

There might have been a thing or two in the bathroom

I'd have taken, but now that Mom was right here, I didn't want to linger. I moved toward the doorway, pulling the suitcase on its wheels, and she backed out, her expression still distraught. She touched my shoulder as I passed her.

"I'm here for you if you do need anything," she said. "I *want* to worry about you if there's reason to."

For a second, I completely choked up. Maybe she meant that, but not enough. Not enough to save me. As far as I could tell, I was the only one who could do that.

"Okay, Mom," I said, because I wasn't here to be cruel to her either. Then I hurried out to my car before the mix of guilt and resentment could grip me any harder.

I had another long drive ahead of me, and this one came with a new set of troubled thoughts. Mom might not have guessed why I was taking this step in the moment, but once she'd had time to mull it over, to talk with Dad about it… would they suspect I was onto their secret? Would Dad decide I was a threat that needed to be eliminated right away after all? Presenting a false heir to the entire community, including the other barons, was an offense a hell of a lot worse than anything Rory was accused of doing.

I couldn't control what they thought or decided to do, only what I did for myself from here on.

Evening set in during my drive. The lights of New York City glowed in the distance long before I passed through the suburbs and crossed the bridge to Manhattan Island. Traffic slowed to a crawl, and Mischief squirmed impatiently beside me, but the bustle of city energy was weirdly soothing. In a place like this, I could disappear at least temporarily.

When I reached my apartment building, I left the car in the underground garage and hauled my suitcase and the bag I'd brought from school to the elevator. My familiar bounded along ahead of me. The elevator dropped me off on the second highest floor, and my ferret and I walked into the apartment together.

Crisp filtered air wafted over me in the sparse modern space that belonged to no one but me. Mischief let out an excited chortle and scurried across the hardwood floor to make a full exploration. A smile crossed my lips as I stopped by the broad windows overlooking Central Park. It wasn't a huge apartment, but I'd been willing to splurge a little for this view.

The combined living-dining room had enough seating for six around the TV and at the dining table. Maybe someday I could invite all the scions over *here* for a proper hang-out. The thought of Rory nestled on the corner of the sofa made me giddy.

I wasn't sure how I'd explain this move to the others, though. The thought of telling them the truth about my parentage still sent a shudder of panic through me.

Why the hell would they want to hang out with an imposter, a guy who wasn't even one of them? Would they have given me the time of day in the first place if I hadn't been thrust into their midst under false pretenses?

I inhaled slowly, letting the clean lines of the furnishings calm me. I didn't have to find out the answer to that question yet. Maybe I never had to. For now, I needed to take every step I could to make sure I kept this new life.

As I opened my bag, the conducting pieces I'd carefully shaped clicked against each other. I picked up the first one, sat down on the sofa, and began the slow process of casting a protective ward strong enough to buy my escape if Dad happened to come calling.

CHAPTER EIGHTEEN

Rory

A s soon as I started looking for Cressida instead of
avoiding her the way I normally did Victory and
her best friends, it became very obvious that *she* was
avoiding me. Very effectively, too. No matter what time I
left my bedroom in the morning or popped back into the
dorm during the day, I never bumped into her. Our paths
never crossed on the green or elsewhere around campus.
So far she hadn't even been in any of my classes.

After getting nowhere for a day, I knocked on her
bedroom door the next morning. No one answered, but I
had no idea whether that meant she was in there ignoring
me or had already headed out. At this point, both
possibilities seemed equally plausible.

As I went about my day, still without so much as a
glimpse of her white-blond French braid, the sense grew
that this couldn't be coincidence. She was staying away

from me on purpose. And why would she be keeping such a careful distance from me unless she knew something to do with me that she didn't want to have to face?

I couldn't believe she was simply terrified that I might really have murdered Imogen. She'd seen just as much as Malcolm had that I wasn't the type to lose my temper violently even under extreme circumstances.

Her two cohorts, Victory and Sinclair, hadn't taken any jabs at me since they'd gotten back from break, but they weren't dodging me either. I came into the common room in the middle of the afternoon to find the two of them sitting on one of the sofas murmuring over a fashion magazine, and a prickle ran up the back of my neck. Normally Cressida would have been perched there with them. Was she just not around… or had she been alerted to my arrival somehow and ducked away before I'd walked in?

The last thing I wanted to do was ask my long-time nemesis for help, but I could bite the bullet when my ability to prove I wasn't a murderer was on the line. I strode up to the sofa and waited until Victory raised her eyes to meet mine.

"Where's Cressida?" I asked. Might as well cut to the chase and keep this conversation as brief as possible.

Victory wrinkled her nose. "I'm not her keeper. And why should I tell you even if I know—so you can go harass her?"

I restrained myself from rolling my eyes. I'd never done anything remotely close to "harassing" Victory and

her friends, unless you counted paying them back in kind
for the ways they'd harassed me.

"I need to ask her about something important," I said.
"I'm not looking to argue with her or whatever."

Victory shrugged and turned back to her magazine.
"You really should ask your fellow scions for help, since
you're all so close these days."

Obviously she was still pissed off at me because
Malcolm had interrupted her plan to feed Deborah to her
cat familiar. I wavered, wondering if there was any other
tactic I could try, but the only things I knew Victory
wanted from me were to see me crushed or disgraced,
neither of which I could offer up. She'd probably rejoice if
I failed at the hearing.

In the end, I grabbed a book on insight magic from
the library and took it out onto the green to read where I
could watch for Cressida coming or going. She had to
have classes sometime. I didn't think she could make it
from the dorms to Nightwood Tower without me spotting
her.

The first hour or so passed pretty uneventfully. Other
students claimed spots on the grass between the paths,
some of them eyeing me before moving a little farther
away, but no one interrupted my reading. Cressida didn't
make any appearance either, though. I'd gotten through a
couple chapters with my broken attention when mocking
laughter reached my ears from across the green.

I shifted position surreptitiously and peered toward
the sound with my head still tipped toward the book.
Shelby and two other Nary students from the music

program had just left Nightwood Tower, and a few
fearmancer students had closed around them. One of
them was the Cutbridge guy who'd argued for fearmancer
world domination in Physicality the other day.

The girl beside him made a subtle gesture with her
hand, and Shelby's feet flew out from under her as if she'd
tripped. She sprawled on her hands and knees, her cello
case landing with a thump that made me wince. Cutbridge
laughed again.

"Leave us alone," one of the other Naries snapped at
the mages.

"We didn't do anything," Cutbridge said in a sly voice.
"It's not our fault if just being around greatness makes you
clumsy."

Behind the Naries, another of the fearmancers twisted
his fingers. The Nary guy's ankle jerked at the same time,
and he stumbled.

I scrambled onto my feet with a hiccup of my pulse.
The fearmancer students liked to hassle the Naries, sure,
but I'd never seen them toe the line of revealing their
magic so blatantly. They were *pointing out* the fact that
they hadn't needed to touch the other students to assault
them. Was Cutbridge trying to force some kind of reveal
with his talk about greatness?

Shelby had said the vibe between the scholarship
students and the regular ones had become more tense.
How long had stuff like this been happening?

I wasn't sure how much I cared whether Naries knew
magic existed or not, but I wasn't going to sit around while
a bunch of bullies tormented my friend and her

classmates. I shoved the book under my arm and marched over.

Shelby was just pushing herself upright when she looked around and saw me. A relieved smile touched her lips even as she blushed with embarrassment. The fearmancer girl who'd tripped her, currently leaning over the cello case, caught her glance, raised her own head, and yanked herself backward at the sight of me.

"It's Bloodstone," she murmured. "Holy shit." Her face paled, and her shoulders came up defensively. A waft of fear rolled off her into my chest.

The smack of emotion made me queasy. I held up my hands to show I was coming over peacefully, but the movement made the girl flinch. The other guy was backpedaling too with another wave of panic. Cutbridge held steadier, but his jaw had clenched tight.

"I'll just remind you that there are witnesses," he said stiffly.

Witnesses? So that I'd think twice if I'd been planning on murdering him? Frankly, that comment made me *want* to murder him more than anything else this bunch had done. I settled for letting my voice come out sharp and tart.

"Why don't you all go find something more productive to do? You've got better ways to make yourself feel big than this, don't you?"

I waved my hand vaguely toward the other buildings, and the girl lurched away with a yelp as if I'd cast something at her. Fresh fear raced into me so swiftly it quivered all the way up my gums.

"I didn't—" I started, not knowing how to deny I'd done something that I wasn't allowed to admit was even possible in front of Shelby and the other Naries, but the girl was already spinning and dashing away.

"Bitch," Cutbridge muttered, and stalked after her. The other fearmancer guy fled in the opposite direction.

Shelby straightened the rest of the way up, brushing off her clothes. "Thanks. I don't know what trick they were pulling there. That was almost spooky."

"Seriously," the guy said with a shudder.

My gut twisted, but I didn't know what was disturbing me more—how blatantly the other mages had flouted university rules or how terrified they'd been of me. I'd known people were more nervous of me than before, but… were there really students who'd seen how I'd behaved in the five months I'd been going to school here and still thought I might slaughter one of them in the middle of the green?

The worst thing was, they weren't even completely wrong, were they? Being my friend, helping me in any way, could get you killed. Ask not just Imogen but Professor Banefield too. Could I even keep the Nary girl in front of me safe, really?

"I'm glad you're okay," I said quickly, and swiveled to hurry off in the direction of the Stormhurst Building, for no particular reason other than I was sure the Naries wouldn't be heading there too.

I was about halfway there when I noticed the thud of footsteps behind me. A moment later, Declan caught up with me, his black hair windblown. When he stopped, his hawk familiar circled overhead and dropped from the sky to perch on his shoulder. I guessed he'd been out letting it stretch its wings.

"Hey," he said quietly. "I caught the end of that confrontation on the green. You looked pretty upset."

"I wasn't going to hurt them," I blurted out.

Declan gave me such an incredulous look that I immediately felt ridiculous for even saying that. "Of course you weren't," he said. "I wanted to make sure *you're* okay."

"Yeah, I mean, I guess. I'm a lot more okay than Imogen is." I managed a weak laugh. "Which is obviously what's on everyone else's mind too."

He glanced around and motioned for me to follow him. "Come on. Let's go somewhere quiet, and you can talk about everything that's bothering you. You're going through a lot."

I didn't have the wherewithal to argue with him. I wasn't sure I really wanted to.

We wandered down toward the lake, where the breeze carried the fresh watery scent and a chilly tinge that had put an end to most swimming expeditions. Declan made for the boathouse, giving his familiar a gentle rub to its chest that must also have served as a command. As he opened the boathouse door, the hawk lifted off him with a flap of its wings and soared over the roof.

My heart skipped a beat before I followed Declan inside. He had no idea about the heated and then chilling encounter I'd had with Malcolm in here. That was weeks ago now, though. I *wanted* to move past it.

The dim space felt different now with the cool of the approaching autumn instead of mid-summer humidity. The boats creaked in their moorings with the lapping waves. Declan pulled a couple of plastic crates away from the wall and pushed one toward me. He sat down on the other.

"It's getting to you," he said. "The way people are reacting because of the accusations."

I sank onto my makeshift stool. "I know there was the arrest and everything, but it's hard to see how people could think I'm this violent person after everything I've done *not* to lower myself to really fighting since I got here. Even if I'm acquitted at the hearing… do you think they'll assume I just cheated my way out of the sanctions? Will they still be scared of me?"

Maybe they'd be even more scared, thinking I'd not only murdered a fellow student but gotten away with it.

"They might," Declan admitted. "But it's fearmancer nature to assume the worst of people, to always be suspicious and wary. No one knows you all that well except for, well, us scions I suppose. You'll have more chances to show them the longer you're here."

I lowered my head into my hands. "I just wish all this craziness was done already. It feels like every time I think I've found my footing here, someone pulls the rug out from under me in some new way. I'm *tired*, Declan."

His crate scraped against the boards as he scooted closer. He touched my shoulder with a reassuring stroke of his thumb. "I know. I'm trying to make it easier for you any way I can. We'll get through this, and when we're both in the pentacle of barons, we can start changing things. That's why they're pushing so hard at you now, you know. Because they're scared of what will happen when you really have power."

That idea provided a comfort all of its own, but only a small one, considering I wasn't sure I'd make it to that future. It seemed awfully distant right now.

"I guess I shouldn't be complaining to you," I muttered. "You've had to fight to keep your position for *years*."

"I worked up to it. You were thrown into the deep end. And I've never had to deal with attacks as intense as they're aiming at you."

"So, I'm just special."

"Yes," he said with a smile I could hear. "You are."

I looked up at him so I could see that smile, a little crooked on one side. The affection shining in his eyes wasn't quite enough. I shifted forward on my crate so I could lean into him, giving him what I'd meant to be a quick hug. But once his arms came around me, it was incredibly hard to let him go. I pressed my face into his soft shirt and drank in the cedary smell of him.

One of his hands came up to brush over my hair. An electric tingle shot through my skin. Heat pooled in my lips, and I pulled myself back before I was any more tempted to act on that attraction.

"I'm sorry," I said. "I just—I needed that."

"It's okay," Declan said, but I saw the conflict in the tensing of his face. He stood up a little abruptly. "I think

I've found a source for some more information on the joymancers, if you still think that would help."

It took me a second to catch up with the abrupt change in subject. "I—Yeah. Yeah, it still might. And I'd like to know everything I can about them anyway." If I was going to turn to these people, I'd better know who I was really dealing with.

Declan nodded. "I'll meet you in the scion lounge tomorrow morning at nine?"

"That works."

He tipped his head to me again and headed out, so briskly I couldn't help feeling I'd somehow ruined the moment between us on top of everything else.

CHAPTER NINETEEN

Declan

I ended up in the scion lounge a half hour before I'd told Rory to meet me. Restless, I managed to kill several minutes fiddling with the espresso machine Jude had requested a couple years ago. It finally produced a cup of coffee that tasted like coffee. As I sipped the bitter liquid, I wandered through the room.

The envelope I'd left on the sofa felt way too flimsy to really help Rory. It was good for her to know what the people who'd stolen her away were capable of, but I wasn't sure reading those horror stories would block enough of her long-held sympathies for her to get past the judge's scrutiny if he started along that line of questioning. She shouldn't have to be worrying about how much she might have misjudged the community she'd grown up in on top of everything else going on.

And even if the material did protect her from accusations of treason, it wasn't going to do anything to absolve her of the murder charge. We only had a few days left, and I hadn't made much progress at all.

I couldn't let the other barons win against her. It was that simple. I just... didn't have any idea how I could ensure that *we* won yet, and that fact niggled at me more and more with each passing day.

I'd finally sat down on the sofa when Rory slipped into the room, just before nine. She smiled at me, so goddamn grateful for the little I'd managed to accomplish—grateful that I was here at all—and my stomach clenched up even as my heart skipped a beat.

"So, what have you got for me this time?" she asked in a casual tone that I suspected took some effort. She dropped onto the other end of the sofa.

I nudged the envelope toward her. "These files took a little more digging to uncover. Not because they're top secret or anything, but because the authorities didn't consider them to be of the same level of concern. But... I think you might find them even more concerning than what I've shown you before. They're reports on incidents when the joymancers' efforts to interfere with fearmancer activities didn't result in any of us being harmed, but bystanders were."

The envelope creased where Rory's fingers tightened around it. "They hurt Naries?"

"Sometimes, if those people were in the way to getting at us. Looking over the reports, I'd say it was accidents or carelessness in the moment, not planned callousness, but still. The ones who stalk us think screwing us over is worth a little collateral damage."

I could tell how much that thought disturbed her from her hesitation before she opened the envelope. The uneasy sense crept over me that I should leave her to do her reading in private, but she hadn't given any sign she wanted to be alone. The least I could do was be here for her if she needed someone to talk with to process everything in those files.

As she looked over one report and then another, I returned my attention to my coffee. Her mouth pursed tighter with each page she read. After several, she set the sheets down and pressed the heel of her hand to her forehead.

"There'd be no reason for them to lie about or exaggerate those accounts, would there?" she said, her voice gone hollow. "The fearmancers writing the reports obviously didn't care about what happened to the Naries either—they were just being thorough in noting everything that happened."

"That would be what I'd assume." I didn't believe the blacksuits and other authorities who'd written up attacks where fearmancers *had* suffered would have exaggerated those accounts either, but I couldn't say it wasn't possible a few liberties had been taken here or there to emphasize a case. With the Naries... No, most of my fellow mages saw them on the same level as public property that'd been damaged.

"Some of those situations were so pointless." Rory let out a rough breath. "If they'd just waited for another opportunity, they might have gotten a better one, *and* there wouldn't have been any Naries around. What's the point in trying to stop harmful fearmancer activities if you're going to cause a bunch of harm yourself along the way? Those people who ended up in the hospital… That family whose store was destroyed…" She shook her head.

I grimaced in sympathy. "I know. I'm sure not all joymancers would be that single-minded, just like not every fearmancer is a total asshole, as I hope you're convinced of by now. From what you've said about your adoptive parents, they were good people. I'd never try to convince you that their entire community is evil or something like that. But some of them have gotten so caught up in their campaign against us, I'm not sure they're really thinking things through anymore. Kind of like how Malcolm got in his feud with you."

Rory winced at that reminder. "Okay. That kind of single-mindedness can obviously happen on both sides." She gazed down at the papers with a sort of hopeless expression that squeezed my heart. Maybe there really wouldn't be much loyalty to the joymancers left in her by the time the judge might be poking around inside her head. In this moment, I was finding it hard to consider that a victory.

"Are there *any* mages who don't go around wreaking havoc on regular people?" she asked. "Is that just what all kinds of magic do to you—make you power-hungry and arrogant?"

"I don't know," I admitted. "That seems to be how it works around here, anyway. I'm not sure if the mages in other cultures around the world approach the situation differently… We don't have very close contact with other fearmancer communities outside of a few in western Europe."

"I guess there are mages all over the world, huh?"

"As far as I know." I rubbed my mouth and then let myself add, "That's something I've always wanted to do—travel around and get to know the different communities, find out how they work, see if there are things we could learn from them."

An eager light came into Rory's eyes. "Why haven't you?"

I made a sweeping gesture with my hand to indicate the responsibilities all around me. "I can't afford to take my attention off the barony for that long. Maybe once I'm full baron and more established—once the older barons have retired and I don't have to worry about them undermining me as much… Of course, there'll still be my aunt to keep an eye on. Lord knows how long she'll keep coveting the role."

"I don't suppose she's had any criminal dealings we could sic the blacksuits on her for like we did with my grandparents?"

My lips twitched with a wry smile. "No, she's too careful for that. Which I should probably be thankful for, because if she were bolder with her attempts at sabotage, I might not still be here."

"I won't argue against that." Rory sighed and shoved

the reports into their envelope, which she tucked inside her purse. Then she tipped her head back against the sofa. She frowned at the ceiling. "It seems like every time I turn around, there are fewer people I can count on."

"You've got the scions," I said. "Well, maybe not quite Malcolm yet, but Jude and Connar. And me. I'm not going anywhere."

"As long as the barons don't ramp up their scheming to try to crush you too."

There was so much guilt in her strained words that my throat closed up. I eased closer to her on the sofa, my knee brushing hers with a faint warmth. "Not going to happen. I've got way too much practice at dodging those kinds of threats."

She turned her head to face me, her brow knitting. Her hand slid across the cushion to find mine. An eager quiver shot over my skin at the feel of her fingers twining with my own. "But who's going to look after you while you're so busy looking after me?"

I couldn't have said exactly what broke the dam inside me. Maybe it was the compassion glowing in that gorgeous face of hers, part of what had drawn me to her in the first place. Maybe it was the fact that she could still worry about what happened to me even when her entire future was on the line. Or maybe I'd simply been holding myself back so long my self-control had worn thin.

"I happen to be very good at multitasking," I said, my voice dropping low of its own accord, and before I could think better of it, I'd brought my mouth to hers.

How many weeks had it been since I'd last had this

pleasure? I'd forgotten what kind of heaven kissing Rory was. Especially when she kissed me back, with a soft little sound of encouragement that sent a jolt of lust straight to my groin. Her fingers teased into my hair, and her warm lips moved against mine, deepening the kiss. Just like that, I was lost in the taste of her, in the berry sweetness lingering in her mouth.

Her other hand clutched my shirt, tugging me closer. My breath stuttered with the press of her chest against mine. I gripped her waist, a thrill racing through me as the silky fabric shifted to offer a strip of bare skin.

In that instant, I wanted nothing more than to lay her back on the sofa and rediscover the blissful rush that came with the joining of our bodies. So what if the door to the lounge wasn't locked? Let the other guys stumble on us and see that she wanted me too.

My hand slid higher up her side, her fingers tightened in my hair, and a spark of warning finally penetrated the haze of my desire. I could fuck everything up if just one person stepped over that threshold and saw us—fuck it up not just for me but for her.

I yanked myself back, my nerves raw with the sudden loss of contact and my chest heaving. Rory stayed where she was, even more beautiful with that flush in her cheeks and the hungry glint in her eyes.

"I'm sorry," she started.

I cut the rest of her apology off with a shake of my head. "No. You didn't do anything wrong. I shouldn't have — *I'm* sorry."

It wasn't just for school policy, I reminded myself. I

couldn't have her. Not in the long run, not the way I already wanted her, not without losing the barony and throwing my little brother into the fray. It was easier if I never got involved with her this intimately in the first place.

That was the logic I'd been using from the moment I'd realized I wanted her. Suddenly it struck me as absurd. I *was* involved—Rory Bloodstone was tangled all through my mind and my heart, and I'd be lying to myself more than anyone if I denied it. Sure, it'd be painful letting her go later if I gave in to those feelings wholeheartedly now… but every time I stopped myself, every time I pulled away, was plenty painful too. What was I really sparing myself from?

None of that mattered right now, though. Rory needed a friend, someone to help her through the awful situation she was facing, not another lover. The rest of those thoughts… the rest I could sort through later.

I exhaled slowly and brought my attention back to the reason for this meeting. "Do you think you'll want more of those reports?"

Rory looked down at her purse. She hesitated for a second before accepting the change of subject. The flush was already fading from her cheeks. "No, I think—I think this is enough to color my opinions in the right direction."

"Is there anything else I can look into or try to dig up that would help?" The need shot through me, sharp and searing, to do *something* more than I'd managed so far. "Really, anything at all, even if you're not sure I'd be able to. I do have more access to the professors and the administration in general…"

Rory's face brightened abruptly. "There actually is something. Can you get your hands on a student's class schedule for me? There's someone I'm having a lot of trouble tracking down."

CHAPTER TWENTY

Rory

"I feel so stupid," I said to Deborah as I flopped back on my bed. "I never even met any joymancers other than Mom and Dad, and I just assumed they were all peaceful and kind and, I don't know, focused on joy."

Deborah scurried along my arm to nestle her warm furry presence against my shoulder. *You weren't wrong. The Conclave's main objective is to see us spread as much joy as we can.*

"And to get in the way of the mages who are stirring up fear instead, by whatever means necessary, no matter who's in the way."

I don't know much about the active hostilities between our people and the fearmancers, but I'm sure they always weighed the risks carefully—

"How can you be sure if you don't know much about

it?" I reined my temper in and sighed. I had to remember to keep my voice quiet when I was talking to her to make sure no one overheard. If I concentrated, I could make out the murmur of a few of my dormmates talking in the common room on the other side of my door.

"I'm sure they believe they're doing the right thing," I went on. "They probably have all sorts of justifications. I'm just starting to think they weigh the factors in the situation differently than I would. At least, when it comes to the ones that come up here basically hunting fearmancers, even though the fearmancers leave them alone."

They don't come after the fearmancers to protect themselves. It's for the Naries' sake.

"Then I don't see why they're so reckless about hurting the Naries who happen to be nearby."

Maybe the joymancers who fought those battles told themselves it was on behalf of people without magic, the people the fearmancers exploited… but the records I'd seen made it hard to believe that. How much were they trying to make the world more joyful, and how much did they simply take joy in eliminating mages they disagreed with, no matter who else paid the price along the way?

I wasn't going to say the fearmancers were *better* on average, but…

"How can I go to them to take down the school when I don't know how they'll handle that fight?" My throat tightened. "They might decide even the people who want the fearmancer community to be better, like Declan, are a threat. They might hurt the Nary students while they're destroying everything here they can. I don't want to cause some kind of slaughter."

If you laid it out for them—if you explained things—they'd understand.

"Maybe. How much will they even listen to me, when I'm one of those fearmancers?" I grimaced. "They didn't even trust me staying with my parents once I got old enough to come into my magic, when I'd never done anything wrong and they were suppressing my powers the whole time."

Deborah didn't seem to have any answer to that. She nuzzled my shoulder.

Whatever happens, I'll stand up for you however I can. I know you're more joymancer than fearmancer at heart.

That reassurance only made me queasy. I wasn't so sure anymore that I *wanted* to be more like the joymancers. I wanted to be like my adoptive parents—but as people, not as mages. When it came to my magic, I wanted to be *me*.

A fearmancer could do good for the world. A fearmancer could care about other people. I had more than one example of that just among the scions.

The peal of my phone's ringtone broke through my uneasy reverie. I rolled over to grab it out of my purse.

"Rory!" a cheerful voice said when I answered. "It's Maggie. I'm glad I could catch you."

It took me a second to recognize the voice and the name. Then my body tensed against the bedspread.

Maggie was Lillian Ravenguard's assistant. I hadn't

heard from Lillian since our tense conversation on the green. I'd found her employee pleasant enough to talk with in the past, but now the brightness of Maggie's voice, as if we were all such good friends, rubbed me completely the wrong way.

"Hi," I said warily. "What are you calling about?"

Maggie's tone became more subdued as if she'd noticed my hesitance. "Oh, it's kind of silly." She let out a brief self-deprecating laugh. "I was just wondering if Lillian had come by to see you in the last couple days."

Wasn't knowing Lillian's schedule part of her job? The inquiry set my nerves even more on edge. "I haven't seen her since Monday."

"Ah. All right. Did she mention anything she was planning, maybe to do with your case, when you saw her then?"

"No, not really." And if she'd worked any magic on me, the other scions hadn't been able to detect it.

I wasn't inclined to give Maggie the details of our conversation if she didn't already know them anyway. I frowned at the phone. "Shouldn't you be asking Lillian this stuff?"

Maybe my tone was a little more brusque than was necessary. Maggie paused for a moment before answering, and her voice came out with a slight edge to it beneath the brightness. "I would, but she hasn't been in touch for a few days. I'm a little worried, considering her line of work, that's all. I thought she might have said something to you."

Lillian was probably off figuring out all the ways to ensure my murder charges stuck. "Well, she didn't, so I can't help you," I said. "And actually, I've got to get to class."

My jaw clenched as I tucked the phone away. Maggie was worried about *Lillian* and asking me for help, when I was the one just a few days away from losing the whole rest of my life? She had to have some idea what her employer was involved in even if she didn't know all the specifics. I didn't like being rude, but if I'd offended her and she didn't call again, I couldn't say I minded.

I hadn't been lying about having a class to get to soon, although it wasn't my own. Thanks to Declan's consultation of the student records, I happened to know that Cressida would be getting out of an Illusion seminar in just fifteen minutes.

"Wish me luck getting some answers," I murmured to Deborah, who bobbed her head encouragingly.

I got to the classroom on the fifth floor of the tower several minutes early, but that was fine. For all I knew, Cressida might have tried to sneak out early. I waited, leaning against the wall outside, until the door swung open and the students filed out.

Cressida was in the middle of the pack. She was just opening her mouth and raising her hand in what looked like the start of a casting when I snagged the sleeve of her blouse. Her mouth snapped shut at the sight of me.

"Hi," I said with a tight smile. "I think we need to talk."

Her lips pressed into a flat line. "I don't think we have

anything to talk about," she said stiffly as we headed down the stairs together.

"Well, why don't I ask you a few questions, and we'll find out whether that's true. Consider it a request from one of your future barons."

I didn't expect that angle to necessarily work. As we left Nightwood Tower, I kept a casting on the tip of my tongue in case I needed to hold onto her magically. But Cressida apparently wanted to keep a certain appearance of dignity, because now that I'd found her, she made no moves to bolt for the hills.

"Where are we having this conversation?" she asked.

I wanted privacy, but I didn't want to have to travel very far while counting on her compliance. After a moment's deliberation, I headed toward the kennel. No one was hanging out on the field nearby, and Malcolm's familiar was the only animal currently residing in the small building.

After a quick peek into Shadow's stall to confirm the Nightwood scion wasn't around—which earned me a pleading whine from the wolf—I turned to Cressida. Her nose had wrinkled as if the incredibly faint doggy smell offended her.

"You were in Ashgrave Hall when Imogen was killed," I said. "I passed you on my way to the stairs—and she was already dead when I got up to the dorm."

Cressida lifted her shoulders in the most subtle of shrugs. The dim daylight that streaked through the kennel's few windows washed out the purple and pink streaks in her white-blond hair. "That doesn't sound like a question."

She sounded as if she didn't care about the topic at hand, but a flutter of fear passed from her into me. She'd seen something she was afraid to talk about.

I willed my hands not to clench in frustration. "What were you doing up there? I'm going to assume the actual murderer didn't let you wander into our dorm while she was toying with Imogen."

"I was going to grab something from my room but realized I didn't really need it. Nothing particularly shocking about that."

I studied her expression. She'd kept a casual air, but her stance had tensed. Under my scrutiny, she narrowed her eyes at me. "I hope you're not trying to accuse *me* of killing her."

"No," I said quickly. "Of course not. I know it wasn't you. The point is, I think *you* know it wasn't *me*. And it's kind of important to me that I don't end up sanctioned for a murder I didn't commit."

"Well, I can't say I care either way." Cressida flicked her braid over her shoulder with obvious contempt.

Keeping my cool was getting harder by the second. "Maybe you'd care if you realized how much I already know. You went into the dorm room under ours, didn't you?"

Her eyes didn't give away more than a twitch, but a sharper jolt of anxiety hit me at the same time. I'd been right. She'd been the one who'd made that sound right after Imogen's attack. And why would she be scared of me revealing that if she hadn't heard evidence of the murder?

"What makes you say that?" she hedged, crossing her arms over her chest.

Of course, I didn't have any evidence I could put on display. "I put the pieces together," I said. "Other people might too. Won't you get in trouble if it turns out you were keeping quiet about important evidence that could exonerate a scion?"

"Is that a threat now?" She cocked her head. "I think if you had any real leverage, we wouldn't be talking about this in the doghouse. I have no idea what the hell you've gotten yourself into, Bloodstone, but you obviously have a lot of people out to tear you down. It'd be pretty stupid of me to do anything other than stay as far away from that mess as I possibly can, don't you think? Why the hell should I put my neck out for you? What the hell have *you* ever done for me?"

I hadn't hit back at her for all the ways she'd tried to undermine me with Victory or on her own, which I thought was pretty generous. Clearly Cressida didn't agree.

"Why make this about me?" I tried. "The whole fearmancer community is going to be affected if a soon-to-be baron goes down for a crime they had nothing to do with. Do you really want the kind of assholes who'd set me up like this to win?"

"If they win, then you don't deserve to be baron anyway," Cressida said tartly, and spun with a swing of her braid. "You asked your questions, and I answered them. We're done."

"Cressida." I took a step after her, but I really didn't have anything else I could say. All I could do was glower at her back as she sashayed away.

Her testimony could be the deciding factor in my hearing. The confirmation that she knew something gave me hope, but not enough to lift my spirits.

How the hell could I convince her it was worth the risk of giving that testimony?

CHAPTER TWENTY-ONE

Rory

"I don't know much about Cressida's family," Connar said as we ambled together across the green. "The Warburys are definitely respected, but they're a little distant from the other top families. They always give off a vibe like they prefer to stick to their own inner circle."

I made a face at the building in front of us. "So you don't have any idea what they might want that they don't already have."

"They seem to have pretty much everything they could want. I mean, maybe they'd want to mingle with a barony if they had the chance, but Cressida's never pushed the flirting all that hard, so I'm not sure—and anyway..." He trailed off awkwardly.

I gave him a playful tap of my elbow. "Don't worry, I won't try to marry off you or the other scions to clear my name. There's got to be something other than that."

"The trick will probably be getting her to tell you. If you could get a peek in her head with an insight spell, that might help."

"I don't think I'm going to win any points with her if I start stealing her thoughts without permission. She'll only hate me more."

"I don't think she hates you," Connar said quietly. "The crap she and the other girls pulled—it's all the same power struggle, you know. Jockeying for position, making themselves look powerful to anyone watching. Pretty much everyone here does it if they can get away with it. She thought she could lord it over a scion." He shot me a quick grin. "Clearly a major miscalculation."

It was hard to get into that fearmancer mindset—to understand the ways they might think automatically that were so different from how I'd been raised. I rubbed my forehead as the warm September sun beamed down on us.

The day was gorgeous, between that sun and the woody scents of the forest carrying in the air. I'd have been able to enjoy it a lot more if the problem of convincing Cressida to speak up for me hadn't been gnawing at me.

We came to a stop by Killbrook Hall, Connar tucking his hand around mine. We'd just left an early afternoon class, and I didn't have another today, but I couldn't summon any enthusiasm for heading back to my dorm— where Cressida would be hiding from me again, no doubt. There wasn't any point in making another attempt at talking to her until I'd figured out a better strategy anyway.

As I stood there waffling, Declan came out of the

building with a couple of the professors. He nodded at something one of them was saying and then offered a remark that made the other chuckle, carrying himself with ease. But I recognized the strain in the slight stiffness of his posture, the flicker of fatigue that crossed his face when it was partly hidden as he swiped his hand up over his hair.

If I felt trapped by this situation, how much more confined must he feel, working himself to the bone to keep up appearances and prove himself every second of every day since he'd been a child. Even the brief respite I'd given him at the nearby Bloodstone country property had ended with more stress.

He deserved better than that.

The idea sparked in my head and traveled to my tongue before I had a chance to second-guess myself. "Connar," I said, squeezing the Stormhurst scion's hand, "I think we could use an escape, don't you? And Declan could definitely use one too. Why don't we all go up to the cliff for a little while and leave this place behind? Maybe getting away will give my mind a chance to come up with some brilliant plan."

Connar hesitated. The cliff where the two of us had first talked—and first a lot of other things—had been his private place for a long time, from what I'd gathered. I didn't think any of the other scions had ever joined him there before I'd stumbled on the spot. But he only balked for a second, and then he nodded. "Yeah. Why not? I'm sure a little time away would be good for him. I'm still impressed he managed to talk circles around the blacksuits to get you out of their custody in the first place."

Declan had just parted ways from the professors. Connar raised his hand with a quick wave. "Declan! We're going down to the lake. Why don't you take a break and come along?"

The Ashgrave scion's expression turned a bit puzzled at the invitation. As he seemed to waver, I smiled at him. "You don't have any classes to run off to, do you?"

"No," he admitted. "I'm not in much of a mood for a swim, though."

"We're just going to take a walk," Connar said, lowering his voice as we came up beside Declan. "There's a great spot a little ways down the shore that's great for just… thinking, and putting all the campus's tensions aside for a while."

The other scion didn't look any less bemused, but he nodded. "All right. You've been holding out on the rest of us, huh?"

The teasing was gentle, but a faint flush colored Connar's face. "None of us have many places we can feel are just ours."

"No denying that. I guess I didn't realize…" Declan trailed off as if recognizing that he couldn't end that sentence in a positive way. He hadn't realized that Connar was sensitive enough to be bothered by a lack of privacy? None of the scions had really seen the big guy as anything other than a musclehead. The Ashgrave scion course-corrected quickly, though. "You don't have to share it now."

"I want to," Connar said firmly. "I think... the last few months have proven that we have to be able to count on each other if we're going to get through this."

Declan gave him a longer, considering look, and a more relaxed smile crossed his lips. "Yeah." He caught my eye for a second, extending the smile to me, and I had the urge to reach for his hand too. But I knew better than to attempt that when we were in full view of the green.

We meandered past the campus buildings toward the lake and then veered down the path that rambled through the east woods. Connar walked with the confidence of a guy who'd taken this route dozens of times in the past.

He left the path with an assured turn of his heel, and Declan and I followed through the brush, up the forested slope. The leaves rustled overhead, and birds called to each other in the distance. As we neared the top, I made out the hiss of the lake's waves washing against the base of the cliff now far below us.

When he stepped from the line of trees at the edge of the clearing, Connar let out an audible breath. The brightening of his face made me wonder how much *he'd* needed a break too.

Declan stopped beside me, taking in the stretch of grassy ground along the cliff, the fallen log that bisected it, the warble of the water below, and the warm waft of the breeze. His stance relaxed by increments.

"This is nice," he said with a bit of awe in his tone. "I can't believe I didn't know this clearing was here."

Connar smiled with obvious satisfaction. "I stumbled on it when I was hiking around burning off steam. I'm sure I'm not the first person who's ever come up here, but most people don't go far off the paths."

"No, I guess they don't." Declan moved forward cautiously, as if he thought he might overstep in some way, but after a moment he headed over to the log and sat down on it to gaze across the lake. Something in my own chest released seeing him relax, if only for a short time.

"We should cast a spell to make sure we have this place to ourselves right now," I said to Connar. "I don't really trust the appearance of privacy these days."

"I'll cast it," he said. "Who knows what the blacksuits would make of that spell if you did?" He tipped his head toward the cuffs circling my wrists.

"Good point."

As he murmured a spell to block anyone from roaming this way, I wandered farther into the clearing, soaking in the sunlight and the fresh air. Other than the light weight of the cuffs, there was nothing here to remind me of everything I wanted to escape back in the real world.

Declan glanced over at me, his expression turning thoughtful. "You've been up here before," he said, not even a question.

"Just a few times." Who knew what he'd make of that.

Connar hunkered down in his favorite spot with his back against a tree trunk, and I walked all the way to the cliff's edge. I sat down there with a little thrill at letting my legs dangle over the distant water beneath. If the most nerve-wracking thing in my life had been this thirty-foot drop, I'd have been ecstatic.

After a while, the tug of the wind right over the water

became too insistent. As I got to my feet, Connar did too. He came to join me in the middle of the clearing, setting his hand on my waist. I let myself lean back into his solid frame at his soft tug, but my senses sprang into sharper awareness of Declan several feet away. I didn't want to remind him of what he'd decided he and I couldn't have.

Connar touched my jaw to turn my face toward him and leaned over my shoulder to steal a kiss. I couldn't help melting into it for the few seconds before I eased away. My gaze twitched toward Declan, who'd turned to look at us. Connar followed my gaze.

"It's okay," Declan said. "Don't worry about me." That last bit he obviously meant more for me than Connar. His tone had stayed even enough, but his throat bobbed with a thick swallow, and there was enough hunger in his eyes to heat my skin. My mind slipped back to the other day in the lounge, the delicious burn of his kiss, over too soon.

Maybe I made some motion I wasn't aware of, or maybe Connar could pick up on at least some of what'd passed through Declan's expression. It wasn't as if he hadn't seen how much I enjoyed having the attentions of two guys at the same time before. The Stormhurst scion considered his friend for a long moment, and then he said, low but steady, "You could always join in."

A deeper flare of heat unfurled inside me at the thought, with a pang at the thought that Declan would refuse. His eyes widened, and he wet his lips, the brief movement of his tongue setting off all kinds of sparks through my nerves even across that distance.

To my surprise, he got up. "You're sure no one's going to make their way up here?" he said.

"If someone breaks the spell I put up, I'd feel it well before they got to the clearing," Connar said.

Declan's attention shifted to me. Our gazes locked, a quiver of anticipation racing through me. I lifted my hand toward him. If he'd changed his mind about what he was willing to let himself get into with me, I was totally on board.

He crossed the last distance between us and twined his fingers with mine. "Rory," he said, his voice raw, before he dipped his head to kiss me.

It wasn't like our kisses before. So many of those had been hasty, lust on the verge of being reined back in again. Even when we'd had sex in the country house, every caress had come with the sense that our time together was strictly limited.

This kiss captured my lips with a tender pressure that spoke of an expanse of pent-up desire, desire that could go on and on without fading away or being tamped down. As if Declan were offering himself up to me as he was, no boundaries or restrictions—all of him. A heady flutter passed through my chest.

Another set of lips brushed my skin. Connar kissed his way across my shoulder, adjusting the neckline of my dress for better access. His fingers trailed over my stomach. As he stepped around me, Declan pulled back from the kiss with a wildness in his bright hazel eyes that I'd never seen before. He seemed to waver for a second and then pressed his mouth to the side of my neck, leaving my lips for Connar to reclaim.

As their mouths sent heat searing through my body, I released their hands to curl my fingers into both of their shirts. Just having them on either side of me—these guys I wanted so much and was coming to care about so deeply —made me tingle from head to toe.

Connar's tongue slipped past my lips, and his hand came up to cup my breast. The swipe of his thumb pebbled my nipple in an instant with a jolt of pleasure. Declan grazed his teeth across the crook of my neck. At my ecstatic shiver, he stroked his fingers over my other breast.

The contrasting sensations of Connar's firm caresses and Declan's light teasing brought a gasp to my throat. The tingling condensed between my thighs. I wanted so much more than this—I wanted all three of us gasping—I wanted the pleasure to carry me away from my worries completely if only for a few moments.

My grip on their shirts tightened. As if picking up on my growing urgency, Connar reached for the hem of my dress and eased it up, letting the smooth fabric trace a path over my thigh. He released my mouth to nibble along my jawline, and Declan was there to catch my lips with his.

Connar's fingers settled over my panties. Bliss careened from my core. I made a hungry sound against Declan's mouth and stroked my hands down both guys' chests, wanting to pay back the sensations they were provoking in every way I could. They both stood several inches taller than me, but their differing frames, brawny and slim, felt like the perfect combination.

When my hand brushed over the bulge in Connar's slacks, he growled against my neck. The circular motion of his fingers between my legs intensified, each pulse of pleasure making my knees wobble. I traced my thumb over Declan's erection, taut against his fly, and his breath stuttered as he deepened our kiss.

Connar gave my clit one last flick of his thumb and yanked down my panties. I squeezed him through his pants encouragingly. His next growl turned a groan.

"Down," he murmured, half command and half plea, with a guiding nudge of his hand. I sank onto a grassy bit of ground on my knees, and he dropped with me, slicking his fingers over my arousal from behind. I rocked into his touch.

"Yes," I gasped out as his forefinger dipped right inside me. At the same time, I gripped Declan's pants, tugging both him and them down to my level. He knelt in front of me. As I flicked open the clasp and delved inside to free his cock from his boxers, he inhaled sharply.

"Rory?"

I gazed up at his face, reveling in the bliss thrumming from my core with each pump of Connar's fingers, in the silky stiff feel of the cock I held in my grasp. Nothing in Declan's expression looked anything but eager other than a hint of concern about me. As if I hadn't wondered what he'd taste like from the first moment I'd touched him like this months ago.

Slowly, deliberately, with a smile of anticipation, I

brought my mouth to his cock. His hips jerked at the slide of my lips over the head. "Fuck," he muttered, the curse a strangled sound. He grasped my hair, his fingertips skimming my scalp in giddying ways.

The sound of a zipper opening behind me made me quiver with my own eagerness. I took more of Declan into my mouth, swiveling my tongue around his sweetly musky length, and Connar's cock grazed my entrance. Need throbbed through my sex. I pressed back toward him in encouragement.

He murmured the necessary spell, ran his hands over my ass, and then gripped my thighs as he thrust inside me. I cried out over Declan's cock. Riding the surge of pleasure that filled me, I closed my lips again and sucked even harder.

We rocked together in a perfect symphony of bliss, Connar plunging in and out of me with deeper and deeper strokes that fanned the flames inside me higher, my body swaying with his rhythm and carrying it into the bob of my head over Declan, Declan's hips pumping in time, his fingers stroking over my head.

As I felt the wave of release building inside me, I squeezed my mouth tighter around Declan's cock and sped up, urging him to join me. His fingers tightened in my hair. "Fuck," he said again in a strained voice. "I'm almost there. Rory, you don't have to—"

But I wanted to. I slicked my tongue around him as firmly as I could, and his voice broke. He came with a salty flood in the back of my mouth. As I swallowed, he drew back and urged my head up so he could kiss me.

As our breath and tongues twined, Connar sped up his thrusts too. A sound escaped me that was almost a whine. Connar's cock pumped into me even deeper, and he tucked his hand around me to rub the sensitive nub just above where we joined. The mastered strength in his powerful body radiated through me.

I shattered, leaning forward into Declan, every muscle shaking. In the rush of ecstasy, the hitch of Connar's chest told me he'd followed me over.

My head slumped against Declan's shoulder, my body slack in the aftermath. He slipped an arm around my back, and Connar hugged me from behind with a kiss to the base of my neck. All I could do in that moment was wonder at the fact that I'd gotten so lucky to have moments like this at all—and whether I could really hope for that luck to last much longer.

CHAPTER TWENTY-TWO

Rory

The vines rose up around me, clutching my limbs, squeezing my chest. Their thorns jabbed through my skin. I winced and gritted my teeth, willing myself not to yelp at the pain.

Professor Razeden's voice reached me distantly. "None of it is real. You can fight them off. How can you destroy them or slip free?"

That was the question, wasn't it? I had no doubt at all about what was being symbolized by the tangled thicket I'd found myself in for this Desensitization session. The dark chamber around me was meant to use a combination of insight and illusion to throw my worst fears at me so that I could practice tackling them. And yeah, I was plenty afraid of forces beyond my control constraining me and dragging me down. I was just glad the chamber hadn't produced a more literal illusion this time.

Well, other than the cool chuckle that echoed off the walls, mimicking Baron Nightwood's voice.

I'd slowly been getting better at fending for myself in these sessions, after the initial few when Razeden had needed to rescue me from my own mind. Conquering the agonizing sensations still wasn't anywhere near *easy*, though.

Dragging in a breath, I retreated farther into my head. The pain dulled with the distance. The vines squeezed tighter, but they weren't really there. They were just illusions—illusions I *could* change with the right spell.

They wanted to strangle me? I'd loosen them right up.

"Expand and open," I murmured, focusing on the tight coils. I pictured the loops stretching and releasing. Magic danced behind my collarbone, but at first the vines didn't budge. My pulse stuttered with the suffocating pressure.

Frowning, I spoke the words again, imbuing them with a harder push of magic. Sweat beaded on my forehead—and the friction around my limbs released. I scrambled away from the illusionary brambles before I lost control and they snatched at me again.

My feet skidded on the smooth floor, and I tripped onto my ass. Not my most graceful moment. But the prickly vines dissolved once I'd gotten my distance. The light blinked on overhead, revealing the domed room with every surface painted black, and nothing around me except Professor Razeden in his spot near the door.

"That one took you a little longer than last time," he said, checking his watch, "but not by a lot."

"I feel like it's a success any time I don't need you to step in," I said with a weak laugh as I pushed myself to my feet. "That's enough of a victory for me right now."

"Fair enough." He gave me a mild but genuine smile. "You've needed increasingly less intervention as we've gone on. Do you think you're ready to return to the usual group sessions?"

A twinge of guilt shot through my gut. Normally Desensitization was run with four students at a time, three observing while each struggled through their fears. Dealing with the potential distraction and embarrassment of those witnesses was part of the learning experience.

Because I'd had so much trouble with my initial sessions—and maybe because the images summoned up, like those of my parents' murder, had been so traumatic—the headmistress had switched me to solo sessions. But that obviously meant extra work for the professor.

The thought of my peers getting a glimpse of the things that terrified me made my stomach knot. But really, that was even more reason I should come to grips with the idea. They all had their fears exposed to each other on a weekly basis. And mine had been coming out more metaphorical recently, which was a small comfort.

"All right," I said. "If you think I'm ready."

"I'm sure you are, Miss Bloodstone," Razeden said. "But I don't resent giving you time to catch up at your own pace. It's hardly your fault you came to your studies so late and with so little preparation."

No, it was the joymancers' fault. Razeden didn't belabor that point, which I was grateful for. I nodded. "I appreciate it. I think I can handle group sessions now. I guess I should talk to Ms. Grimsworth about adjusting my schedule?"

"I can bring it up with her." He motioned me over to the door. "You obviously have much larger matters occupying your mind for the coming week."

Today's metaphors hadn't been particularly subtle, had they? Razeden must have been able to read between the lines.

He paused as I reached him, his hand resting on the door handle but not turning it. For a few seconds, he just studied me, his gaunt face even more solemn than usual.

"I can't imagine the pressure you're under at the moment," he said. "So I don't know if this will provide any comfort. But I'd like you to know that there are many of us in the school and farther abroad in the community who have certain standards of fairness and justice, even if they're not quite what you grew up with, and who wish to see you acquitted of this crime. If I can contribute toward your hearing, or if there's any other way I can assist you with this or future troubles, it would be my honor to serve my future baron."

He spoke in his usual measured voice, no outburst of emotion, with a matter-of-fact tone about the "future troubles" as if he took it as a given those would appear. Still, the unexpected declaration of loyalty brought an awkward flush to my cheeks.

How much did he know about the scheming behind the scenes? How much was he risking by making this statement to me?

Unless he was with my enemies, and this was a ploy to get past my guard? I didn't get that impression, though. He wasn't being pushy about helping or prying for information, just stating his position for the record.

"Thank you," I said past the tightness in my throat.

Razeden dipped his head in response and opened the door for me.

The Desensitization chamber was located in the basement of Nightwood Tower, and it had a typical basement vibe. As I climbed the stairs to the main floor, the air turned crisper and warmer, and more sunlight splashed across the walls from the windows above. The knowledge that I might have more supporters than had spoken up warmed me a little too, but it was hard to get much relief when there was no concrete way for those people to get me through the week ahead.

Jude had suggested we grab lunch in town after my session, so I headed around the tower toward the road into town. I expected to meet him at the path that ran through the woods alongside the road, but instead I spotted his dark copper hair halfway across the west field, where he was striding toward a cluster of students.

It only took a second and a gleam of the leaf pins on a couple of the figures' clothes for me to figure out that the fearmancers were up to their usual bullying tricks. Or the not-so-usual tricks, actually. A group of fearmancer students were surrounding the two Naries. As I veered over to intervene, one of the bullies stepped to the side to reveal another boy sprawled on the ground. The Nary guy was trying to push himself up, but his arms kept giving as if a force was pressing him down.

A force the fearmancer student was directing with subtle flicks of his hand. As the other Naries knelt to try to help their friend, the bully's lips moved with a softly spoken spell. Just like the bunch who'd harassed Shelby and her classmates the other day, these fearmancers were toeing the line of just how much magic they could get away with using without making their supernatural powers totally obvious.

Jude reached the group several strides before me—and caught the main bully's wrist in mid-flick. As the Killbrook scion faced the guy, I caught Jude's expression: jaw clenched and eyes dark with anger.

"I think that's enough," Jude said in a cuttingly flippant voice. "If you pump your ego up any bigger, it just might pop, and then everyone will see how small you actually are."

The other guy flinched, shifting into a defensive stance but shrinking a little just staring down the scion. When I caught up, his posture deflated even more.

"I wasn't *doing* anything," he said, giving us a pointed look as if *we* needed reminding that we weren't supposed to acknowledge the existence of magic. "The kid is such a weakling he couldn't manage to get himself up."

The "kid" in question, who looked about seventeen, had scrambled onto his feet now that he wasn't being magically restrained. "You were doing *something* to me," he accused, looking a little terrified at his own daring.

A chill shot through me. The fearmancer students

really had stepped awfully close to the line for him to speak with that much certainty.

The main bully paled slightly himself, but he raised his chin with a snort. "I was just pointing out feebleness where I see it." He strode off without another word, his friends hurrying after him.

Jude and I exchanged a glance. He didn't look any happier about the situation than I was. I'd known he'd been working on his attitude toward the Naries, that he'd gone out of his way to help Shelby after the accidental injury he'd caused her, but I still wouldn't have expected him to defend a bunch of strangers from fellow mages. A flutter of affection rippled through my uneasiness.

The Nary guy was wiping off his jeans, his friends standing close with concerned murmurs about his wellbeing. I wasn't sure there was anything else we could do for them now. Would the professors care if we reported how bold some of the mages were getting with their magical harassment? I could just picture Ms. Grimsworth saying, "If we haven't heard anything worrisome from the Naries, then the other students must have disguised their magic well enough."

Jude was obviously thinking along similar lines. "Hey," he said to the Naries when their hushed conversation fell into a lull. "Has that kind of thing been happening a lot since the term started?"

"People have been pretty weird," one of the guy's friends said, hugging herself, her gaze and her tone wary.

"I've seen it before," I said quietly.

Jude frowned. His expression turned oddly

contemplative for a moment. Then he snapped his fingers. "I've got a strategy you could try if the regular students get 'weird' like that again."

The guy considered him with narrowed eyes. "Why should we listen to *you*? Maybe you're setting us up for some other trick."

I shook my head. "We want to help. If Jude's got an idea, it's probably a good one." I didn't think he'd be offering it if he wasn't fairly confident it'd help.

The guy stayed skeptical, but his other friend cleared his throat and tipped his head toward me. "She's okay. I've seen her standing up for us to the assholes around here. I think we should at least listen."

Jude spread his hands. "You can give it a shot, and if it doesn't work, well, you at least shouldn't be any worse off."

"Okay, let's hear it, then," the guy said.

"It's very simple. Bullies are cowards underneath, you know. They like seeing you scared or upset. So what you do, next time someone's messing with you—stare right at them. Don't stop looking at their face. Show them you're not going to cower, and I bet you they'll back down."

Understanding clicked in my head. "Yeah," I said. "Stare them down. They'll hate that."

"Worth trying, I guess," the girl said with a shrug.

They all ambled back toward the green. Jude beamed at me. "You get it."

"If the Naries are watching their faces, they can't cast anything without giving themselves away. They've got to speak to get a spell out."

"Exactly! That doesn't mean they won't go back to old

methods, but I think it'll cut down on some of that really overt torment." He glanced at the spot where the Nary guy had been pinned down and grimaced. "The general jerkishness of the student population does appear to have escalated. Something in the water?"

"I wish I knew," I muttered.

"Well, I hope the next time the bastards try that on our scholarship students, they find themselves unpleasantly surprised." He grinned again, looking incredibly pleased at the imagined triumph he might have manufactured for the people that just a few months ago he'd sneered at.

The flutter came back into my chest. I stepped closer to him and pulled him into a hug. Jude's arms came around my shoulders, his voice amused but happy. "What's that for?"

"Do I need a reason?" I mumbled into his shirt, my nose filling with the spicy smell of him, like peppered coriander. But the truth was, I did have a reason. A very big one.

He hadn't done any of this for me. He'd already been charging over to the Naries' rescue before I'd been nearby. Protecting them really had mattered to him for their own sake.

He wasn't the same guy who'd mocked me during my first month here, not at all, and there was something miraculous about that transformation.

I lifted my head, and he pressed a quick kiss to my forehead. Emotion swelled in my throat. It wasn't just for him—Lord knew I felt a hell of a lot for Connar and

Declan too—but I was completely sure about these words in this moment.

"I love you too," I said.

A wider smile leapt across Jude's lips. His embrace tightened around me, and he ducked his head lower to capture my mouth. Right then, all I could feel, taste, and smell was him, and I was okay with that.

"Of course you do," he said, but he couldn't quite smooth the tremor out of his voice. "I'm eminently lovable."

I swatted him, and he laughed, his eyes shining with affection. He pressed one last kiss to my temple, holding me as if he couldn't convince himself to let me go just yet.

"If love were enough to protect you from the assholes after you, I'd have you covered," he murmured. "You'd never have to worry again."

If only we had a solution that simple when it came to my enemies.

CHAPTER TWENTY-THREE

Connar

U p in the cliff-side clearing, the morning breeze was a little biting, but I got all the warmth I needed from Rory nestled against me. She leaned her head on my shoulder, gazing out over the rippling expanse of the lake and the clear blue sky above, and sighed.

"It's too bad I can't just hide away up here for a few weeks and have the hearing blow over."

"Not much chance of that," I agreed with a grimace. I pressed a kiss to the back of her head in a way I hoped was comforting.

Having her like this was bittersweet. I couldn't think of much I enjoyed more than the simple pleasure of getting to hold her in my arms, inhaling her scent as sweet as toffee, knowing she had enough faith in me to completely relax in my embrace. But at the same time I was sharply aware of how ineffective all the muscles I'd built in those arms and the rest of my body were when it came to defending her from the greatest threat she was facing.

I could hold her right now, comfort her right now, but I couldn't fight or intimidate her enemies into fleeing. Why should she rely on me when I couldn't offer anything better?

I shoved those uneasy thoughts down and focused on the softness of her body against mine. Rory stayed cuddled there, the tree I was leaning against shading us, for another few minutes. Then she checked her phone. With a groan, she pulled away from me.

"I've got my mentoring session with Professor Viceport. She'll never forgive me if I'm even two seconds late."

Guilt jabbed through my chest. The Physicality professor hadn't exactly been warm toward Rory from the start, but the way I'd subtly sabotaged some of Rory's spells a couple terms ago hadn't helped the situation.

"Has she at least lightened up on you now that she's gotten a better idea of your abilities?"

Rory smiled crookedly. "She's not as overtly hostile as she used to be. I still don't think she likes me very much, for whatever reason. I guess there's not much point in worrying about that with everything else going on."

Before I could apologize again for the crap I'd put her through, she twisted around to kiss me, so tenderly I didn't need to hear the words to know she'd completely forgiven my transgressions. I wasn't sure I'd ever completely forgive myself, but I shouldn't put the burden of my guilt on her.

"I'll see you later," she said, getting up. As she moved toward the forest, another figure slipped through the trees toward us. My eyebrows rose at the sight of Declan hesitating at the edge of the clearing.

He glanced from me to Rory, his stance a little awkward, no doubt thinking about the unexpected intimacy we'd shared up here just a couple days ago.

"Hey," Rory said easily, as if it wasn't any big deal, and his shoulders came down. "I've got to get back to campus."

He nodded. "Can you meet me at the Stormhurst Building this afternoon? Let's say two? There are some things about your hearing I think we should discuss."

Rory's smile fell at the mention of the hearing, but she dipped her head in agreement. "I'll be there."

She brushed her hand against his before heading down the slope. Declan ventured farther into the clearing, some of his earlier awkwardness coming back. He cleared his throat and looked at me. "I wanted to talk with you too."

I shrugged. "Sure. This is as good a place for a chat as any."

The corner of his mouth quirked up. He cast around and ended up sitting down against a tree a few over from mine, his long legs sprawling in front of him. His gaze drifted toward the horizon as he ran a hand through his hair.

"I probably don't need to tell you this, but what happened up here the other day—no one can know that there's anything going on between Rory and me. Not while I'm still an aide, anyway."

Something about his phrasing made me wonder how much had been "going on" between the two of them before that afternoon. It'd been clear from the way he looked at her that some kind of feelings had been developing for a while, and Rory had seemed nothing but eager about him joining in, but I hadn't seen any hint of a more than friendly connection between them before. I wasn't sure whether that was my own obliviousness or Declan's usually excellent self-discipline.

"Of course," I said. "Even if you weren't working for the university, I'm not really the type to go around gossiping."

"I know. Discretion just seems particularly important right now." He let out a ragged breath. "Maybe I should have walked away. But it was starting to feel so pointless, pretending not to want… what I want."

He fell silent. Declan didn't talk about his feelings in general all that much, at least not with me, so I didn't have a clue what kind of response he'd be looking for. I fumbled for the right words and finally settled on, "She's something special."

His whole mouth curved with a smile then. "Yeah, she is."

It was an awfully strange situation when you looked at it, him and me and Jude all caring about Rory the way we did, and her seeming to share that affection, but none of us really being in a position to make anything permanent out of it. Maybe that was why it only raised the smallest prickle of jealousy to think that she might have had something going with Declan that I'd had no idea about. We were all in the same boat. And we were all on her side.

"The things you need to go over with her about the hearing…" I said. "Have you come up with a new strategy that could help?"

"Not exactly. More like damage control." His smile turned pained. "These aren't the easiest opponents to go up against."

As I knew from personal experience. I hadn't meant to say anything about it, but his comment brought out the ache in my stomach that I'd been suppressing since I'd gotten the text last night. In some ways, Declan had a better idea of how to deal with the barons than the rest of us scions, even if they were family. Maybe he'd have some wisdom that would bolster my confidence.

"I'm supposed to meet with my parents later today," I said. "They're going to hassle me about Rory not taking their deal, I assume, and who knows what else." Just saying it aloud made my gut clench tighter. I'd stonewalled their suspicions briefly, but I wasn't used to playing mind games. What if I fucked something up this time? I hadn't forgotten my mother's clear threat about Holden. Of course she'd drag my brother into this situation too.

"And you're obviously not looking forward to that meeting," Declan said mildly. He looked down at his hands where he'd rested them on his knees and then glanced over at me. "You know, I think I've made assumptions about you over the years that weren't really fair, based on seeing what *they're* like. Malcolm was right about at least one thing—we need to stick together as scions. I should have paid more attention to *you*, and I'm sorry about that. For what it's worth, now that I am paying attention, it couldn't be clearer that you're nothing like them."

The words might not have given me an answer to my most pressing problem, but they were worth a lot all the same. Some of the uncertainty I'd felt about him and his apparent wariness of me crumbled away. I couldn't really blame him for keeping a certain distance given my parents, the stories about me, and the aggressive front I'd often let myself put on.

"I appreciate that," I said. "Hopefully you won't ever need to testify to that effect on my behalf."

He let out a rough bark of a laugh. "I'll be happy if the word 'hearing' never comes up again in the rest of my life in relation to any of us."

He'd been open enough with me that I decided to press the issue a little further. "Why the need for damage control for Rory? What's going on with her hearing?"

Declan paused, and for a few seconds I thought he might decide he couldn't trust me enough to tell me. Then he sucked in a breath. "The blacksuits have assigned a different judge at the last minute. Under pressure from the other barons, I have to guess. The new one—he's known to insist on extensive insight interrogations of the accused, often going far beyond the boundaries of the case to seek out other possible crimes."

A chill trickled through me. "We already figured it was

possible they'd dig deeper into Rory's thoughts and memories."

"Yeah, but now it's basically certain. I think her attitudes about the joymancers have shifted, but the wrong piece of a memory, the wrong emotional impression in a situation… The barons want to dredge up anything incriminating they can. It's going to be awful for her, and I think it's pretty likely they'll find something they can spin against her with the lengths this judge goes to."

"Fuck. And she can't get some kind of exemption for privacy's sake, being the only heir of Bloodstone?"

He shook his head. "I get the sense there are a fair number of people even in the blacksuits who are wary of her because of her upbringing. I don't think the barons have had much trouble getting their way with the hearing. A lot of fearmancers would rather have one point of the pentacle dulled than potentially 'contaminated' by attitudes they don't approve of."

The idea set my teeth on edge. "If they'd just give her a chance…"

"We didn't really when she first got here, did we? It's only because we had to interact with her so much that we started to see her as she really is instead of through the biases we've had ingrained in us. I'm not sure how we'd get the wider community to that point. I'm not saying everyone's against her or anything, only that it's not going to be the smoothest road. If we can even get her past the current roadblock."

"Yeah." That was the problem right there.

We just sat, quietly contemplative, for a little while.

Declan got up with a sigh and said, "I'll leave you to it. Good luck with your parents."

As he left, my spirits sank again. I focused on the glimmer of sunlight on the water and thought back over everything he'd told me.

A flicker of inspiration lit in my mind. Maybe there was something there I could use to my advantage. The meeting with my parents might not be a total disaster. I just had to play it right... and I had managed to play them once before, if on a smaller scale.

I turned the possibility over in my head as I lingered in the clearing, and kept mulling it over on my way back to campus. Was it really the best choice I could make? I could be shooting myself in the foot.

But I had to come to my parents with something, or God only knew how they'd take out their disapproval and frustration on me—and my brother.

My heart thumped hard as I drove through town and onward to the country inn restaurant farther down the highway where my father liked the food. I got there early, but their car was already in the parking lot. I squared my shoulders and strode inside.

My parents had only just gotten their drinks: a Bloody Mary for my mother and a whisky sour for my father. The thought of adding alcohol to the churn of my stomach made me queasier. I sat down at their table and asked for a root beer.

They didn't even give me a chance to pick up the menu. "You appear to have overestimated your influence over the Bloodstone scion," my mother said in a low but caustic tone, ripping one of the bread rolls in half. "Given the evidence, I wouldn't be surprised if she's learning more from your slips than you're managing her behavior. At this point, the most useful thing you could do is break her heart the morning before the hearing and let her go with that shaking her up."

She watched me from the corner of her eyes as she jabbed butter across the roll, evaluating my response to that suggestion as much as waiting for my agreement. My skin prickled.

"Rory had already talked to Baron Nightwood before I had a chance to see her that day," I said. "Once she'd made her decision, it'd have been humiliating for her to run back to him begging to take the deal after all. I don't think *anyone* could have influenced her that far."

"Nonetheless—"

I barreled ahead before she could pitch her heart-breaking plan again. "I might not have been able to talk her into accepting your deal, but acting like I'm on her side means she lets all kinds of things slip to *me*. I don't think that's a benefit we should be so quick to throw away."

My mother snorted. "And what great insights have you picked up that would be of any use to us, Connar?"

I forced myself to smile. "Just today I found out something I think you'll want to hear about this new judge who's been assigned to her case."

CHAPTER TWENTY-FOUR

Rory

T he chlorine smell tickled my nose as I followed Declan down to the boiler room near the Stormhurst Building's pool. The hum of the pipes filled the dim space. It felt even more eerie than when we'd come down here with Jude and Connar to tell them about their parents' role in the conspiracy against me. Declan hadn't said yet what he wanted to talk to me about, but it was obviously something perilous if he felt the need to bring the conversation here.

He crossed the small room and came to a stop by the large pipe at the far end. One of the maintenance staff had left a bucket there. He flipped it upside down and nudged it toward me with his foot. "You can sit if you want. This will probably take some time."

"*What* will?" I asked. "What's going on?" The worries that had been nipping at me ever since he'd asked me to meet him here clamored louder. "Have the barons come up with more made-up evidence against me or something?"

Declan shook his head. "It's not exactly a new threat, just one that's escalated. The original judge has been replaced with one who's known for extensive insight interrogations. I'm sure the barons set that up to maximize their chances of uncovering something damaging in your own thoughts or memories. We have to assume at this point that the questioning will go far beyond the scope of the case."

"Shit." I rubbed my face with a rising sense of exhaustion. "I think… I think I should be okay now as far as the joymancer stuff goes. Unless they're going to hold the fact that I still care about my parents against me, but there's nothing I can do about that. There might be other things, though." Deborah, in particular. "The judge or whoever's doing the interrogation will ask specific questions, though, right? Not just go rummaging around at random?"

"It'll definitely be a directed questioning. We just don't know for sure what questions they'll ask—or what might come up in your mind in response. That's why I thought we could try a practice run, if you're okay with that. I've come up with a list of the questions I think they might use that would pose the most risk, and I can ask you them using insight to see what they provoke. If anything shows up that I think could be a problem, we have a few days to figure out how to handle it."

My pulse stuttered at the thought of even Declan

making a thorough exploration of my mind. There were things he still didn't know about me, things I didn't think he'd approve of. But... If *anyone* out of all the fearmancers I'd met was going to accept the secrets I'd been keeping, it'd be him. Better I found out what might emerge now in his company than during the hearing.

"I guess there's not much chance I could simply decline the interrogation altogether?" I said without any real hope.

Declan made a face. "Not without looking incredibly guilty. The best defense we have is the use of the casting word in the illusion, and we've got no proof of that unless you let the judge see it. If you refuse to allow other questions, the barons or the blacksuits on their side will spin that hesitation against you in an instant."

"Okay." I exhaled slowly. "Let's try the practice interrogation then." I wasn't sure what a judge might ask that would uncover any sign of Deborah's true nature anyway. Maybe it'd turn out I was safe after all. The questioning might reveal some of my antagonistic feelings about the fearmancers, but only in the context of my parents' murder or the harassment at the hands of students here. It wasn't as if I'd taken any active steps toward taking down the community so far.

I sank onto the up-turned bucket. The ridged plastic surface pressed through my dress pants in a way that wasn't exactly comfortable. Declan took a step toward me, just close enough to graze his fingers across my forehead and brush my hair farther aside. It'd been a perfunctory gesture, but a tingle of warmth shot through me anyway.

For an instant, I was back by the lake with his mouth and hands—and Connar's—on me.

A question of my own tumbled out. "Are we ever going to talk about what happened on the cliff?"

We'd left the clearing in a sort of blissful daze, and I hadn't seen Declan the day after. Since meeting up today, he hadn't made any mention of the encounter or any move to touch me other than that brief motion just now. I wasn't even sure whether he was glad he'd surrendered to the moment or full of regret.

Declan's body went still. His mouth opened, closed, and opened again. "We will," he said, in a slightly rough tone that sent a flutter through my stomach. "But I think maybe we should leave a discussion that potentially intense for after the hearing. And… it's better not to mix any of that part of our relationship with preparing for the hearing."

Because we wouldn't want the judge stumbling on *those* memories either. Concern shot through me. "You don't think—he won't ask about my dating life, will he?"

Declan gave me a crooked smile. "I'd say it's unlikely. But even if he does, anything he sees of us will only reflect badly on me. By the time you're in the hearing, I'll already have supported you every way I can. Even if you lose my testimony, you've got Jude and Connar too."

"I don't want you getting in trouble either," I muttered.

"It was my choice. On the off-chance it does come up, you can always say those were only daydreams."

My lips twitched in amusement. "I just fantasize about you a lot. Got it." It wasn't even a total lie.

"Are you ready?" he asked.

I steadied myself on my makeshift seat. "I'd better be."

I closed my eyes to try to focus on my own internal sensations, not that I'd be able to detect exactly what Declan picked up. He stayed where he was a couple feet away from me, a solid presence even when I couldn't see him.

The lilt of spell-casting came into his voice. "How did you interact with Imogen Wakeburn in the months before her murder?"

A quiver of magic rippled through my head. Then there was only stillness. I trained my attention on the rhythm of my breath until Declan must have seen everything he thought he'd get and moved on.

"What was your relationship like with your other dormmates?"

My enemies might get some mileage out of that, but not anything I could imagine anyone seeing as a criminal act. Victory and the others had done a lot worse to me than I'd ever done to them.

Declan went on through his list of questions, and I gradually relaxed. Nothing he thought the judge might ask seemed to bump too closely against the things I'd rather keep hidden. I was just starting to feel a little relieved when he said, "Have you ever intended to cause anyone at the school harm?"

My body tensed instinctively for a second before I willed myself calm again. What could he see in my impressions that would give away any of the plans I'd only considered, without any chance to put them into action? And I'd never really wanted to see anyone *hurt*, only... stopped.

But that might not be good enough. Declan was silent for a longer stretch than before. When he spoke, there was a note in his voice that made me nervous all over again.

"Rory."

I opened my eyes and looked up at him. He was studying me, his brow knit, the brightness of his eyes shadowed with concern.

"When I asked that question, I mostly got fragments of times when you pushed back against Victory's hassling," he said quietly. "Nothing unusual there. But there was also —some time when you were with Connar, at night—I think it might have been up on the cliff—you were asking him about the school's wards. About the joymancers trying to find us. Why would that have come up?"

My heart sank. It'd come up because when I'd asked Connar those questions, I'd been trying to figure out how I could help the joymancers get past the wards and attack the school. I'd forgotten about that short conversation— forgotten that I'd pursued the idea of destroying the school that far in an overt way.

Declan has asked whether I'd intended to cause anyone harm. Could I explain away that memory somehow without admitting why I'd really brought up the subject of the wards? I groped for an excuse, but nothing came to me. The drone of the pipes echoed through my head.

Declan crouched down in front of me, taking one of my hands. His voice stayed gentle—as gentle as it'd been the first time I'd met him, when he'd tried to reassure me in the midst of my parents' murders.

"Whatever it was, we need to talk about it now. If you freeze up during the hearing like you just did with me, the judge will double-down on the questioning in an instant. I know it couldn't have been anything that bad, Rory. I know *you*. You can tell me."

I swallowed thickly. He didn't know me as well as he thought. Looking back on those moments when I'd been so sure that bringing the joymancers charging into the university was the right thing to do, I had to suppress a cringe. The situation, the people here and there, the history between the mage communities—it was all so much more complicated than I'd realized.

I could tell him that too, along with everything else. He deserved to know, didn't he, before he tangled his life even more with mine? Maybe it was wrong that I'd let him stick his neck out so far for me without telling him how many traitorous thoughts I'd entertained.

"It is pretty bad." My gaze dropped to my hands. "I— You have to remember that when I first got here, all I'd seen was fearmancers murdering people and then acting like bullies. As far as I was concerned, calling this place 'Villain Academy' was totally accurate. Compared to that, and knowing what my parents were like, I had to think the joymancers were the heroes."

"That makes sense," Declan said. "You didn't exactly get the most pleasant welcome into the community."

A halting laugh made its way up my throat. "No. And I—all I wanted to do was get back home to California. To be with people like my parents again. And to get justice for my parents against the people who'd killed them—to get justice for the Nary students here for the way everyone seemed to treat them—to stop all the lessons about how to terrorize people…"

My throat closed up for a second. Declan waited patiently, his grip steady on my hand.

I made myself look at him again. "I decided I was going to find a way to give the joymancers access to the school: figure out how to disable the wards, or something like that. And then I'd run back to California and use what I could tell them as proof that I wasn't a villain like the rest of you. And let them take down the school."

I had to suck in a breath before I could go on. "But I never thought—I had no idea the joymancers might be so *vicious*, that they might kill people indiscriminately just for being fearmancers. I didn't want some kind of slaughter here. And I was going to make sure people like your family were protected. But after seeing all the reports, and remembering how my parents kept me apart from the rest of the joymancers, I don't want even that anymore. That conversation with Connar—it was months ago. I haven't done anything to undermine the school."

Declan's expression had tensed. My gut knotted at his reaction. "I'm sorry," I added. "I just wanted to *stop* more people from being hurt."

"Oh, Rory," he said in a tight voice. I braced myself

for an accusation or recrimination, but instead he simply leaned forward and hugged me.

I hugged him back automatically, burying my face in his shoulder. "I don't want anything to happen to you," I said. "Or Jude or Connar or… so many people here. I'm not sure what I want to do if I can make it through this hearing, but I'm not running back to the joymancers. I promise you, I wouldn't put you all in that kind of danger."

"I know." Declan eased back a bit so his head bowed next to mine. He paused, his jaw working.

"I never told even my father about this," he said. "Back when I was around fifteen, when I was getting more access as baron-to-be and I saw the full report on our parents' deaths… There was a while when I kept picturing how I could encourage the other barons to launch some kind of assault on the joymancer community. It ate at me so much that they were getting away with what they'd done and with so many other attacks on us too."

A lump rose in my throat. "That makes sense."

"Well, once my anger settled down, I felt ashamed that I'd let that impulse for revenge get a hold on me. But if I'd had the opportunity, I might have acted in the moment."

"You were younger. Fifteen's practically still a kid."

He shook his head. "That's not the point. *You* saw the people you think of as your parents killed right in front of you and had people at school pushing you around. All I did was read a report and look at some pictures. If your response means something awful about you, then I must be the most wretched human being ever."

Every particle of my body balked at that judgment, which I guessed had been the point Declan was trying to make. "So you don't hate me for what I wanted to do?"

"Not at all." He pulled back completely to look me in the eyes. "But the other barons and the blacksuits won't see it that way. We need to come up with a reasonable answer if they stumble on that memory."

"I couldn't think of anything except the truth to tell you."

He gave me a wry smile. "I appreciate the honesty. What if… what if we lean into the protectiveness you feel now for at least some of the people here? You could say you were imagining that if joymancers came onto the campus, you'd have to hurt them to defend us. That's still harming someone who in the scenario would be at the school."

The idea of joymancers storming the school did send a jab of anxiety through me now. "Do you think they'd buy it?"

"If you let your real emotion come through, yes. Nothing else emerged that would suggest you were sabotaging the school. You didn't take any concrete steps toward putting that plan into motion, did you?"

I shook my head emphatically. "It was just asking about the wards, and, I mean, I thought about how I could do it. But you can't read specific thoughts in memories, right?"

"Definitely not." He sat back on his heels and then straightened up. "We'd better make sure nothing else jumps out like that. Are you good to keep going?"

"Yeah," I said, but as I adjusted my position on the bucket, an ache crept through my chest.

Declan had accepted the plans I'd been making in this moment when he was set on exonerating me. Would he be so forgiving when he'd had more time for what I'd told him to sink in after the hearing was over?

CHAPTER TWENTY-FIVE

Rory

S taying in the university library instead of studying in my dorm had plenty of upsides. I got immediate access to all the books in the place without hauling them up multiple flights of stairs. If I found a good nook, it was often quieter. And there was something soothing about the high ceilings in the expansive room. Sometimes my little bedroom started to feel claustrophobic.

Of course, the library also had its downsides. Not least of which was the fact that if someone noticed me in whatever secluded corner I'd holed up in, the illusion of privacy could vanish in an instant.

It started with the page I was looking at in the book open on my lap abruptly slipping from my fingers. As I flinched at the sudden movement, more pages started flipping over as if in a strong gust of wind, though I didn't feel anything on my skin. I stared for a second before my brain caught up. It was a spell, obviously.

I jammed my hands down on the book to try to hold it still, but jerked them back at the first sound of tearing paper. I didn't want to ruin this magical text because of someone else's stupid prank. Instead, I settled for tipping it off my lap onto the floor. As soon as the cover thumped shut, it lay still.

Before I could decide whether it was worth trying to pick the book up again—or try any other—a slim, leather-bound volume tumbled off a shelf above me and smacked me right on the top of my head.

Pain spiked through my scalp, and a yelp slipped from my lips. I scrambled onto my feet, just as a heavier volume careened toward me. I jerked my arm up just in time, wincing at the slam of the edge just below my elbow. That was going to leave a bruise.

What asshole had thought it'd be a good idea to pull this stunt? Assaulting a scion and supposed murderer didn't seem like the wisest move ever. Another dare between junior students who were immature enough to ignore the possible consequences?

I braced for another blitz from above as I marched down the aisle toward the open area of the library, but the next projectiles came from the opposite shelf instead. Three books hurtled at me in quick succession from slightly different angles. This time, at least, I was prepared enough to snap out a spell to form a protective barrier around me. The books bounced off it and thudded to the floor.

When I emerged from my aisle, it was just in time to see a familiar but unexpected figure charging into the row of shelves next to mine. In the brief glimpse I got of him, Malcolm's eyes were so fierce beneath his golden hair that you could forget about the divine part—that was all devil. A second after he'd barreled out of view, someone let out a squeak of pain.

I hurried over to find him holding a girl, who did look young enough to be a junior, by the collar of her blouse.

"What the hell family did you grow up in that you figure attacking a scion is a good way to make a name for yourself?" he demanded, glaring down at her.

The girl had blanched. "I'm sorry," she mumbled. "I was just—my mother said everyone would be safer if someone proved the Bloodstone scion would lash out again, so she'd have to leave school—"

Her gaze flitted to me, and a rush of fear hit me from her, so sharp I almost bit my tongue with the impact.

"Let her go, Malcolm," I said evenly. "She was just trying to impress her parents. You should know something about that."

Malcolm grimaced at me, but he released the girl's shirt, still glowering at her. "Didn't you ever think that if *you're* the one throwing books around, if someone did lash out, it'd be at *you*? I don't think anyone will be impressed if you get yourself killed. Not that Rory would have done that anyway. In case you haven't noticed, she's a hell of a lot more forgiving than I am."

The girl cringed against the shelves as if expecting him to hurl a spell at her. I slipped past him to face her. The comment about her mother had sent my thoughts spinning. I couldn't help remembering Cutbridge and his campaign against the Naries.

"What's your name?" I asked her.

She wet her lips nervously, hugging herself. "Penelope Villia," she said after a moment's hesitation.

Villia. That name had been on Professor Banefield's list too. Yeah, provoking me into a show of force, especially against a junior, would only have solidified the case against me, which of course the barons' allies would want. This kid was only a tool.

"I'm not going to hurt you," I said, and shot a pointed glance at Malcolm. "And neither is he. But I'd appreciate if you didn't dive bomb me with books any more in the future, all right? Go study for your classes or something."

"Yes. I'm sorry." She bobbed her head and bolted past Malcolm out of the aisle.

The Nightwood scion shook his head. "You go easy on them, and they'll just come back worse."

I narrowed my eyes at him. "Where the hell did you come from all of a sudden anyway? Have you been following me around?" Interrupting the guys outside our dorm rooms had been reasonable enough, but this situation was more of a stretch as a coincidence.

"Why would I do that?" Malcolm said. "I was walking by, and I heard the commotion. You're welcome, by the way."

"I don't think yanking her around solved anything. And I'm really supposed to believe you just *happened* to be passing by at the right moment?"

Malcolm let out a huff of breath. "If we're going to argue about this, can we at least do it somewhere less public? You can tell me exactly how horrible it is that I saved you from an avalanche of textbooks in the scion lounge just as easily as here."

He might have a point. An argument between scions, especially when one of those scions was me, could draw attention I didn't really want just two days before my hearing. I gritted my teeth and nodded.

Malcolm didn't say anything else until we'd descended the stairs to the basement room. The lounge was empty, but the hint of coffee scent in the air suggested someone had been enjoying the space recently.

The Nightwood scion ambled around the pool table with a drum of his fingers against the wooden edge. He tucked his hand into the shoulder bag he was carrying and drew out an ancient-looking book.

"I do actually care about my classes. I was in the library grabbing this book for a Persuasion theory essay I'm supposed to write."

"Oh." A significant portion of my annoyance dissolved. I rested my hands on the end of the pool table, keeping several feet of distance between us. "Sorry for the stalking accusation, then. You do still need to back off if you notice someone hassling me, though. I'd much rather handle it my way—and I *can* handle it."

Malcolm frowned. "We're scions. That means we look out for each other."

"Because you think if I look weak, somehow that'll make you look bad too?" I restrained myself from rolling my eyes. "I don't totally know why you've decided *you're* not going to attack me anymore, but heroics on my behalf really aren't necessary."

"Even if I want to jump in and give you a hand?"

"Why would you? You don't even like me."

For a second, Malcolm just stared at me. Then he let out a sputter of a laugh. "For Chrissake, Rory."

He snatched up one of the nearby balls and dropped it on the table with a thunk. The other balls rattled as it connected with a cluster. His gaze followed them across the green surface.

"You've got official confirmation that you're the most powerful mage in the school," he said, his voice dropping lower, "but you still blush a little whenever any professor compliments your spellwork. When you're concentrating hard on figuring out what to cast, your mouth sets with a little crease at the corners, and that's when anyone who's been tangling with you should know to watch out. When you're scared, you lift your chin as if you can intimidate the feeling into going away. But the best moments are when you totally commit to whatever cause you're championing next. There's this light that comes into your eyes, so fierce and unwavering…"

He looked at me then, with an expression I couldn't read but an intensity in *his* eyes that made my breath catch in my throat. "I don't *like* you. I fucking adore you, Rory."

It was my turn to stare. My jaw had gone slack, but I couldn't have missed the affection that had run through every observation he'd related. He meant it.

I had no idea how to react to that. Confusion and

wariness, sure, but the idea that I'd provoked that much fond emotion in him also sent a weird sort of thrill through me.

I snapped my mouth shut, and then managed to say past the thumping of my heart, "You haven't acted like it."

His mouth twisted. "You could say it crept up on me. And it's not as if you haven't been incredibly frustrating at times too. Maybe I tried so hard to break you because I thought we needed to remake you before I could let myself really want anything. But I don't believe that anymore. I'm starting to think you might be exactly what I need as you are."

My fingers had curled around the lip of the table, clutching it tight. I forced them to release. So many feelings were colliding inside me that I could hardly identify all of them, let alone tell which was winning out.

This was Malcolm Nightwood—the bully, my tormentor, hater of joymancers and mocker of good intentions. But... I kind of understood his rancor toward the joymancers now. I even sort of understood how he could see his treatment of the other students as a guiding and strengthening force, as part of his role as scion, rather than real attacks, even if I didn't agree with his approach.

He'd recognized at least some of his mistakes and taken steps to make up for them. He was trying to protect me now, with the same passionate loyalty he had for the other scions. Within the vicious bully was a devoted friend, a determined leader, an affectionate master to his familiar... and just remembering kissing him set off a flare of heat over my skin.

So no, Malcolm wasn't evil. But he was still that bully at the same time. He *had* still tormented me, in all kinds of ways I couldn't forget.

"Why are you telling me?" I said finally. "What are you expecting to happen?"

"Because it seemed like something you should know. And I'm not expecting anything. I'm *hoping* that you've got enough goodness in your heart to give us a chance to be whatever we could be, together."

His dry tone with the last sentence brought back all the times he'd called me Glinda as a jeer. I sucked in a shaky breath.

"I don't know if that's possible. I don't trust you—I'm not sure I'm ever going to really trust you, after everything."

"I can work with that." He took a careful step toward me. "I've spent my whole life so far proving myself every way I can to a man who's never satisfied and barely deserved the effort. Proving myself to you sounds like a much better deal. I broke your trust—I'll rebuild it just like I figured I'd rebuild you. You'll see."

He took another step, almost close enough that he could touch me now. A quiver ran through my body in awareness of him. Part of me clamored to flee, but a larger part was determined to see how far he'd try to take this moment.

I was just as much a scion as he was, and the heir of Bloodstone didn't run away.

"There goes that chin," he said softly, with so much

tenderness my throat closed up. "All glorious defiance. I swear, the last thing I want to do now is hurt you, Rory."

Maybe some part of me *wanted* him to convince me, to prove to me that all that past between us didn't have to matter. That the good in him could override the rest. In that moment, I could imagine that being possible, even if I wasn't there yet.

With a click, the lounge door opened behind me. I glanced back to see Jude on his way in, his stride casual until he caught sight of the two of us. Something about the vibe in the air made him hesitate. Then he started to backtrack, reaching for the door. "Never mind, I can see you're busy."

My head jerked around in time to catch the glower Malcolm had been shooting his way. My hackles rose with my own protective instinct. I marched across the room to catch Jude's arm.

"This is your lounge too. *I* don't want you to leave."

He stopped, his gaze flicking to Malcolm and back to me. At my expression, his shoulders came down. He eased closer, taking my hand. "Well, in that case…"

Malcolm cleared his throat with a disgruntled sound. I gripped Jude's fingers and turned to glare at the other scion.

"You want to prove yourself?" I said. "The first thing you've got to demonstrate is that you can handle me having other guys in my life. Because if you try to tell me who I'm allowed to care about or make out with or anything else—if you try to make me choose between you and everyone else—then I'm going to choose the guys who aren't making up rules about how I live my life."

Jude ducked his head. "Well said, Ice Queen," he said in an amused tone, but the squeeze of his hand told me how much the declaration had meant to him. I didn't imagine he was used to being valued over the Nightwood scion.

I bobbed up on my toes, and he met my kiss, no hesitation in him now. My other hand slid around his neck as I leaned into the embrace. The thought of Malcolm watching, of him deciding how he was going to respond to my statement, somehow made the kiss even hotter.

If Malcolm still had any illusions of me kowtowing to him, he'd better get rid of them fast.

Jude slipped his arm around me as I pulled back from the kiss. I tipped my head against his chest and looked toward Malcolm.

He was watching not me but Jude, with an expression that looked almost startled. Had he ever seen his longtime friend look actually content? I wasn't sure Jude had ever *been* content from the moment he'd discovered his father's secret until finally admitting that secret to me. It had burned too deep a hole in him.

Jude gave my hair an affectionate ruffle. "It's no good loving a wild thing if you're going to stick it in a cage."

"Wild?" I said in mild objection, and he chuckled.

"Only in the best possible ways."

Malcolm's gaze had come back to me, with a heat in it that was nearly scorching. "No, I suppose it isn't. I can handle starting on the sidelines." He folded his arms over his chest and nodded to Jude. "Let's see how well you can drive her wild, then."

Jude hesitated. "What do you mean?"

Malcolm tipped his head, considering. "Go down on her. Get her off."

Jude's eyebrows leapt up. He wavered for a second and then glanced at me in question. Desire had already lit in his eyes.

An unexpected giddiness ran through me. I'd been with two guys at the same time before, but they'd both been participating. To have Malcolm, lord of the scions, exercising the self-control to stand back and watch his friend do what I suspected he'd have liked to do himself... I guessed that would prove something. It made the temptation to go along with his suggestion that much more delicious.

Why not? What did I have to hide? If he was going to melt down over seeing me with Jude after all, it'd be better to find that out now and lay any question of us getting together to rest.

Okay, maybe I was a little wild.

I teased my hand down Jude's chest, and he grinned, obviously taking that as answer enough. As he captured my lips again, he walked me a couple steps backward so my shoulders touched the wall. He held me there, kissing me so thoroughly my mouth tingled, while he trailed his fingers down my side and over my thigh, and then around to the already eager place where my legs joined.

My hips swayed toward him as he stroked my clit

through my clothes. He smiled against my mouth. With tantalizing slowness, he undid the zipper of my pants and drew them down until they fell the rest of the way to puddle around my ankles. Leaving my mouth to kiss my neck, he hooked his fingers around my panties. With each inch he tugged them down, he descended twice as quickly.

He pressed his lips to my sternum and my belly button through my blouse. When his breath spilled over my sex, I tipped my head back. Anticipation hummed through me, almost as heady as the pleasure to come. I braced one hand against the wall and curled the other into Jude's hair.

He lowered his mouth to me with a swipe of his tongue that sent a bolt of bliss through me. A moan vibrated from my throat. He worked me over gently and then more determinedly, increasing the pressure with every sound that escaped me. Pleasure rippled up from my core in sharper and sharper waves.

As he teased his tongue around my clit, Jude stroked his hands over my thighs and then up to my opening. He suckled hard and dipped a finger inside me at the same time, and I let out a noise like a growl, all wanting. My hips jerked.

Oh, fuck, that felt good—but somehow not good enough at the same time. I wanted to be really full, full of him.

Malcolm didn't get to call the shots, not in any of this. I had the final say in how my lovers came to me—and how they made me come.

My fingers tightened in Jude's hair and urged him up. "Jude. I need more."

He caught my eye, his smile coming back with a flash. In an instant, he'd straightened up. His hand dropped to help me as I fumbled with his zipper. I wriggled my panties the rest of the way down to my feet.

Malcolm let out a wordless sound of protest, but I didn't give a damn. I clutched Jude's shoulders, and he lifted my thighs, molding them around his hips as he plunged into me with a hastily cast spell. I cried out at the burst of pleasure. My legs squeezed around him, holding me up and holding him to me. With each rock of his hips, fresh bliss swept through me.

Jude kissed me roughly on the mouth, his control starting to wobble. I arched into him, and he thrust deeper to hit just the right spot to send me spiraling higher.

"Love you," he murmured in a hot rasp by my ear. "Love you so fucking much."

With those words, I shuddered right into ecstasy. The crackling of pleasure raced through me, jolting another moan from my throat and setting every nerve singing.

As I clutched onto Jude, his breath broke, his rhythm turning jerky. With a groan, he spilled himself inside me.

We came to rest against the wall, my legs still clasped around Jude's hips, his head tucked against mine. I touched his cheek and turned his face for another kiss, long and lingering. Only after that did I look to where Malcolm was still standing.

The Nightwood scion's hands and jaw had clenched,

but his eyes were outright blazing, and not, from the feel of them, with anger. Especially not when paired with the bulge that had formed against the fly of his slacks.

Without letting myself rethink the impulse, I reached out to him. After a second, he stalked over. I let my feet sink to the ground, but I kept my other arm around Jude. He nuzzled my neck as I held Malcolm's gaze.

"Not what you asked for, I know," I said. "You might be the king of Blood U, but you don't rule over me."

"Point made, loud and clear," Malcolm said, with a rawness that sparked one more wave of desire through me. That and the fact that he'd accepted our deviation from his orders with relative grace brought my hand to the front of his shirt. I grasped it and pulled him to me.

If Malcolm objected to kissing me while I was still partly entwined with another guy, he didn't show it. His mouth claimed mine with all the searing confidence I remembered. I was breathless when he eased back, but from the hitch of his chest, so was he.

"I'll take that for now," he said, with a look so heated it promised a hell of a lot more to come, if I decided I'd take him.

If I was free enough in two days' time to take anyone at all.

CHAPTER TWENTY-SIX

Rory

The dynamic between Malcolm and I might have been shifting, but the lines drawn in the past hadn't completely dissolved. When Declan called a last-minute meeting of the scions to discuss my hearing, this time over breakfast in a corner booth at one of the restaurants in town, he didn't include the Nightwood scion in that invitation.

As I slid onto the bench next to Connar, I couldn't say I wished Malcolm were there. He could talk all he wanted about "adoring" me, but I hadn't seen any evidence yet that he'd risk his standing in his father's eyes to help me in any public way. Sharing one kiss with him was a heck of a lot less risky than sharing the details of my planned defense.

The waitress started bringing over plates and glasses a

minute later, the rich doughy smell of fresh waffles filling my nose along with the savoriness of crisp bacon. Declan, who'd arrived just after me, blinked at the spread as he sat down across from me next to Jude.

The Killbrook scion leaned back in his seat with a smirk at his neighbor. "I took the liberty of ordering for all of us. I figured once you got here, you'd be all talk and forget about the fact that breakfast generally includes eating. Grab whatever looks good. I think we can share."

He rolled the last word off his tongue with a sly glance at me. Warmth tickled through me despite the anxiety balling my gut, but only for a moment.

My hearing was tomorrow. This was our last chance to prepare. But Jude was right—better not to do it on an empty stomach.

I lifted one of the waffles onto my plate and garnished it with a dollop of syrup. The anxious pressure inside me made me stick to only a small bite to start, but the fluffy sweetness offset some of my queasiness.

Declan gave Jude a bemused look, but that didn't stop him from taking toast and bacon for his own plate. "I've actually got good news," he said as he scraped butter over the toast. "I still think the practice session we did was worthwhile, Rory, but your judge has been replaced *again*. The new one is much less Insight-leaning."

"Really?" Connar perked up, avid interest gleaming in his light blue eyes. A smile slipped across his face that looked more triumphant than I'd have expected.

Declan lifted his gaze to contemplate the other guy.

"Do you know something about this? It's pretty unusual to have a change like that so close to a major hearing, let alone two."

Connar's grin stretched a little wider. "I wasn't sure it would even work. It was a gamble." He glanced at me. "My parents insisted on meeting with me a couple days ago. They still think I'm going to help them undercut you. So… I told them you were glad to hear about the new judge because you thought what he'd glean from intensive insight would push the case in your favor."

Jude let out a low whistle and a laugh. "Look at the heir of Stormhurst turning schemer. The rest of us better watch out."

Connar started to glower at him, but I grabbed the bigger guy's arm with a grateful squeeze. "Thank you. Obviously they bought your story. You might have just saved me a whole lot of trouble." I paused. "Are you going to get in trouble with them when you speak for me at the hearing?"

He shook his head. "I already prepared them for that. I told them I'd need to testify on your behalf to keep up the 'ruse' of being on your side, but that I wouldn't say anything too concrete." His mouth slanted. "Unfortunately that's mainly because I don't have any concrete testimony I *can* give."

"I still appreciate it. Every little bit has to help."

Looking at him and around the table, an unexpected sense of conviction settled over me even though I still had a long, uncertain day ahead of me tomorrow. The four of us were working as a real unit now, not just as lovers but as the colleagues we were meant to be for the rest of our lives. Despite our rocky beginning, our goals had ended up aligning. Even Malcolm was starting to reject his father's ideals, if only in private.

For the first time, the sense of what it might be like to rule alongside these men really hit me. We could do a hell of a lot when we were all barons. We could change the whole direction of fearmancer society into something much less villainous.

It didn't matter what the joymancers had done or how much I could trust them—I didn't need them. I didn't *want* them involved. I had all the support I needed to tear down the toxic parts of the community right here with me, ready to work from the inside.

As long as I was still free to do that work after tomorrow.

A thought that was obviously on Declan's mind too. "Not that you're out of trouble yet," he said. "But you definitely have one problem off your plate. Have you made any progress with Cressida? If she did hear or see something, *her* testimony could be all you need."

I grimaced, poking at my waffle. "She's still avoiding me. I don't know how I could convince her to stick out her neck. She obviously doesn't see any benefit in it for her, and it's not as if I have anything she doesn't have that I can offer her." Money meant nothing to someone whose family was already rolling in it. I hadn't established any real connections in business or politics yet. Mostly what I brought to the table were enemies.

Jude waved his fork at me. "You have the barony. She's got nothing like that."

"I can't exactly give *that* to her," I replied. "And I don't have much official power yet anyway."

"You will, though, if you get through the hearing. Maybe you can work with something there."

"There was—" I cut myself off, hesitating. I'd come across some magical theory in yesterday's studying that could apply to this situation. A way of guaranteeing Cressida a future reward dependent on future needs. But it'd been so open-ended that my instinctive reaction had been to reject the idea.

She'd helped Victory with the other girl's campaign of harassment against me. She clearly didn't have any interest in supporting me for my sake or doing the right thing. How the hell could I trust *her* with any kind of open-ended deal?

But maybe it was time to take that gamble, just like Connar had with his parents. Owing Cressida some uncertain price was better than becoming the other barons' virtual slave.

And really… a few months ago, I hadn't trusted any of the guys sitting around me. As I'd just been thinking, they'd changed so much, revealed depths I hadn't suspected.

Most of my fellow students had to be more than simply villains. I could be cautious, but maybe I should give more of them the benefit of the doubt. These were my people. I was going to lead them one day—soon, as long as I didn't let the older barons win.

That girl in the library yesterday had outright attacked me to try to get me re-arrested, and I'd been willing to forgive her. I had no idea what pressures Cressida might be operating under, did I? *What have you ever done for me?* she'd asked, and from a fearmancer perspective, that was a totally valid question regardless of the stakes.

The guys were watching me with open curiosity, waiting for me to finish. I pushed a piece of my waffle across my plate. "I think I'm going to have to take a leap of faith."

Since our initial talk, Cressida hadn't been going to quite the same lengths to stay away from me. This time, waiting for her to come down from her afternoon class, I lingered in the first floor landing rather than right outside the door.

Despite the lesser intrusion, she stiffened as soon as she saw me standing there. She picked up her pace as if to stride right past me, but I stepped over to block her as unaggressively as I could manage.

"You said I've never done anything for you," I said quickly, pitching my voice low to avoid the curious ears of the students filing past us. "And that's true. What if I could do something that would make it more than worthwhile for you to get involved in my 'mess'?"

She stayed tensed, but something shifted in her expression, a hint of eagerness that gave me hope. I motioned her to the side, away from the other students.

"We could talk downstairs? There's no Desensitization session going right now." I'd checked.

Cressida's mouth tightened before she exhaled in a rush. "All right, fine. Let's hear this. But it'd better be good. People will notice that you're even talking to me, you know."

Exactly why I'd already planned a nearby private spot for that conversation. We tramped down the stairs into the cool basement air and its thicker silence.

The waiting area outside the Desensitization chamber wasn't exactly comfortable, not much more than half a room with a wooden bench on either side. With a little luck, this conversation wouldn't take very long. I said a few words in casting to make sure no one would follow us down while we were there and sat on one of the benches.

After a moment's hesitation, Cressida sank down opposite me. "So?"

"Have the other barons ever done anything for you?" I asked. "Is screwing me over going to get you anything from *them*?"

She scowled at me. "What does that matter? I'm not staying out of this to get some reward—I'm trying to make sure whoever has it out for you doesn't put me and my family in their crosshairs too."

Nothing about her response gave me the impression that the barons had approached her or that she knew they were the ones who wanted to undermine me. Her family's name hadn't shown up on Professor Banefield's list. That wasn't any kind of guarantee, but it gave me the confidence to continue.

"It matters because if I make it through this hearing, I'm going to be a baron soon too. And I've got to think that having one baron in your corner is better than none."

Cressida let out a scoffing sound. "That's an easy thing to say when you're backed into a corner. We're not friends. I've got no reason to think you'd actually follow through on any promises once you're past this."

I swallowed hard and clasped my hands together. "What if you didn't have to count on promises? What if we magically sealed the deal?"

That flicker of eagerness came back, but her skepticism hadn't vanished. "What do you mean? You can't give me anything right now, and you don't know what you'll be able to offer in future."

"No. So you could think of it as me writing you a blank check. I think I found an approach that'll let me offer you one favor if you testify at the hearing tomorrow. You'd be able to come to me at any time during the rest of your life and ask for one thing, and I'd have to do that for you, whatever it is."

Just saying the words made my chest clench up. Cressida's eyes widened as the enormity of what I was proposing sank in. "Are you serious? You lay down magic like that, and—I could ask you to actually murder someone. I could ask you to give me your entire estate."

Of course she'd immediately see the ways the spell could be exploited. I gave her a slanted smile. "I was planning on including a couple of caveats about the favor not being a criminal act and not doing me or anyone else direct harm, so the really questionable stuff would be out.

But yes, I know it's a risk. I'm willing to take that risk, because I'm asking a big risk of you. It's only fair, don't you think?"

Disbelief lingered on her face. I'd be surprised if most fearmancers would ever have considered putting themselves at another person's future mercy like this. But I wasn't an average fearmancer, as she should know by now.

"Do I have to decide right away?" she asked.

I shook my head. "We can cast the spell now—you need to contribute a little to confirm your end of the deal —but it's conditional. If you don't show up at the hearing tomorrow and share everything you know that would help my case, then I won't owe you the favor. You can make up your mind on your own schedule."

She paused for a moment, her gaze going distant as she took that information in. Her lips pursed and relaxed again. She shifted her focus back to me.

"All right," she said. "What do we have to do to work this spell?"

Relief washed over me. I got up, infinitely glad that I'd spent all my time between breakfast and this meeting studying the magical techniques involved.

"We can cast it right here. All we have to do is agree on the exact wording of what we'll each offer, and the rest is actually pretty simple."

"And you won't tell anyone else we made this deal, whether I go through with it or not?"

She was still nervous about the repercussions. I couldn't blame her for that. "I won't," I said. "I know you don't have the highest opinion of me, but I think you've at least seen that I'm not in the habit of publicly airing private business."

"Then we'll put the spell in place," she said, getting to her feet. "And I'll decide about the rest... when I'm ready to decide."

CHAPTER TWENTY-SEVEN

Rory

The hearing room in the blacksuits' building looked a lot like a regular courtroom, at least from what I'd seen of those on TV. A raised seat with a sort of podium for the judge stood in the middle of the far wall, two lower seats on either side of it, and several rows of benches filled the other end of the room. All of the furnishings gleamed with dark hardwood. An inoffensive beige hue colored the walls.

Someone had cranked the air conditioning even though it was a cool September day outside. I'd worn a jacket over my blouse and dress pants, and I left it on, restraining a shiver, as I walked with Declan to the judge's end of the room. Our shoes tapped eerily loud on the polished floor. I curled my fingers around the hem of my jacket, resisting the urge to hug it closer around me.

Several people were already taking spots on the

benches: Jude and Connar, the professors who'd agreed to testify about my temperament and approach to casting, and a number of blacksuits, including a few I recognized from my arrest. How many of them really believed I was guilty?

I dragged in a shaky breath as we came to a stop at the seat to the left of the judge's spot.

"This is where you'll sit for the entire hearing," Declan said in a low voice. "Anyone else giving testimony will come up on the other side. You've got about fifteen minutes before they'll get started—the blacksuits are usually pretty prompt. We'll get through this."

I wished the steadiness of his voice was enough to reassure me. I nodded and sank into the chair, resting my forearms on the narrow desk-like protrusion in front of me. My thin cuffs clinked against the wood.

Declan went to join the other two scions. A few more blacksuits arrived, including Lillian. She caught my eye and strode over. I tried not to tense too much at the thought of talking to her.

"Is there anything you need before we get started?" she asked. "Even a glass of water?"

I grasped my purse. "I brought a bottle of water. I can't think of anything else at this point." I hadn't been sure I could trust anything the people here might give me to consume. And really, I just wanted this day to be over. I didn't think Lillian could give me that, at least not with the outcome I wanted.

A woman built like a football player marched into the room and up to the judge's podium with barely a glance around. She didn't even seem to make note of me. Maybe this one wasn't an Insight enthusiast, but she still looked awfully intimidating.

The next figure to step through the doorway unsettled me even more. Baron Nightwood stalked over to a bench at the back of the room and settled onto it, resting his hands on his lap. Apparently he wanted to watch over the proceedings he and his colleagues had set in motion first-hand. I was probably lucky I didn't have to stare down all three of them.

A different venomous trio arrived a couple minutes later: Victory and her two best friends. I couldn't take any comfort from the sight of Cressida in the room when it was in the company of my long-time nemesis. I guessed the blacksuits had wanted them here to give their account of my earlier conflict with Imogen.

I watched Cressida cross the room, waiting to see if she'd give me any sort of sign of whether she meant to go through with the deal we'd set up, but she kept her gaze averted. That alone made my heart sink.

Reflections of the assembled figures wavered in the mirror that stretched along one side of the room. Declan had told me that observers, mostly blacksuits, often watched from behind that one-way glass, some of whom the judge might consult with for a second opinion if she felt she needed one. The thought of the gazes that might be following me from behind that surface made my skin itch.

The judge clapped her hands together, and the murmured conversations on the benches fell completely silent. "Judge Blazehed, bringing the proceedings to order. We're here today to consider the case of the murder of a Miss Imogen Wakeburn, contended to have been carried out by Miss Rory Bloodstone." Finally, she turned her dark gaze my way. "That would be you, I assume."

"Yes, Your Honor," I said, falling automatically into courtroom lingo.

I thought the corner of her mouth twitched at the title, but so briefly I couldn't tell whether it had shifted up or down. She set a sheaf of papers on the podium area in front of her.

"I've read over the written reports, but I'd like to hear directly from those involved. I also understand both the prosecutor and the accused have witnesses to offer support to either side of the case." She turned to the blacksuits sitting on the front bench. "Let's begin with your account of the discovery of the murder and the arrest."

The blacksuits got to give their version first? That didn't strike me as particularly fair.

I willed myself to sit still without fidgeting as one of the men who'd arrested me took the seat on the other side of the judge, where I couldn't even see him. Maybe that was the point of this layout—to ensure the witnesses couldn't be influenced by anything they saw of the accused. But the situation gave his voice an oddly disembodied quality as he recounted the call they'd received from a fellow student, their arrival at the scene, their observations of Imogen's body and my behavior, and how they'd taken me into custody.

The judge took all this in with nods here and there and

an occasional question. When she was satisfied, she dismissed the blacksuit and turned to me.

"Miss Bloodstone, can you give me your account of the events leading up to and around Miss Wakeburn's death?"

My chest constricted with nerves, but I cleared my throat and started speaking. I gave her the same story I'd given the blacksuits—the party, noticing Imogen was missing, going back to my dorm to get better shoes for driving, finding her body, being gripped by magic as illusions bombarded me.

"I see," the judge said, with no indication in her expression of whether she believed me. "And will you allow me to verify this version of events as well as I can with an insight spell?"

"Yes, I'll allow that," I said, and remembered to add, "One thing you should make note of that I realized afterward—in the illusion of me casting the killing spell, I use a casting word. That's part of my evidence that those are illusions and not memories. Because I only came into the magical community recently, I'm not yet at the point where I feel comfortable working magic by using my own invented words. I pretty much always use literal words to fit the intent of the spell. Some of my professors are here today to confirm that."

"Noted for the record."

The judge's seat swiveled with her so she could face me straight on. I kept my head turned toward her, my pulse thudding as I willed down my instinctive mental shields. She focused her gaze on my head and asked the question charged with magic: "How were you involved in Imogen Wakeburn's death?"

Like with Declan, I had no sense of her intrusion into my mind other than a faint shiver of energy. I held still and tried to keep my breath even. After several uneasy minutes, the introspective haze cleared from the judge's eyes, and she leaned back in her seat.

"All right," she said. "I'll hear from your professors next. Before I do, is there anything else you'd like to offer in your defense?"

I'd rehearsed this speech in my head over and over. To my relief, it spilled out easily.

"Imogen was my friend. Even if I'd been arguing with her, I wouldn't have hurt her. I haven't hurt *anyone* since I arrived at Bloodstone University, even though people have done a lot worse to me than argue. A few of my fellow scions who are also my classmates have come to vouch for that."

The judge's expression stayed impassive. "I'll hear from them after the professors, then. Thank you, Miss Bloodstone."

My fingers twisted together in my lap as Professor Viceport, Professor Burnbuck, and then Professor Crowford went to the other side of the podium and testified that during class, they'd only heard me using real words that literally fit the spell I was casting. Viceport even submitted herself to an insight question so the judge could check her memories. I couldn't tell how much weight this one detail was being given, though. It sounded so small when they talked about it.

The judge called the scions up next. Declan came first and gave a firm, articulate declaration that he'd never seen me to be anything but fair and even-tempered, sometimes to my own detriment. Jude followed and said he agreed with everything Declan had mentioned.

"I gave Rory a hard time when she first got to the university," he added. "The fact that she not only took that treatment in stride but had the generosity to set the past behind her and consider me a friend is all the proof *I* need that she'd never lash out at someone in violence."

He shot me a quick smile as he went back to the bench. Connar passed him to take the same spot.

"I haven't always been the kindest to Rory either," he admitted in his statement. "There were times I was horrible to her. But when she was hurt or angry with me, her reaction was to stay away from me, not to attack me. I've never seen her show any aggression that wasn't in immediate self-defense, and even then, she's moderate about it."

As he returned to the others, one of the blacksuits stood up. The judge nodded to him.

"I'd like it noted on the record that by multiple accounts from their peers, Mr. Killbrook and Mr. Stormhurst have both appeared to be romantically involved with Miss Bloodstone, and as such their opinion of her is likely to be biased."

The judge glanced toward the guys. "Would you dispute that fact?"

"That my feelings for Rory go beyond friendship?"

Jude replied. "No. I dispute the bias. I'm hardly so starry-eyed I'd somehow miss murderous rages."

Connar nodded. "I don't feel my relationship with Rory has affected my ability to see her actions clearly."

"All right. I'll take that all into account." The judge shuffled a few of her papers to the side and looked to the blacksuits again. "You have your own witnesses to make statements?"

"Yes," the man who'd given the initial testimony said. "I'd like to establish the underlying tension that had existed for some time between Miss Bloodstone and Miss Wakeburn, and I have three of their dormmates here to recount their experiences."

This should be fun. I clasped my hands together tighter as Victory came up to speak.

She and Sinclair didn't say anything I couldn't have expected. Victory explained how Imogen had spilled the beans about my familiar, leading to Deborah's being stolen by the scions—playing down the threats she'd used to get that result, unsurprisingly. They both commented on the chilliness between us in the days right after that incident and the distance that had never quite disappeared. None of it sounded like the prelude to a violent murder, at least.

When Cressida walked over, my heart pounded faster. She vanished from my sight on the other side of the podium. I waited, forcing my breaths to stay even. If she was going to speak up about what she'd observed during Imogen's murder, this would be the time to do it.

"Tell me about what you saw of Miss Bloodstone's associations with Miss Wakeburn," the judge said.

Cressida inhaled audibly and repeated most of what the other girls had said in her own words. Then she paused.

The judge cocked her head. "Is there something else you'd like to add, Miss Warbury?"

I braced myself. And Cressida said, "No. That's all."

My spirits sank as she sauntered away without a backward glance. She'd decided even with my "blank check," telling the truth to save me wasn't worth the risk.

My freedom depended on the testimony of three guys the judge could easily dismiss as biased and one minor detail of the illusion.

I swallowed hard, fighting down a swelling sense of hopelessness. Baron Nightwood hadn't stirred from his spot at the back of the room, where he was watching the proceedings with a small smile. He thought he'd already won. He might be right.

"Have you found any evidence of anyone else who might have been present in the room during Miss Wakeburn's murder?" the judge was asking the blacksuits, with a shake of the lead guy's head in response, when a door at the opposite end of the room swung open.

Malcolm Nightwood stepped in and strode right up to the judge's podium, his handsome face set with total determination. I stared at him for a second before my gaze darted to his father... who was no longer smiling.

The judge looked a little startled too. "Mr. Nightwood," she started.

Malcolm lifted his head at a typically cocky angle. "I apologize for the delay, Judge Blazehed. I have a few things to say in regards to Miss Bloodstone's character." He didn't so much as look at me.

A chill crept over my skin. Had all that fuss about wanting to prove himself to me been a front? Was this some kind of coordinated assault arranged with his father?

But as the judge waved Malcolm to the testifying seat, the baron's face only tightened. He was keeping his cool, but I'd swear he was upset. He definitely didn't look as if he'd expected this.

"Go ahead," the judge said to Malcolm.

I caught a flicker of movement, as if the Nightwood scion had waved his hand in the direction of the benches. He must have been indicating the scions, because the first thing he said was, "Those two told you how harsh they were on Rory when she arrived at the school. But they'd have to admit that the way they cracked down on her was nothing compared to my offensives. The truth is, Miss Bloodstone challenged me and insulted me on her first day at the school and refused to back down, and I couldn't let that kind of disrespect stand."

"I see," the judge said. My stomach churned with the uncertainty of where he was going with this. His testimonial didn't sound all that complimentary yet.

Malcolm's voice stayed confident, but I caught a hint of rawness creeping into it, like the other day in the lounge. "I intended to break her down, and my actions in pursuit of that goal were undeniably cruel. As a few examples, I forced her to walk to a high window using persuasion and threatened to make her jump out. I organized the stealing of her familiar and the trick to make her think it'd be killed. I conjured nightmares so wrenching she woke up screaming several nights."

The memory made me cringe inside. Malcolm kept talking.

"Through all that, no matter how badly I hurt her or terrorized her, she never *once* inflicted the slightest harm on me. Not a single bruise or scratch, not the slightest emotional scar. She refused to back down, but she also refused to fight on my terms. Even when I mocked her to her face, I never once had to fear for my safety."

"With all due respect, Mr. Nightwood," the judge said, "your situation and Miss Wakeburn's may not be entirely the same."

"Of course they aren't," Malcolm said, his voice turning derisive. "I'm the heir to a family second only to Rory's. The Wakeburn girl couldn't possibly have dealt the same kind of damage I'm capable of. There's no doubt in my mind that it's impossible for Rory to have injured her, let alone murdered her."

I couldn't help glancing at Baron Nightwood again. He kept strict control over his expression and stance, but he couldn't completely hide the furious glint in his eyes. No, this hadn't gone according to his plan at all. My stomach listed with a nauseating combination of gratitude and fear.

Malcolm's father looked ready to rip *someone* apart. And I didn't think it'd be me this time.

Malcolm got up to sit on the bench behind the other scions without acknowledging his father. He met my eyes for just a second, with the slightest tip of his head as if to say, *I owed you.*

It probably wasn't enough. The judge hadn't sounded convinced. But it might make a difference—and it mattered more than I could say that he'd even tried.

And it seemed his show of courage had affected more than just me. As the judge shifted in her seat as if to call an end to the hearing, Cressida shot to her feet.

"I have something else to say," she blurted out, ignoring Sinclair's gape of bewilderment beside her. "I know that Rory didn't kill Imogen."

The judge's eyebrows leapt to the fringe of her bangs. "And you didn't think to include this information earlier?"

"I… I'm including it now," Cressida said, her hands clenching at her sides.

"Well, come up here and let's hear it, then."

There was a stirring among the blacksuits as Cressida recrossed the room. Her face was nearly as pale as her hair, but she walked steadily enough.

"This is what I know," she said after she sat down. "The day Imogen died, I left the end-of-term party early because I was tired and wanted to head home. I just needed to get a few things from my room. When I tried to go up the stairs to the fifth floor, a strong emotion came over me that I needed to be somewhere else. As I backtracked, I realized it had to be a spell compelling me away."

She paused and then soldiered on. "I was suspicious. I —I actually wondered if Rory had something to do with it, because the three of us had been hassling her quite a bit, and maybe she was taking some kind of revenge. I went into the dorm room under ours and cast a spell to bring out any sounds from above to try to hear what was going on up there."

The whole room was dead silent when she stopped to gather herself. "I assume you did hear something," the judge said, with an unexpected softness.

"I did," Cressida said, quietly but clearly. "At first there wasn't anything I could really make out, but then I heard a sort of scuffing noise like shoes on the floor. All of a sudden, someone cried out, and there was a heavy thump. It startled me so much I flinched and hit the coffee table behind me. That made me nervous that whatever was going on upstairs, the person or people responsible might realize I'd heard. So I hurried out of the building as quickly as I could… and I passed Rory after I came out on the first floor. There's no way she could have been the one who did it. She wasn't anywhere near our room when it actually happened."

Her voice had turned strained with the finale of her confession. The judge peered down at her. "Would you allow me to verify your statement using insight?"

"Yes," Cressida said, even more quietly. That had been part of our deal—that she had to offer direct proof of her statement for it to count. "I'm ready."

I fought the urge to squirm in my seat as the judge delved into Cressida's mind. While my dormmate had spoken, Lillian had disappeared from the gathering of blacksuits. Interestingly, Baron Nightwood was gone as well. Had they slunk off somewhere to brainstorm urgent damage control?

If they had, they didn't make it back in time. The judge straightened up and dismissed Cressida back to her bench. She turned to me with the first glimmer of sympathy I'd seen from her.

"I apologize for everything you've been through, Miss Bloodstone," she said.

The realization that this horror show was actually finished swept through me so suddenly tears sprang to my eyes even as I smiled.

The judge turned toward the rest of the room. "I've now been faced with overwhelming evidence that Miss Bloodstone had no part in Imogen Wakeburn's murder. Which means I do hope the blacksuits will quickly apply themselves to discovering who not only killed one of our own but attempted to damage the reputation of a soon-to-be baron at the same time. Rory Bloodstone is innocent. This hearing is over."

CHAPTER TWENTY-EIGHT

Malcolm

Watching the blacksuits detach the silver cuffs from Rory's wrists gave me a sense of elation that overwhelmed even the dread expanding in my stomach. I held on to that feeling as they escorted her, with due deference this time, to the exit, but the moment she passed through the doorway, my relief had already started to fade. The other scions were heading over to follow her. I got up too, but more slowly.

My friends glanced back at me, obviously assuming I'd join them. That subtle show of solidarity nearly broke my resolve, but I gave them a brief shake of my head. Though Declan looked a little concerned and Connar hesitated a beat longer, they went on without me when I didn't move toward them.

The dread rose up to fill my chest as well. I'd done what I could for Rory here, however much difference it'd made. Now I'd face the consequences. I'd rather not face even a fraction of them in front of her, especially when that might make both our situations worse.

Dad had left his seat at the back of the room at some point during the final testimony. I wasn't sure where he'd gone, though no doubt he'd find me the moment he wanted me. He had to be fuming about this outcome. Maybe he'd stalked off to take his first round of hostility out on his blacksuit co-conspirators?

One battle for Rory's freedom was won, but the war was hardly over. It'd be useful to know which of the blacksuits or other leading fearmancers the barons had far enough in their pocket to involve them in the highest level of treason.

Rory and the others had disappeared by the time I came out into the hall. A few blacksuits lingered near the office doors farther down the brightly lit space with its khaki-green walls, but my father wasn't among them. I strolled over as if I had every right to be nosing around the blacksuit headquarters.

"I don't suppose any of you know where my father wandered off to?" I asked in a blasé tone.

One of the women motioned toward the other end of the hallway. "I think I saw Baron Nightwood going into Ravenguard's office."

I bobbed my head in thanks and ambled on. Blacksuits were trained to pick up on suspicious body language or any other sign of ill intentions. I didn't want them to see anything besides a scion looking for his dad.

"...was quite a mess," one of the other blacksuits

muttered behind me as they went back to their conversation. "Can you believe— Someone should have found that witness before the hearing."

Yeah, I'd bet this catastrophe would haunt the blacksuits who actually cared about justice for quite a while. Now they had to sit with the fact that they'd wrongly accused and almost wrongly sanctioned a baron-to-be. Was it too much to hope that a few sanctions be laid out on some employees around here?

I found the office labeled with a Lillian Ravenguard's name just around the corner. The murmurs of the other blacksuits had faded away—this stretch of hallway was empty and silent. No sound filtered through the closed door either, unsurprisingly. If blacksuits couldn't handle their own security, what the hell was the point of them?

None of them could quite match a Nightwood's power, though. We were a ruling family for a reason.

I glanced around, weighing my options. If someone came by, which was totally possible, they'd catch me eavesdropping in an instant. Maybe I should take a page out of Cressida's playbook. Making use of available nearby space had worked for her, even if what she'd heard hadn't been what she'd have wanted to.

I moved to the office next to Ravenguard's and sent a quick querying spell inside to confirm it was empty. Then I tested the lock with a casting. The physical mechanism had a complicated winding of magical strands reinforcing it, but not quite as treacherous as the wards I'd disabled on my father's home office. I could handle this one as long as no one interrupted me.

I bowed my head next to the door and murmured one casting word after another, gradually unwinding the spell. At the sound of footsteps in the distance, I froze and edged to the side so I could pretend I'd just been standing here waiting, but the person stopped before they reached the bend. With a thankful exhalation, I returned to my work.

God willing, my father and the blacksuit and whoever else might have joined their meeting wouldn't already be done talking by the time I made my way inside.

Finally, the lock clicked over with the twist of my fingers. I ducked into the dark room, leaving the light off in case it'd be visible from beneath the door. A thin illumination seeped through the closed blinds on the tiny window at the far end.

I moved to the wall between this office and Ravenguard's and came to a halt beside the shelving unit against it. Training my gaze on the bare stretch of wall, I cast my way through the plaster.

Ravenguard had a silencing spell embedded in the boundaries of her room. My awareness nudged against it cautiously. I didn't want to *break* it, because she'd definitely notice that, but if I could just scrape a little gap in it…

I worked at it as slowly as I had the patience for, my skin prickling in recognition of the minutes slipping away from me. It took at least ten before I'd worn the silencing spell thin enough that the amplifying cone I conjured in the air brought faint voices to my ears.

The first one I heard I easily identified as my father's. "…taken due precautions."

A woman's voice answered. "We've been over this. It was a delicate balance. The more variables you control, the more likely your control will be noticed."

"That's simply not good enough."

"Well, what do you expect me to do, baron? I can hardly arrest her all over again for a crime it's been proven she didn't commit."

"Perhaps you should have had a more extensive back-up plan."

"There wasn't any sign we needed one until the last minute."

Any last lingering hope I'd had that Rory and Declan's insinuations were wrong, that my father hadn't crossed the line into overt treason and murdering random mages after all, crumbled away. The murder and the false arrest had been *his* plan, clearly. And the blacksuit he was talking to was one of those who'd helped him carry it out.

"What about the other avenue you said you were investigating that might solve our problems?" Dad asked, and I perked up again, shoving down the admittedly rather feeble flicker of disappointment. I didn't hear any indication of others in the room, just him and this Ravenguard woman. Was she his main contact here, then?

"I'm continuing to pursue it," she said. "I don't have definite information yet, but we're getting closer. I'd rather not raise expectations until I know for sure what we're dealing with."

"I'd better be the first to hear all the details."

"Of course, baron. I'll actually be taking the next step shortly."

Her tone indicated that she had nothing else to say on the matter. The conversation was winding down. I'd better get going before they came out and potentially noticed the nearby intrusion.

I slipped out of the office and engaged the physical lock with a jerk of magic. There wasn't time to reconstruct the rest, but I could hope the caster's comings and goings had become so automatic that they wouldn't notice if their dispelling casting had nothing to catch onto. I strode off down the hall, slowing at the click of the other door behind me.

Dad's voice carried to me, managing to contain an edge with just two syllables. "Malcolm?"

I turned and gave him a mild smile. "There you are. I wasn't sure where you'd gone off to."

He was alone—Ravenguard had stayed in her office. Which might have been worse for me, because there were no witnesses as the baron stalked along the hall to meet me. I drew myself up a little straighter, bracing myself.

I could have run back to the school and waited him out. I could have bought myself some time. But over the years I'd decided that when the axe was going to fall, it was better to get it over with as quickly as possible rather than wallow in the dread.

I came up with a quick excuse for why I'd been looking for him, but apparently Dad had too much on his mind to care about those technicalities. He gripped my elbow for one painful moment to spin me around and push me forward.

"I think you'd better come back to the house with me. We've got a lot to talk about."

His voice was flat and sharp as a razor. I kept pace with him, keeping up my oblivious front. "I drove here from school. My car—"

"You'll ride with me. We can have someone deal with your car later."

I shrugged. "All right, if you think that's really necessary."

Perhaps the shrug was a little too much. The tendons in Dad's jaw flexed. He marched me out into the cool, gasoline-tainted air of the parking lot just a hair's breadth from looking as though he were taking *me* into custody. Although in a way he was.

"In," he said when we reached the car.

I dropped into the passenger seat, he got in behind the wheel, and the doors slammed closed. His knuckles stood out against his skin as he grasped the wheel. But my father was nothing if not conscious of appearances. He didn't lay into me until we'd left the blacksuit headquarters behind.

"What the hell was that display during the hearing about?" he snapped. "Why would you get up there and speak *for* that girl?"

I gave him my best puzzled look. Having a plausible story wouldn't prevent retribution, but it would make the difference between him seeing me as inept rather than an active opponent.

"From what I saw and heard around campus and my

own experiences with her, it was obvious she couldn't be responsible. Obviously we wouldn't want one of the barons handicapped unnecessarily. You want to be able to bring her around so you can use her power, not have it suppressed."

Because I wasn't supposed to know that he'd intended from the start to use the unjustified sanctions to get her under control. That he might actually prefer her weak and out of the way after the defiance she'd already shown. He hadn't trusted me enough to fill me in on his real plans, and he could hardly blame me for not reading his mind.

He couldn't even tell me now exactly why he was so furious. "You couldn't have known for sure," he bit out, taking a turn just a tad too abruptly. The engine roared as we sped onto the freeway. "If you'd been wrong and your testimony had swayed the judge—"

"But I wasn't wrong," I said matter-of-factly. "It's a good thing I showed solidarity."

I shouldn't have rubbed it in. Dad's eyes flashed with an anger that crackled through the car.

"Your job is to focus on solidarity with your own family first. I shouldn't have been finding out that you meant to step in when it happened in the middle of the hearing."

All right, valid point. Even if he hadn't been a traitor, he'd have a right to be upset about me surprising him like that. Of course, *I* hadn't known I was going to burst in there until seconds beforehand.

I hadn't known if I'd need to. I'd come just to watch, to see how the hearing would play out from the observation room. But it'd been obvious that the other guys hadn't convinced the judge, and Rory must have known Cressida was keeping something vital to herself, because she'd looked so hopeless in the moment after the other girl left the witness chair…

There'd been a small chance my words would tip the balance, would make the difference between Rory continuing to grow into her power as the magnificent mage she was already becoming and seeing her greatness cut off at the knees, and in that moment it hadn't really been a choice at all. I knew which woman, which baron, *I* wanted to stand beside when it was my turn at the table of the pentacle.

And having that woman would be worth whatever Dad intended to do to burn my regret over my "mistake" into my memory. I owed Rory, didn't I, after all the unnecessary pain I'd caused her?

"I'm sorry," I said to Dad, not meaning it at all. "I wasn't thinking."

"Clearly. I'm going to make sure that next time you will."

CHAPTER TWENTY-NINE

Rory

Professor Burnbuck raised his eyebrows when he answered his office door and found me standing outside.

"Miss Bloodstone," he said, flicking his scruffy hair farther out of his eyes. "It's good to see you unencumbered." His gaze dipped to my now bare wrists and back to my face. "Is there something I can help you with?"

I resisted the urge to rub the unencumbered skin, to revel in my new freedom as I had a whole bunch of times since yesterday's release. As I drew in my breath, my nerves jittered.

There'd been a Burnbuck in Professor Banefield's notes, but she was his aunt, not even part of his immediate family. If the Illusion professor had been conspiring with the barons, surely my mentor would have known?

In any case, I'd have Jude examine the spell I was about to ask for before I trusted it completely.

"I've decided on my prize for the summer project," I said. "At least, I think I have, if it's possible. And I'd like you to cast it."

"Something to do with illusions, hmm?" His eyes lit with eager interest. "I don't usually get asked since the winners tend to be looking for permanent effects. Come in and tell me what you're thinking."

Like his hair, his office had a scruffy look to it, books stacked in front of other books on the shelves even though there were gaps here and there where they could have been tucked in, the desk's finish worn down in patches. The pendulum on the dusty grandfather clock in the corner clicked as it swung. The room smelled fresh enough, though, with a grassy scent that carried through the half-open window from the field beyond.

I sat down on the slightly lumpy armchair. "I'm hoping you can cast a sort of charm for *detecting* illusions. A spell that would allow me to tell when something I'm seeing or hearing or whatever isn't actually real."

It wasn't the kind of spell I'd have most wanted as a prize. If one of the professors could have given me an "out to destroy the Bloodstone scion" detector so I knew exactly who to trust and who not to from here onward, that would have been perfect. But since there was no chance of that, I'd stick with something that could have come in handy multiple times since I'd arrived here. Even if I'd have to keep using my wits to figure out *who* to trust, at least I'd have a tool to help me figure out *what* to.

If I was going to stay here and fix the toxic parts of the fearmancer community myself, I had a feeling I'd need a tool like that.

The professor rubbed his narrow chin. "I can imbue an object with a spell for that purpose, but I should warn you that it wouldn't operate on a continual basis. You'd need to activate it to test a particular stimulus, and each test would drain some of its power, because the function requires that the magic leave the enchanted object to interact with the outside world."

"How many uses would I get?"

"It depends on how big and subtly cast the things you're testing are. Several at least, perhaps even dozens, depending. Is that adequate?"

I hadn't thought of any other prize I could ask for that would be half as good. I could accept what he was proposing. Hopefully by the time I'd used up the spell's magic, I'd be advanced enough in my studies to re-cast it myself.

"That's fine." I reached to undo the clasp on my necklace and slipped my glass dragon charm off the chain. My chest clenched as I handed it to Burnbuck. It was my last remaining token of my life with my real parents, and I hadn't let it out of my sight since I'd arrived here. But it was also the only object I could be sure of having on me when I needed it. "This is what I'd like you to place the spell on."

Burnbuck nodded. "I can have that ready for you by our class tomorrow morning. I'll attempt to give it as much potency as possible. It'll be an interesting challenge."

He gave me a smile as if he was pleased to tackle that challenge.

When I left the Illusion professor's office, Declan was heading my way from farther down the hall. When he saw me, his gaze darted around us, instinctively checking for witnesses, but he gave me a little smile and didn't object to my waiting for him so we could walk together.

"Who were you calling on?" I asked.

"Professor Sinleigh." He paused. "I stepped down from my position as teacher's aide."

"Oh?" My heart skipped a beat. I hadn't expected that —he hadn't even hinted he was considering it. "Any particular reason?"

Declan's smile turned a bit wry. "I told her I felt as though I needed my full focus on my other responsibilities for my last few months here. There certainly have ended up being… many more factors demanding my attention than I anticipated when I took the job."

I might have laughed if another part of his comment hadn't struck me. "You're only here a few more months?"

He nodded. "I'll have finished my full education by the end of January. Then I'll take over the Ashgrave barony completely."

How long was *I* going to have to stay at the university, considering all the catching up I needed to do? Were they going to make me continue classes even after my twenty-first year since I'd missed so many before? That was, assuming I made it through the next year without finding myself in cuffs either literal or metaphorical again. As relieved as I was to have the hearing over and my innocence established, I found it hard to believe the battle between me and the barons was anything close to finished.

Declan couldn't answer those questions, though, and his decision mattered in other ways. I smiled back at him with a tingle of warmth. "I'm sorry your life has gotten so hectic, but glad you'll have fewer... constraints on your time." Not to mention on who he spent that time with and how.

We came down the staircase to the main floor of the building and veered out a side door onto the green. "I was thinking now that I've settled that and your most immediate problem is dealt with," Declan said, "maybe we could have that talk about—"

He cut himself off at the sound of my name called across the green. Shelby was bounding toward us, grinning.

"Guess what!" she said. "One of the restaurants in town invited the music students to perform tonight. They're even paying us!" Her ponytail bobbed with her excitement. Then her eyes widened. "I don't know what to wear for something like that. They're probably expecting everyone who's from the university to dress all fancy."

The conversation with Declan about what exactly we were doing with our relationship could wait until this minor friend crisis was over. I caught his eye, and he nodded with obvious amusement.

"Let's take a look in your wardrobe, and I'll help you pick," I told Shelby. "And that's awesome! I guess you were right about the program here being good for your career."

"One more year and then I can start making applications to orchestras."

She practically bounced up the stairs to our dorm room. As she pulled out her key card, my gaze caught for a moment on the door next to ours that led into Malcolm's dorm.

I hadn't seen the Nightwood scion since yesterday at the hearing. Maybe he'd needed a little space to figure out how he was going to proceed now that he'd put himself out there in opposition to his father's interests.

A twinge ran through my chest. I wasn't totally sure what I'd say to him, but we definitely needed to talk. At the very least, so I could thank him. Taking that stand couldn't have been easy. And I'd been suspicious of him even after he'd started his testimony...

This once, I might owe *him* an apology. If I was coming to know anything about Malcolm Nightwood, it was that he kept his word, and he'd said he'd prove himself to me. I couldn't really have asked for a clearer show of loyalty.

Shelby tugged me into our room, away from those conflicted thoughts. As we examined her clothing options, I let myself become absorbed in her giddy chatter. After the weeks of worrying and uncertainty, there was something blissfully normal about hanging out with a friend who had no part in the conspiracies around me and talking about something as mundane as appropriate work attire.

In the end, we settled on a pearl-pink blouse and dark wash jeans, since Shelby didn't have any dress pants or skirts. "I'm sure they care a lot more about how the music sounds than what you're wearing," I reassured her. "Anyway, who'll be able to see your pants past the cello?"

"Good point," she said with a laugh.

My good mood lingered as I crossed the common room—and vanished when I opened my bedroom door to find Lillian Ravenguard standing by my desk. My pulse hiccupped, and my fingers tensed around the doorknob. I hadn't even noticed that the magical defenses on my room had been breached. But then, this was a top blacksuit I was dealing with.

"I'm sorry for the sudden visit," Lillian said, obviously noting my surprise. "It's a rather urgent matter… and one too discrete to discuss by traceable methods or in public." She stepped away from the desk and raised her hand. "I'll make sure we won't be overheard here."

As she cast the silencing spell, I sank down on the edge of my bed. Deborah darted across the bedspread a moment later, tucking herself behind me. I moved to gesture to her to hide herself somewhere farther away, since we couldn't be sure how sensitive Lillian might be to my familiar's unusual state.

Before I could, Deborah's voice traveled into my head, faintly as if at a whisper. Whatever she had to tell me, it was important enough for her to risk discovery.

Watch out, she murmured. *I got a whiff of that woman as she was waiting for you. I'd swear she's the one who murdered your friend.*

My stomach lurched. I'd known Lillian was almost certainly involved in the plot to frame me, but the possibility that she'd killed Imogen herself had never occurred to me.

Deborah scurried away. Lillian turned, finished with her casting, and my mouth went dry.

The woman aiming that concerned look at me hated me so much that she was willing to kill to cut me down.

"What's going on?" I said, scrambling to think of an excuse to get out of this room, somewhere we wouldn't be alone. Somewhere I'd have a chance of getting help if she launched another attack of some sort.

Lillian leaned against my wardrobe, partly blocking my way to the door. Not that I could have made a run for it without revealing a whole lot more about what I knew than I wanted to just yet. She lowered her head with a ragged sigh. Then she looked at me again.

"I don't know how to tell you this," she said. "If it's true, I'm ashamed that I missed it for so long. Rory... We've found evidence that your mother is still alive."

ABOUT THE AUTHOR

Eva Chase lives in Canada with her family. She loves stories both swoony and supernatural, and strong women and the men who appreciate them. Along with the Royals of Villain Academy series, she is the author of the Moriarty's Men series, the Looking Glass Curse trilogy, the Their Dark Valkyrie series, the Witch's Consorts series, the Dragon Shifter's Mates series, the Demons of Fame Romance series, the Legends Reborn trilogy, and the Alpha Project Psychic Romance series.

Connect with Eva online:
www.evachase.com
eva@evachase.com

Made in United States
Troutdale, OR
04/02/2024